SOLDIERS NEVER SLEEP

A Story of Love and War

HAWK KIEFER

ISBN 978-1-964462-19-6 (Paperback)
ISBN 978-1-964462-20-2 (Ebook)

Inquiries and Book Orders should be addressed to:

Leavitt Peak Press
17901 Pioneer Blvd Ste L #298, Artesia, California 90701
Phone #: 2092191548

To Professor Emeritus Sue Kimball, who edited and critiqued; to Shirley Harrison and Lucy Johnson, who gave me feedback; to Virginia, who put up with me; and to all who encouraged me, I am grateful.

CONTENTS

SOLDIERS NEVER SLEEP

"Until the Great Spirit sends the wind and the rain no more and the sun does not warm the Sioux, fires of Red, Yellow, and Black will consume all warriors who bear your name and grant them no rest."

Sitting Bull to Joseph Walker,
September 5, 1890.

The Walker Family

Joshua Walker eloped with teenager *Sara Austin* around 1835. They had one child, *Joseph Andrew Walker*, who was born around 1842.

Joseph Walker married *Ida Sanford* in 1865. They had one child, *Joseph A. Walker Jr.*, who was born in 1867.

Junior Walker married *Kate Beirne* in 1890. They had three children: *Jeanette*, who was born in 1892; *Rose*, who was born in 1894; and *Andrew*, who was born in 1903.

Andrew Walker married *Penny Nugent* in 1925. They had two children: *Sanford*, who was born in 1926, and *Kathleen*, who was born in 1927. After *Penny's* death in 1973, *Andy* married *Helen Vincent*.

Sandy Walker married *Nancy Down* in 1948. They had two children: *Walter*, who was born in 1949, and *Sara*, who was born in 1950.

Walter Walker married *Cathy Plummer* in 1967. They had two children: *Paul*, who was born in 1968; and *Beth*, who was born in 1969.

Paul Walker married *Jo Weibel* in 1987. They had one child, *Steven*, who was born in 1988.

PROLOGUE

Around 1835, Joshua Walker spirited young Sara Austin from the Southwest Virginia mountains named after his family and set out through the Cumberland Gap to central Kentucky where they intended to homestead, settle, and farm fifty prime acres. Once there, however, Joshua discovered that Indian raids were frequent and militia protection was far away. Soon Sara became sick, and Joshua found that competent medical help was nonexistent. Much as he loved the land, Joshua was not comfortable with multiple threats to his wife's safety, and, after five years of hardship and struggle, he moved his family farther west to Cincinnati.

Joshua was attracted to the city because it was well on its way to becoming a major center of commerce. President Jefferson had consummated the Louisiana Purchase, dispatched Lewis and Clark up the Missouri River to find a passage to Oregon, and opened the Northwest Territories to settlement. Cities like Cincinnati that bordered navigable waters became gateways to the West and magnets for investment. Joshua quickly found employment as a trader in the marketing of agriculture products. His wealth and reputation grew rapidly, and soon he started his own firm. He prospered and Sara was happy.

Joseph Andrew Walker was born in 1842. His arrival delighted his parents, but the birth was difficult and Sara suffered so much that Joseph became Joshua and Sara's only child. As the heir of a self- made investor and financier, Joseph studied in preparation for becoming a banker. In 1861, however, when the Civil War broke out and President Lincoln issued his first call for volunteers, Joseph changed his life forever by rushing to enlist as a private in the Guthrie Grays, then the National Guard of Ohio. His mother tried to dissuade him, but he insisted on serving, inspired by an intense patriotism to defend and preserve the Union. In so doing, he became the first of a long line of Walker men to serve their country through the military.

Joseph turned out to be a good soldier. In February of 1862, he was with General—and future President—Grant at Fort Henry in Tennessee, where the explosion of a three-inch shell rendered him unconscious and caused a concussion. Not seriously injured, he was among the first in his unit to be decorated for bravery. Based on his performance, moreover, General Grant awarded him a commission as a Lieutenant of Infantry. Quickly healed and back in the line, now as a company commander, he was once more with Grant in April at Shiloh, where his leadership and courage caused his superiors again to cite him for bravery and promote him to Captain. That December, he joined General Phil Sheridan for three terrible days at Stones River, where Confederate General Braxton Bragg failed to follow up his initial success and lost over nine thousand men. In the heart of that costly battle, in a place that came to be called the Slaughter Pen, a Confederate twelve-pounder exploded near him and seriously mangled his right leg. The injury marked the end of his active duty in the Civil War. While Joseph was in the field hospital at Nashville, too weak to be moved, General Grant came to his bedside to thank him for his service, present him the newly created Medal of Honor, and award him the brevet rank of Major.

Joseph's wound was severe, and for two years, first in that primitive field hospital and then back in Cincinnati, he struggled to recover the use of his shattered limb. Were it not for strength of his will and the support of his family and friends, he might have lost the leg. His childhood sweetheart, Ida Sanford, nursed him through that difficult and painful time and vowed she would never permit him to leave her again. She must have helped, for by the spring of 1865, Joseph's wound had sufficiently mended for him to resume more normal activities, although he would limp for the rest of his life. Shortly thereafter, their relationship having been strengthened by his ordeal, the lovers married.

The family has kept the tintype: he seated and she standing at his left with her right hand resting lightly on his shoulder as if her role was to restrain him. With a firm jaw, piercing gaze, and aquiline nose, he wears a high collar and a string tie. His dark hair is neatly parted on the right, and his full mustache curves on either side of his thin lips. His stern countenance radiates aggressive confidence, as always, and he looks like a leader that men will follow. She wears her black hair in a bun on the top of her head, and her prim, white, full-length dress has long sleeves with lace at the neck and wrists. As beautiful as she is, she seems far too fragile for the dangerous life she is about to lead, but her dark eyes glow with love and hint at the tenacity of a tiger.

Having faced the elephant, Joseph could not assume the life of a banker. Thus, when his doctors determined he was well enough to return to full active duty, he requested and the War Department awarded him a commission as a Captain of Infantry in the Regular Army. He and Ida then moved from Cincinnati to spend the Christmas of 1865 on the banks of the Missouri River at the headquarters that commanded the Northwest Territories. This was the famous Fort Leavenworth, already an historic place and destined to become more so. Forty years before the Walkers arrived, the Commanding General of the northern Louisiana Purchase lands had sent a Colonel Henry Leavenworth to establish a fort on the west bank of the Missouri between the Kansas and Platte Rivers. He took four companies of infantry with him and selected an excellent location. Indians may have helped in that choice by solemnly assuring him first that a tornado had already hit the site and secondly that tornadoes would never hit the same place twice. The latter promise soon proved false. At any rate, the selected fort became the installation most responsible for operations along the Oregon Trail and against the Plains Indians. Colonel Leavenworth had earlier fought alongside the Sioux against the Rees. His new fort would thenceforth be critical in campaigns against his former allies. As a reward for his outstanding efforts, the Army promoted Henry to Brigadier General. Before word of his new rank reached him, however, he sustained severe injuries in a fall from his horse and died. The fort is today the home of the Army's Command and Staff College and largest prison.

The newlyweds arrived at Fort Leavenworth just as the Army was preparing to move west for campaigns against the Sioux, Cheyenne, and Arapaho. Those savages had been left largely to their own devices during the Civil War years and had roamed freely and violently where the United States now wished to expand. The year before, General Connor had failed in an attempt to pacify them along the Powder River in Dakota Territory. He spent in that futile effort more than twenty million dollars, an immense sum in those days, and lost over a thousand mules and horses without intimidating the Sioux or their allies.

Now, as Joseph and Ida were starting west, those savages were bent on killing, torturing, and robbing every cowboy, prospector, and lonesome straggler who dared travel the Bozeman Trail, and the voting citizens who managed somehow to survive such horrors were complaining. Congress had determined that it needed to assist its constituents, so it had ordered the Commanding General at Fort Leavenworth to provide protection. He decided to build two more forts along the Bozeman in the Sioux's best hunting lands, and the Army's wars against the Plains Indians began in earnest. For the next twenty-five years, mostly in the lands that are now Montana, Wyoming, and the Dakotas, Ida, Joseph, and their only son, Junior, were in the middle of it all. They shared the hardships, dangers, and deep satisfactions of frontier life. In doing so, they lived through many a difficult campaign: from the Bozeman Trail, to the Little Big Horn, and eventually to the tragedy of Wounded Knee.

Over those years, Joseph Walker became widely recognized in the Army of the West for his leadership, skill, and bravery, as he raised his son, loved his wife, and fought the Indians, mostly the Sioux and the Cheyenne. He built a reputation as the best rifle shot in the Army, a valued officer, an independent thinker, and a man who loved his country. After the tragedy at Wounded Knee and Joseph's controversial testimony at the court-martial of Colonel Forsythe that followed, as well as his outspoken criticism of poor treatment of the

Indians, Joseph returned East in disgust. He would not be long in exile.

At the start of the Spanish American War, when combat leaders were desperately needed, General Nelson Miles took Joseph from obscurity, promoted him to Colonel, and gave him first a training mission at Camp Cuba Libre and then command of a Buffalo Soldier regiment at Fort Missoula, Montana. Colored soldiers with white officers, these were the descendents of the two units formed by an act of Congress at Fort Leavenworth in 1868, the same year as the great Treaty of Laramie that ended Red Cloud's War, Joseph's first major campaign after the Civil War. The Buffalo Soldiers quickly gained the respect of the Indians, who named them after the magnificent animal that was such an important part of Indian life. With his son commanding such a company, Joseph led this fine regiment in three years of guerrilla warfare against the rebels of the new Philippine Republic. They were just beginning to celebrate their success when, in 1902, they received a cable that Ida was seriously ill, and they rushed home to her deathbed.

Without her, Joseph lost the will and energy to press on, and after forty-one years, he left the service of his country. Upon his retirement, President Theodore Roosevelt promoted him to Brigadier General. Joseph then undertook a vigorous writing and speaking campaign to bring about changes in military doctrine and improve the lot of the Indians whom he had fought for so many years. In spite of his significant prestige and considerable talent with pen and tongue, he failed. On September 5, 1906, he received word that the Philippine Constabulary had killed nine hundred Moro men, women, and children in an extinct volcanic crater on the Island of Jolo. The news raised terrible memories of frozen bodies at Wounded Knee, and in a fit of depression over those images and the loss of his wife, he killed himself.

CHAPTER ONE

Andrew Sanford Walker, third child of Kate and Junior Walker, was born in 1903 following his father's return from three years of fighting guerrillas in the Philippine Islands. Upset at having been away from Kate, Jeanette, and Rose for so long at such a critical time in his young daughters' lives, Junior decided to leave a promising career in the Regular Army and devote himself to his wife, children, and community. He worked hard at all three and soon became a respected father and successful Cincinnati banker. The family thrived. His daughters were beautiful ladies, and Andy showed promise of becoming a fine young man. As the scion of a respected and prosperous member of the community, he lived in a large house, attended the best schools, loved his family, and yearned to be just like his father. Junior Walker, for his part, seemed content to leave war behind him, discard his military rank, and become a valued member of the Cincinnati community. Even so, he delighted in telling Andy stories about his own father: Joseph Andrew Walker, decorated Civil War hero, famous Indian fighter, and outstanding commander of the Buffalo Soldiers. In return for his father's attention, Andy ignored occasional repetition and understandable hyperbole, for he never tired of hearing about his grandfather, the man whom the Crows honored by naming him "The Angry White Chief who fights the Sioux."

"Tell me how you were born," Andy would plead.

"In 1866, Fort Smith was a small, exposed, and isolated post along the famous Bozeman Trail," Junior would begin, "near the Big Horn River. There, the winter weather was cruel and summer Indian attacks never ceased. As the winter eased and the snow melted, the savage threat increased. More and more, Mom and Dad worried about the harsh conditions at the fort, the fate of her unborn child, the lack of a qualified doctor, and her July due date. In early June, she finally relented and agreed to return to the relative safety and better medical facilities of Fort Laramie. Joseph organized and trained a special force for the trip, knowing full well that the Sioux would seize upon any perceived weakness to harass and attack them.

"The first ninety-mile stretch on the trail to Fort Phil Kearny was the most dangerous. A lone horseman could cover that distance in less than two days, but Joseph's mule-drawn wagons would require at least twice that time. With Ida's safety as his paramount concern, Joseph therefor assigned four supply wagons and forty men to the mission. They traveled in two lines, muskets outward, always at the ready. Fort Smith marked the beginning of friendly Crow territory farther to the west, so as Joseph's party left the fort to the east, it did not fear immediate Sioux attack. Indeed, the initial part of the trail south lay mostly through pleasant, gently rolling grassland, and the fresh scent of wildflowers made for a peaceful scene. Although hostile Indian scouts were clearly evident, the readiness of the soldiers in the wagons must have deterred the savages, for nothing more than a few brief skirmishes ensued until they reached the Tongue River.

"About half way to Fort Kearny, in the very heart of hostile territory at the base of the Big Horn mountains, the Tongue's ford provided fresh water and a shallow crossing, but it also offered easy concealment in the nearby hills and trees along the river. It was thus a favorite Sioux ambush site, and Joseph expected the worst. Before dusk on the second day, therefore, he squared the four wagons there. Selecting a spot with good fields of fire, he watered and fed the animals early and then tethered them within the quadrangle. Placing ten soldiers with each wagon, he ordered that five were to remain on alert at all times.

"At 3 a.m., the neighs, whinnies, and shuffling of their restless mules gave the soldiers ample early warnings of nearby Indians. Shortly thereafter, when howling braves swarmed at the detachment from all sides, the men were ready, and their accurate fire severely wounded several attackers. The fight was quickly over. Joseph had little time to assess damage and congratulate himself, however, for as he turned from his survey of the battle scene in the moonlight, to his horror he saw a Sioux warrior on Ida's wagon with his tomahawk raised over her supine body. Joseph barely had time to turn his pistol and fire, but his marksmanship was true. Ida was shaken and my life was violent before my birth, but she and I were safe.

"The Indians must have been badly punished and realized that this particular convoy was well led and ready to fight, for they did not attack again. Shortly after Joseph's small force arrived safely at Fort Kearny, moreover, he and Ida joined another wagon train on its way to Fort Laramie. Ida's narrow escape had inflamed Joseph, however, and his anger increased when she had a difficult time with my birth a month later. She suffered, and the doctor told Joseph that her near death experience at the ford might have had something to do with the fact that she could have no more children. The diagnosis may have been questionable, but from that time on, Joseph sought revenge with a determination that would gain him a reputation of being possessed. That was when the friendly Crow Indians gave him the nickname that remained with him. In their dialect, it sounded something like *macheechee macheche poomacatee barasoupsque ahumbatsots*. With the increased respect that accompanied such recognition, your grandfather soon became honored among the Crow and Shoshone Indians for his bravery and skill."

"He must have been quite a guy," Andy said. "I wish I had known him. I'm going to grow up like him."

"Then you must learn to lead and inspire men with dedication, skill and bravery. Joseph was the very best at that, and there is no greater calling."

"I promise, but tell me about that trail. You said it was famous. Why was it called the Bozeman?"

"Back in 1862," Junior answered, "out near Virginia City in what is now southwest Montana, prospectors had found considerable quantities of gold. Immediately upon hearing of that discovery, miners, dance hall queens, drifters, and those who prey upon them flocked in great numbers toward those newest gold fields. In doing so, they could take the route Lewis and Clark took up the Missouri River to Fort Benton and then south over a relatively easy trail. But this was a slow and costly journey. On the other hand, they could take the difficult Oregon Trail west to Utah and then cut north on a spur that was lengthy and arduous. The winter after the discovery of gold, however, a man named John M. Bozeman found a route that could save the more adventurous over two hundred miles. He went north from the Oregon Trail near Fort Laramie and then to the east and north of the Big Horn Mountains. From there, he proceeded along the Yellowstone River, and finally through Clark's Pass. In doing so, however, he passed directly through the heart of prime Indian hunting lands, sacred territory that the United States had promised would not be violated. The Sioux had warned many times that they would resist White incursions there. Ignoring that threat, large numbers of eager gold seekers chose to take John Bozeman's new trail, and when the Sioux and Cheyenne saw how many of these latest invaders came, they took to the warpath.

"Under frequent attack, the frightened wayfarers panicked and petitioned their representatives in Washington for protection from the Indians. That was why the Commanding General at Leavenworth had ordered Joseph and his regiment to build and man Fort Smith. Their mission was to police the Sioux and safeguard traveling citizens. And in spite of the very obvious dangers and primitive living conditions, Ida insisted on going along."

"She must have been brave too."

"She was, for that part of the Old West was no place for a lady, but she and Joseph were very much in love and she remembered what had happened to him when he left her to fight in the Civil War. And so she went."

"And Joseph hated the Indians for attacking her?"

"Oh, he hated them well before that," Junior said. "As a matter of fact, there was plenty of hatred on both sides. Shortly before Joseph went west, citizen soldiers had attacked a peaceful Indian village at Sand Creek in Colorado, and General Custer had charged a village along the Washita in Kansas Territory. In both campaigns, most of the dead were Indian old women and children. In retaliation for those and other such atrocities, Indian warriors frequently raped white women, tortured captives, and mutilated our dead. Joseph had learned about such behavior before he left Fort Leavenworth, but you're right when you say that he became angry after the attack on Ida at the Tongue River ford. From that time on, he was a man possessed."

"And he took revenge?"

"Yes, almost immediately. Very shortly after I was born at Fort Laramie and while Ida was still recovering, he hurried back up the Bozeman to Fort Smith to implement an idea suggested to him by the Army's new Springfield carbines. Until then, his soldiers had been armed with muzzle-loading weapons. A quick man could reload in about ten seconds, but he had to kneel to do so, making himself an easy target in the process. A common practice of the Sioux was to draw fire by feinting with a small force and then attacking with their main body while the soldiers were reloading. Many a good man had died under such circumstances. In the Civil War, however, the Army had developed breech-loading, rapid-fire carbines, and quantities of these new weapons were now reaching Fort Laramie. Joseph had plans for them.

"First he smuggled the carbines to Fort Smith by concealing them in bales of hay and other supplies on the usual supply wagons. Then he set a trap. In August, five hundred Cheyenne and Sioux under the command of Crazy Horse fell for his scheme. He dispatched a small hay-gathering detachment from the fort, and the Indians attacked as they had before. First, they sent a small group of taunting warriors, hoping to cause the group of nineteen soldiers to fire their weapons and reload. When that happened, the main body of warriors attacked, seeking to catch the men before they could recover. This time, the fight did not go as planned. To the amazement of the Indians, their assaults were met by volley after volley of intense fire. Again and again, they massed and charged the small force of soldiers lying safely behind and under their hay wagons, only to encounter a killer swarm of unceasing bullets. Finally, after losing many braves dead and wounded, they gave up, gathered their casualties, and retired from the field, puzzled and badly punished from what was afterwards called the Hayfield Fight. I call it Joseph's vengeance, and for him, it was just a beginning. Time and again, he would demonstrate leadership ability by giving his men the means to prevail in battle and then leading them to an inspiring victory."

"But we didn't always win. What happened to General Custer at the battle on the Little Big Horn?"

"No, you're right. We didn't always win, but Joseph was not present at Custer's terrible defeat. He was at the battle on the Rosebud just a week before. He commanded an infantry battalion under General George Crook when in the summer of 1876 they moved north from Fort Fetterman toward Rosebud Creek intending to link up with General Custer at the stream the Indians called the 'Place of the Grassy Grass.' Custer, Old Yellow Hair the Indians called him, was from General Terry's command, which was coming down from the north. In the south, Crook had fifteen cavalry troops, five companies of infantry, three hundred friendly Crow and Shoshone warriors, and assorted civilians, scouts, and observers.

"Altogether, his command comprised more than thirteen hundred men, and by the afternoon of June 16th, General Crook's small army was massed on the south banks of Rosebud Creek. That evening, his returning Crow scouts told him that a large Indian village lay directly ahead of him and that over a thousand Sioux and Cheyenne braves were between him and those lodges.

"At dawn the following morning, General Crook dispatched his cavalry on a great circling movement to the west, hoping to flank the Indian warriors and attack the undefended village. He directed Joseph to distract the Indians' attention by leading his infantry across the little stream to his front and advancing toward the reported village. Barely across the shallow waters, Joseph and his men were amazed to see a large body of mounted Sioux and Cheyenne coming over the hills and massing on the crests. In fact the Indians had about eight hundred braves well positioned on those heights, while in the valley, Joseph had barely three hundred infantrymen. Neither he nor his soldiers had ever seen such a large body of warriors, and smell of death was near. Joseph hastened to organize his men for defense. As he did so, a chief in the center of the great enemy formation gave a signal, and the unified mass began a charge of thunderous momentum toward the dismounted soldiers.

"Around and around the Indians circled the infantry, who were pinned to the ground behind rocks and in protecting ditches. For hours, in the heat, dust, and flies of the Dakota summer, the sweating soldiers fired at the circling savages. With their arms through braided loops in their horses' manes, the Indians clung to the protected sides of their mounts and fired their own weapons under their horses as they rode. The acrid smell of powder and the stench of battle were overwhelming as the tide of conflict ebbed and flowed for more than five hours. Had not Joseph's friends, the Crows and their Shoshone allies, come to the rescue with a great charge at the end, the day might well have been lost, and Joseph might have been overrun as Custer was a week later. Reeling from that sudden charge, the Sioux and Cheyenne broke contact and fled from the field.

"The infantry had prevailed, but only at great cost, losing over fifty dead and wounded, not counting casualties among the friendly Indians. Later, Joseph would say that nothing in his career gave him more satisfaction than the bravery of his men that day. At the time, however, he was livid at the injuries and deaths in his battalion, and he protested to General Crook over the senseless exposure of his men. By separating forces and depriving the infantry of its protective cavalry screen, Crook almost lost half of his command, and the absent cavalry had accomplished nothing. They skirmished the entire day without success against Crazy Horse's mounted braves, who fought with an energy and determination the troopers had not encountered before. The cavalry returned empty handed to the Rosebud at nightfall, having never found the village that had been their objective.

"In the morning, General Crook massed his forces to attack again, but his scouts reported that the great Sioux village had disappeared. Then the Crow and Shoshone warriors announced that they would fight no more and rode off to protect their teepees. At that, General Crook decided to regroup. He declared the battle of the Rosebud a victory because Joseph had held the field. Not true, the Indians had forced Crook to retreat to Fort Fetterman without joining General Terry or even sending a messenger to warn of the large body of Indians he might be facing. Then Crook went fishing while General Custer advanced toward the Little Big Horn. It was a mistake that was to cost old Yellowhair and his men their lives."

"Joseph protested to General Crook?" Andy asked.

"Yes, and in doing so, he put himself at considerable risk, for such Generals do not take criticism lightly. But he did it because it was the right thing to do. Remember, Andy, loyalty goes down as well as up."

"You said Joseph was friends with the Crows?"

"Yes. Back in 1868 after the Hayfield Fight, he realized he needed to be able to communicate with the Indians, so he studied sign language and practiced the Crow dialect. From the Treaty of Laramie, until his campaign on the Yellowstone with Custer in 1873, he had time to develop fluency. The Crows respected him for trying. If you ever serve in a foreign country, Andy, you must learn their language and customs."

"And what happened after Custer died?"

"Until that tragedy, Congress had ignored the Army of the West. But Custer's death and the loss of 250 troopers of the Seventh Cavalry with him shocked the nation, and a public outcry arose to punish the savages. The United States mobilized its forces and took to the field in pursuit. In this effort, Joseph was to serve as a regimental commander under Colonel Ranald S. MacKenzie, a vigorous field general arriving fresh from successful campaigns against the Apaches. MacKenzie fought with a fervor equal to Joseph's, and initial success was not long in coming. On September 8th, 1876, at Slim Buttes, they surprised and overran forty lodges of the Sioux led by Crazy Horse. Their attack was so powerful that many warriors died and the rest dispersed into the hills, unable to muster a counterattack. Joseph lost only three soldiers in the battle, but he felt their loss as much as he had his fifty casualties at the Rosebud. Earlier he had shared the danger on the ground, and he could control the action. Now, as a regimental commander, he was more remote from the fighting, yet at the same time, he was more responsible because every decision he made affected so many. That is an important lesson, Andy. You must stay close to your men, for they are your neighbor's sons.

"In the past after a battle like Slim Buttes, General Crook always retreated to Fort Laramie to recover, but MacKenzie didn't. He continued tracking the Indians for months. On November 25th, at Crazy Woman's Fork on the Powder River, he attacked and destroyed the largest Indian village yet, almost two hundred lodges of the Cheyenne under Dull Knife. MacKenzie's artillery was particularly effective, and when the battle was over, he had deprived over a thousand Indian men, women, and children of food, clothing, and shelter for the winter. After that defeat, the Cheyenne were finished as an effective fighting force.

"Not far to the north, coordinating his efforts with those of MacKenzie in order to deny the Indians any chance to rest and recover, Colonel Nelson Miles was making his reputation in battle. With five hundred men, on January 8, 1877, to the west of Slim Buttes at Wolf Mountain, he attacked a large village at a time when the Indians were usually in camp for the winter. In a driving snowstorm, he used his artillery, the Napoleon cannons, to good effect, demoralizing and routing more than eight hundred Sioux and Cheyenne warriors again fighting under Crazy Horse.

"After their overwhelming defeats at Crazy Woman's Fork and Wolf Mountain, Sitting Bull and Gall fled north with four hundred followers to sanctuary in Canada. On the other hand, Crazy Horse took his depleted forces south to surrender at Fort Robinson. Both choices turned out bad for them, but just then, the departure of Sitting Bull from the Dakotas and the surrender, imprisonment, and subsequent death of Crazy Horse ended the major battles of the Great Plains. The story would not end until thirteen years later, but Colonels Miles and MacKenzie had done their jobs. They had relentlessly pursued the Sioux and Cheyenne warriors, women, and children until the exhausted Indians gave up.

"On May 6, 1877, less than a year after the Little Big Horn, Joseph watched as Crazy Horse led over a thousand Indians and their twenty-five hundred ponies into Fort Robinson to surrender. The mounted braves remained hostile to the end. Three hundred massed warriors defiantly shook their rifles above their heads and broke into a war chant in front of General Crook as Crazy Horse rode up to that General and contemptuously threw his Winchester rifle to the ground, saying he would fight no more."

"And did he?"

"That is a story I will tell you some other time."

"Then tell me now about the Napoleon Cannons," Andy said. "Were they French?"

"The so-called Napoleon cannons may indeed have had a French origin, but they were perfected in our Civil War, and both Lee and Meade used them at Gettysburg. And so in the Plains Wars against the Indians, they were another of the Army's surprise weapons. They fired shot or shell at ranges up to four miles, and canister for close-in combat. The cavalry truly prized them, for the guns could be broken down and loaded on four horses, and could thus accompany the mounted squadrons. Before Custer, the Army had not used such artillery against the Indians, so the Sioux were indeed demoralized by the cannon's devastating fires. No Indian ever fought well against artillery."

"And the surrender of the Sioux at Fort Robinson was the end of Joseph's combat service?"

"No, he fought again in the Philippine Insurrection, at the end of the Spanish-American War. That was when the United States reneged on its pledge to grant Filipino independence and then ignored the protests of their commander, General Aguinaldo. So in January of 1899, he declared war. We had more than fifty thousand men there, left from the war against Spain, so we continued our buildup, and soon we had twice that number. Joseph was part of that force. Earlier, at the start of the war with Spain, General Miles had asked him to train volunteers like the Rough Riders for combat in Cuba, and I served with him on that mission at Camp Cuba Libre, near Jacksonville. That task finished, Miles transferred us to Fort Missoula, Montana, to lead a regiment of the Buffalo Soldiers. Ida, Kate, and the girls joined us there, and we began the process of procuring supplies and equipment, acquiring and testing cadres, training soldiers, and preparing plans for deployment to the Far East.

"We were headed for a dangerous place, and our leaders were ill prepared. The theater commanders, Admiral Dewey and General

Merritt, commonly referred to the Filipinos as 'Indians' who were 'non-people.' As usual, the American soldiers took their cues from their leaders, calling the natives 'monkey men,' 'dirty,' and 'stunted.' They sang a ditty, 'The monkeys have no tails in Zamboanga.' But the little brown men would not give up. Like the Indians of the American West, they knew they could not hope to match the Americans in conventional weapons or numbers, so they fought as guerrillas, much as the Indians had.

"Inspired by Teddy Roosevelt and stirred by Hearst's yellow journalism, American soldiers had only enlisted to fight the evil Spanish. Now that they had won that war, they wanted no part of any ugly, insurgent battles. Above all, they had not joined up to fight in the Philippines. They hated those hot, humid islands, full of strange diseases. To them the 'Gugus' they were fighting were barbaric savages, far worse than the Sioux had ever been. They clamored to leave and wrote their Congressmen in Washington for relief. A major election was coming, and President McKinley wanted to appease certain states, so he agreed, directing General Miles to relieve the volunteers from those states where he needed an electoral boost and to replace them with regulars. Politics is a dangerous game for soldiers, Andy. Remember that.

"The result of the volunteers' departure from the Philippines was final orders for Joseph's regiment. They were to deploy by rail to San Francisco and then by ship to the islands. The family farewell in August of 1899 was hard on everyone. Ida was not well, and she didn't want Joseph to leave her. He was headed for battle in a distant place she knew nothing about. But she consoled herself that she would be with Kate, Jeanette, and Rose, and while I was gone, Kate would need all the help Ida could give. Thus, as Army wives frequently must, she and Kate accepted the situation and endured the parting with brave faces, wanting their men to have fond memories. As Kate's favorite poet has said, life is a continual farewell."

"Who was that?" Andy asked.

"Yeats, my boy, William Butler," Junior said and continued.

"By September, Joseph had moved his regiment to Zambales Province in the Philippine Islands. Their mission was law and order, but their methods were right out of a guerrilla warfare textbook. The regiment performed well. Applying hard lessons they had learned against the Sioux, Joseph's Buffalo Soldiers fought superbly against the Filipinos, and they gradually gained control of the land. In contrast to their White counterparts, colored soldiers mingled easily with the locals and soon gained their trust. They lived in the local villages and married native women. Unorthodox though that practice might have been, it effectively cut off support for the guerrillas.

"We worked hard. Joseph set the objectives, and the rest of us met them. The Philippine Islands were dangerous places in which to fight. Men sickened and died in the harsh environment. The jungle was hostile, and the Filipinos resisted vigorously. As a company commander, I ate, worked, and slept with my men, sharing their fears and discomfort. We went together on night patrols and fought under the most adverse conditions. That is how you must lead, Andy. Learn to listen to your men and share their hardships, and eventually you will win their trust.

"After two years of fighting, Filipino supplies and material dried up, and soon we compelled the surrender of all the insurgent forces in our sector. Restoration of civil authority and good order would take another year, but the difficult part was over. I was exhausted and happy, but most of all I was proud of my Buffalo Soldiers. I could not have asked for a finer body of men to lead."

Were you ever wounded?" "Minor scrapes."

"Tell me again about West Point and how you met mom."

"If story-telling runs in our family, I learned it from Dad. And of all his stories, I remember best the many tales about West Point graduates he had known in the Army, from the Civil War to the campaigns of the West. Early on I decided I wanted to attend the Academy. My lack of formal education was a serious problem, however, for few books and little schooling were available at the frontier Army posts where we lived. I needed a more disciplined preparation before I could hope to pass the entrance examination. I also had to secure an appointment from a member of Congress. We never stayed in one place long enough for me to meet residential requirements, but finally father persuaded the representative from our family home back in Cincinnati to give me a chance if I could pass the tough entrance test.

"I had to leave Fort Laramie, accept assistance from mother's folks in Cincinnati, and then move on to Washington to Mallard's Preparatory School for West Point. Testing there determined that I needed an intensive two-year program of study. Without a solid academic background, I found the discipline to be hard work, but I resolved to justify my father's faith in me. So I stuck with it without a break. Twenty-four months later, in the spring of 1886, together with some two hundred other aspirants, I rode the New York Central Railroad up to West Point. For three days, we were confined to Beast Barracks for the grueling physical and mental examination. God must have been with me, for when the results were announced, I had won a competitive appointment. I entered in the summer of 1886, a member of the class of 1890.

"My educational background may have put me at an academic disadvantage, and I certainly had to work hard at my studies, but I soon discovered that my knowledge of military life and the Sioux wars gave me an edge. Everyone wanted to know about Crazy Horse, Sitting Bull, Red Cloud, and Custer. Upperclassmen who might soon be fighting Indians picked my brains. Initially, hazing was a problem, especially from southern upperclassmen, who apparently resented my father's role in the Civil War. It persisted until one of them 'called' me out for a fistfight, a common practice in those days. My opponent was a large fellow who must have seen me as an easy foe. He could not have known of my many scrapes with wiry Indian boys, and he was as surprised as I was at how easily I beat him.

Several more challenged me, and when I had whipped them all, hazing ceased. Please don't misunderstand me; because of the rigorous requirements of study, athletics, and discipline, Plebe Year was by no means easy. But at the end of that introductory period, I was established at West Point. The following year, I was able to ease up a bit and join the athletic program. I may have been a questionable student of engineering, but I was good at most field competition. Because of my western, Army background, I excelled in shooting, track, and the equestrian arts.

"One Saturday of the summer following my 'yearling' year at the Academy, my life changed during a stroll among the statues and battlements of Trophy Point just above the spot where the Hudson River makes a dramatic turn around Constitution Island. Then as now, as you may find someday if you are fortunate enough to visit the Academy, the monuments, trophies, and cannon combined with the view of the spectacular river valley to make Trophy Point truly awe-inspiring. On this particular afternoon, many tourists were enjoying what is without doubt the most beautiful setting on the Academy grounds. This was the spot where, on my very first day at West Point, I had taken my oath of allegiance to the Constitution of the United States, and thus it held special meaning for me. While I wandered, lost in contemplation of the magnificent river, the cooling breezes, and the green Hudson valley, I suddenly met two young ladies. Smitten by the blond beauty of one, I stopped and stared at her as they passed. When she turned and smiled back at me, I first blushed, then stammered, and finally summoned the courage to introduce myself and ask her name.

"She was Kate Beirne, a Boston Irish girl who was attending Ladycliffe, and I never had a chance. She was the one who first nicknamed me Junior, and initially her friendship and then her love sustained me during my final years at West Point. My studies may have suffered, and my interest in athletics might have waned, but I was in heaven. Your mother was someone a lonely young man from out west had never expected to find, and she made my head whirl. By the time I graduated two years later, I believe I was respected by my instructors and admired by my classmates, but I know I was overwhelmingly in love with Kate. She, her family, and my father were there at June Week to pin on my gold bars, and I took her to Cincinnati for our marriage in June."

Junior's glamorous tales, well polished and frequently embellished were much like bedtime stories to Andy, entertainment a father would offer a child. He sanitized warfare to protect his son. He said nothing of limbs torn and bodies shattered. He never described crying and cowering soldiers blinded by shell fragments. No captives were skinned alive, with their fingers, toes, and ribs broken and their severed penises stuffed into their gaping mouths. None of the dead had names or grieving widows. The good guys always won. Women were brave and virtuous, and romance always triumphed. The grim face of reality never intruded. Andy accepted that vision with no hint of what was to come.

CHAPTER TWO

The summer of 1914 brought war to Europe and conflict on our border with Mexico. Events moved quickly. Germany declared war on Russia and France and then invaded neutral Belgium. Britain in turn declared war and moved troops to France, and trench warfare began. When the British also attempted to blockade the coasts of Europe, German U-boats retaliated by sinking three British cruisers near Holland and then the battleship *Audacious* off the Irish coast. Sensing victory, German cruisers bombarded and raided Yorkshire, and the Kaiser announced a new policy of unrestricted submarine warfare. The Germans courted Mexico, seeking it as an ally. As the war widened, Italy and Turkey joined the conflict. It became a global conflict.

Still in his first term, President Woodrow Wilson urged the heads of warring states to end the war peacefully. That changed when Germany sank the Cunard liner *Lusitania* near the British Isles and 128 Americans were among the twelve hundred who died. The United States was outraged, and Wilson informed Germany that unless they abandoned their inhumane policy of unrestricted submarine warfare, he would bring the might of America against them. When they then agreed not to attack unarmed shipping, the President renewed his search for peace without conflict, and he was able to win re-election in 1916 as a peace candidate. As soon as he addressed Congress at the start of his second term, however, the Germans resumed indiscriminate submarine attacks. In April, after the British uncovered a German plot to reward Mexico for declaring war on the United States, President Wilson informed Congress that we had to enter the war against the hated Kaiser and make the world safe for democracy.

Andy Walker was fourteen when General Pershing called in April asking his father to accept a Colonel's rank, return to active duty, and report to the War Department in Washington. His General's stars were not to be far behind. The rank impressed Andy, for Junior had resigned his Lieutenant's commission after Ida died, and Andy had never seen his father in uniform. To him, Junior was a banker, and that was what Andy had always wanted to be. Up to that point, the war in Europe interested Andy only in that his father said it affected interest rates. Besides, it was spring, and he was on the baseball team. Junior had always come to his games. Now he would be far off in Washington.

"What about us?" he asked.

"The United States has declared war," Junior said. "I'm needed immediately."

"Needed? Who needs you more than the girls and me?"

"The country desperately needs all the good men it can find. General Pershing has placed me in charge of mobilization. We're to raise an army of a million men in less than a year and send them to Europe."

"You, a Colonel? In charge of mobilization?" Andy asked, amazed. "You're a banker."

"I'll be a General if Pershing has his way." "But what will you do?" Andy wanted to know.

"If Congress passes a selective service act, we will have to find a fair way to choose the men who will serve. Then we must train them and form the units in which they will fight. It's an immense task."

"But why you?"

"General Pershing has only a month before he must go to Europe as the commander of the American Expeditionary Force. He has to have a staff here that he can trust. We served together in the past, and he needs me now."

In fact, the American Army at the turn of the century was so small that most officers personally knew almost all their peers. For example, Pershing was the First Captain of the Corps of Cadets while Junior was studying to enter the Academy. Junior first heard about the man when Pershing led the Corps across the Hudson to the town of Garrison and stood them at attention under arms in Full Dress as Grant's funeral train passed. While Junior was at the Academy telling stories about the Indian Wars, Pershing was serving in Arizona with General Miles in the campaigns against the Apaches. This was the same Nelson Miles under whom Joseph served after the Little Big Horn. Soon to be the Army's Chief of Staff, Miles was a man to know. He had made his reputation by chasing Sitting Bull to Canada and capturing Chief Joseph of the Nez Perce. Junior had met Pershing and Miles on the battlefield after Wounded Knee, and he had obviously impressed the General and his soon-to-be aide. Eight years later when the Spanish-American War broke out, General Miles removed Joseph, Junior, and Pershing from desk jobs and sent them to Florida to prepare for the invasion of Cuba. After the quick Spanish surrender there, the action shifted to the Philippines, so he moved them to the Far East. Pershing fought the Moros and then served in the Philippines on and off for the next sixteen years, while the Walkers served three years in Zambales Province.

"But how come Pershing is so important now?"

"He was always a comer," Junior said. "He was twenty-two years old when he went to the Academy, older than most, and everyone looked up to him. After graduation, he served four years with Colonel Baldwin and the cavalry against the Apaches, making his reputation as a fearless and effective officer. He then went to the University of Nebraska, where he revitalized the military training there, even as he earned a law degree. As a result, West Point asked that he be assigned to its Tactical Department, and he was there when war became imminent in Cuba. Sent by General Miles into combat, he won the Silver Star at San Juan Hill, serving with Baldwin's cavalry again and, more importantly, coming to the attention of Teddy Roosevelt. Because of stagnation in the Army, however, he was still a Lieutenant when Miles sent him to the Philippines. He was finally promoted to Captain in 1901, fifteen years after graduation from the Military Academy. He was so obviously outstanding, however, and the Regular Army's system of seniority promotion was so patently unjust, that five General Officers joined together to write a formal request that he be promoted ahead of others less qualified. In spite of that, he remained a company-grade officer.

"Teddy Roosevelt, becoming President after McKinley's assassination, cited Pershing by name in his annual message to Congress, requesting authority to promote outstanding officers such as Pershing ahead of others their senior. Nothing happened until circumstances changed. In 1905, Captain Pershing married Helen Warren, daughter of the senior Senator from Wyoming. The marriage was an astute political move, and in 1906 Roosevelt promoted him from Captain to Brigadier General in one astounding jump over his contemporaries. The selection immediately resulted in a gigantic political uproar over favoritism that Roosevelt and Pershing simply ignored.

"He was still serving in the Philippines when trouble broke out on the Mexican border and General Leonard Wood was the new Army Chief of Staff. Pershing had served with Wood in Cuba and in Moro Province, and Wood quickly brought him home to police our southwest border. When Pancho Villa invaded New Mexico and killed thirteen Americans, Pershing went after the murderers. He took Lieutenant George Patton as his aide and Joseph's Buffalo Soldiers as his infantry. Altogether he had about ten thousand men, almost forty percent of the existing Regular Army. Cursed with obsolete equipment and few supplies, they chased Villa for two years, wounding but never catching him. The campaign was so well handled, however, under such adverse conditions, that Congress has just now promoted him to Major General and handed him a new job. The war in Europe is about to entangle us, and the Mexican expedition has revealed major shortcomings in our organization and equipment. We have waited until the last moment to prepare. Now we must quickly mobilize many men and send them to Europe. For this job, Pershing called me personally. How can I refuse?"

Andy had no answer for that, and so he had to finish his baseball season without his father. All was not lost, however, for on one hot spring evening, as his team played under the waning twilight against a school from Kentucky, he scored the winning run in the bottom of the ninth. Afterwards, as they celebrated, one of the attractive visiting fans who had flirted with him when he was in his left field position implored him to come with her to a cookout on a nearby farm. She said her name was Honey, and she turned out to be the sister of one of the visiting players. She was eighteen years old, and Andy was flattered to be with her. They laughed as she taught him to dance the Flatfoot. Later she led him to a quiet, secluded spot under the stars. In the light of a magnificent full moon and amidst the intoxicating scent of new-mown hay, she produced a small bottle of white lightning.

"This is sour mash," she said. "We make it down home."

"I don't know," Andy said. "I've never tried any of that. Will it hurt me?"

"Nah. It's the smoothest stuff," she said. "Taste it, and you'll see. It makes things right."

When he did so, a warm glow spread over him. She too took a swallow and then kissed him. He fumbled a bit, reluctant to do anything that might offend her. Suddenly, she rolled off him, stood up, and removed her dress. Wearing just a light slip, she knelt over him. He had never seen anything like her, and he pulled her to him. She then reached down, unbuttoned his trousers, and took him in both hands. After a few moments, she guided him into her. In the warm night under a thousand stars, they made love again and again, as she taught him how to please a woman.

"Where did you learn all that?" he asked her as they walked back to the campfires and music.

"We start 'em young down home," she said. Then she kissed him and slipped away to join her brother. She hadn't given him her full name, and he couldn't find her again, hard as he tried.

The following week, he watched in silence as his mother and sisters all gathered in Junior's room to help him pack the great trunk he would take to Washington. Jeanette and Rose were teary-eyed and unhappy.

"Why are we going to fight over in Europe?" Jeanette asked. "Why should we care if they want to kill each other? It's none of our business."

"Their U-boats are killing hundreds of Americans," Junior said. "We can't stand idly by."

"But I'm all set to marry Paul this summer," Rose said, her eyes wet with tears. "And you'll be way off in Washington, and everything is so uncertain. And President Wilson said we must conscript a million soldiers. Paul might well be one of those called. What about our marriage? What will happen to us?"

"If called, he must serve." "That's not fair," Rose said.

"Wars are never fair to the women," Kate said.

The next morning, they all went to the train station to see Junior off for the nation's capitol. Erect in his uniform, he was splendid in high- collared tunic, jodhpurs, riding crop, and gleaming, knee-high boots. Andy was most of all impressed by the rows of ribbons on Junior's chest. Medals from the Indian Wars, the Spanish American War, and the Philippine Insurrection, they included the Silver Star, Medal of Honor, and Purple Heart. Andy was wide-eyed as Junior took him aside.

"I rely on you to help your mother," he said.

Andy fought back the tears welling in his eyes as Junior's train chugged from the station. He straightened his back and resolved to live up to his father's faith in him.

When America entered World War I, one-third of its citizens were immigrants, and eight million of those were Germans. The nation had a history of avoiding foreign entanglements, and public sentiment was against fighting in Europe. President Wilson knew he had to change the mood of America from overwhelming isolationism to one of public support for the United States' intervention in what many citizens considered a European conflict that was none of their business. A week after Congress declared war, he therefore created the Committee on Public Information (CPI) to popularize the war at home. This was the first time that any nation had attempted to shape public opinion on a grand scale. The CPI immediately imposed voluntary censorship and distributed massive numbers of weekly press releases. It also employed scores of cartoonists and filmmakers to portray the Huns as barbaric and to stir up war fever. As sentiment changed in the United States, Congress passed Selective Service, the Espionage Act of 1917, and the Sedition Act of 1918. In early 1918, the government took control of the railroads. We were at war. The country responded quickly to the threat.

Jeanette's husband, Walter, announced he had volunteered and been accepted to serve in the Army as an engineer. Rose's fiancé, Paul, was discussing with the Navy about a commission and going to sea.

"What am I to do?" Jeanette asked.

"Just what I'll do," Kate answered, "and what Ida did for Joseph twenty years ago. You'll kiss Walter goodbye, smile as you wave farewell, and write him every day he's gone."

"I realize now why we must fight," Jeanette said, "but I can't stand the thought of him being hurt. What if he was gassed or maimed, even killed?"

"You mustn't think about that," Kate said. "That way lies madness.

Think only of the good times when he returns."

"But Walter has a skill the Army can use," Rose said. "He can be an engineer. Paul has never been to sea. It makes no sense. He says he's always wanted to be a sailor, and now he's changed. He's going to join the Navy and destroy the U20, the submarine that sank the *Lusitania* and killed all those Americans."

"Maybe that's better than being conscripted," Kate said. "But what should we do?" Rose asked. "Should we marry?" "Do you really love him?" Kate asked.

"Yes, of course."

"Then you should marry immediately and have a baby before Paul leaves. That way, no matter what happens, you'll always have Paul with you through the baby's eyes."

As sentiment about the war rapidly changed in America and isolationism became a thing of the past, Andy began to think that perhaps helping mother was not what a red-blooded American boy should be doing. While he stayed home, everybody else was going off to fight the rapacious Boche and evil Kaiser. Every Cincinnati street corner bore a poster showing a stern Uncle Sam pointing right at him and announcing "Uncle Sam wants you." As his friends left to join the war effort, their baseball team fell apart, and Honey did not come again. Gradually Andy became a patriot, avidly following the course of the war. Two months after Junior left for Washington, the First Infantry Division, the Big Red One, arrived in France. True, they had little equipment, and some soldiers had been with the division only a few weeks, but they were over there. Eager to have men in the trenches, the French quickly supplied the Division with arms and ammunition. Soon they were in combat, and the following May the Americans mounted a major offensive at Chateau-Thierry. General Pershing then told Congress he needed two million men in his American Expeditionary Force. Andy decided not to be left behind.

He was big for his age and well spoken, and he could be pretty cool in tight situations, although he was inexplicably nervous when he entered the Army recruiting station that summer. He took a deep breath, swallowed, and told himself to shape up. He would really have no problem. After all, he may have been only fifteen, but he looked several years older. Surely the Army would take him, and the deed would be done before Kate could stop him. He met obstacles almost immediately.

"Name and address?" the sergeant asked. "Why do you want my address?"

"We gotta tell you where to report," the sergeant said, already suspicious. He had seen the likes of Andy before.

"You mean I have to wait?" Andy asked.

"Sure do," the man said. "You go home, and when we get a large group together, we notify you and everybody ships out together."

What could he do? If he gave a fake address, the whole thing would fall through. He had to give correct information, all except his age. Then he would talk Kate into letting him go. That was the only way. He filled out the form, carefully making himself just eighteen. As he handed it in, the sergeant was contemptuous.

"We'll be in touch, kid," the man said.

He went home, worried about it for a day or two, and then asked Kate for her permission. She reacted sharply.

"You are too young," she said. "I will not let you do it." "But the war will be over before I'm old enough."

"You really want to be in the army?" she asked. "I thought you had your heart set on being a banker."

"That was before General Pershing called and I found out that dad was so respected in the military. I want to be like him. I always have. You know that."

She marveled at the change the war propaganda had brought about in him and everybody else. But she would not allow her son to become cannon fodder. Then she thought of West Point. By the time Andy qualified for the Academy and graduated, the war would be over. The idea appealed. After all, she had met Junior at the Military Academy, and Andy would make a fine cadet.

"Then you must go to West Point," she said.

The idea stunned him. He had never considered the Academy, but the opportunity suddenly seemed attractive. He would be following in the footsteps of men like Pershing, MacArthur, and his father. He would be serving his country in uniform, and he would gain his independence. After graduation, he would receive a commission as a Second Lieutenant. He could stay in the Army and start a career as a Regular Army officer, or he could resign and become a banker. The idea appealed.

"Do you think they will have me?"

CHAPTER THREE

His decision made, Andy had two years to prepare for the West Point entrance examination, and he immediately began a program of study and tutoring aimed at improving his chances of winning a competitive appointment. He balanced that program with a schedule of physical workouts designed to condition him to handle the intense stress of the West Point Plebe Year. Kate too went to work, contacting their Senators and Congressman and requesting each to consider Andy for an appointment. With such a definite goal before him, Andy dismissed the idea of joining the Army to fight the Germans in Europe, and the war went on without him. Time passed rapidly. In eighteen months, the armistice was signed, and the conflict was over.

A month after that, Junior returned to Cincinnati. Andy was disappointed. His father was not a Brigadier General, and he had changed. He was not the cheerful man Andy remembered. Wan and sallow, he appeared exhausted and sickly, and thus the family celebration was subdued. In truth, they had no heart for it, especially Jeanette and Rose, for Paul was still on a destroyer in the Atlantic, and Walter had not returned from France. So the family gathered for a quiet dinner, and Junior was not the animated storyteller he had been. After the meal, he asked to speak with Andy alone in his study.

"Your mother tells me you want to go to West Point," he said. "Why is that?"

"You went there," Andy said. "I want to be an officer." "Are you sure?"

"Yes, I want to be like you and grandfather."

"But there is more to it than that," Junior said, rubbing tired eyes. "Let me try to explain. You don't understand what combat is, and that is my fault. All you know is what I have told you and the propaganda you have read in the newspapers. I painted a positive picture of military service, and I do not regret that, but the truth is that war is not some sort of glory thing. The just concluded Great War in Europe was a bloody, tragic mess that maimed and killed hundreds of thousands of good men and set back Europe for many years. The peace treaty just signed may even have sown the seeds of another war, and that is insanity. I erred by telling you stories meant to entertain, and I gave you a distorted view of the soldier's life. Now you need to hear the other side."

"What do you mean?"

"Let's go back to the Bozeman Trail. Remember that Ida and Joseph were at Fort Kearny just before Christmas of 1866. It was then, on a dreary, cold day that the Sioux were being especially aggressive against soldiers who were outside the walls foraging for wood and hay. Captain William J. Fetterman, a Civil War hero just recently arrived and supremely confident, sought permission to disperse the hostiles. The ambitious Captain had repeatedly boasted that with eighty men, he could wipe out all the Plains Indians. In a strange coincidence, two civilians volunteered to join his force, bringing its number to exactly eighty. As they sallied forth, his veteran commander directed them to remain always within sight and support of the guns at the fort. It was a prudent and reasonable order that the brash young cavalryman promptly disobeyed.

"Taunted by daring and impudent Indian braves, Fetterman and his men pursued the savages over the hills to the northwest of Fort Kearny and disappeared. When his force was well beyond the view of the fort and the range of supporting artillery, more than a thousand savages suddenly charged out of the ravines and trees around them. The soldiers apparently fought desperately but were soon overrun. All eighty men were killed, many of them suffering multiple wounds. A few were even tortured to death. Subsequent examination revealed that the confident Captain Fetterman and his fellow officers had saved their last bullets for themselves. Some of the others had not been as fortunate. They had been alive when they were tortured, skinned and hacked to pieces.

"When the sounds of battle reached the fort and Fetterman's force did not return, Joseph requested permission to lead the relief column, and he was the first to reach the ambush site. He found dead soldiers stripped of their clothing and horribly mutilated, the officers with their penises in their mouths. One of the civilian volunteers had been armed with a repeating Henry rifle, and bloodstains in front of his position revealed the carnage he had wrecked on the Indians before he died. The Sioux repaid him by firing one hundred and sixty arrows into his naked body. Those slaughtered men, Andy, are the reality of war. When eighty of your fellow soldiers are dead and mutilated, you live with horrible memories."

"But we were fighting savages," Sandy said. "And I realize that war is a terrible thing."

"We were fighting Red Cloud and his warriors. And they were defending their lands from invasion. Just as we went to Europe to defend France."

"Our soldiers were doing what they were ordered to do," Andy said. "They had to protect our citizens."

"That is a soldier's role, but in that case, leadership failed. Let's take another example. In December of 1890, shortly after Sitting Bull was murdered, Chief Big Foot, the Minneconjou Sioux who had been with Crazy Horse at the battle of Little Big Horn and may have been the warrior who actually fired the shots that killed General Custer, left his reservation. He took with him some three hundred and fifty followers, of which almost two hundred and fifty were women and children. Our good family friend General Miles wanted to stop Big Foot's band, and he ordered a maximum effort to locate them. When a troop of Custer's Seventh Cavalry caught the Indians at dusk on the evening of December 28th near a creek called Wounded Knee, however, the Indians were not attempting to escape. Big Foot was sick, his people were starving, and he was headed for the supplies and sanctuary of Fort Robinson. Surrounded by the cavalrymen, he did not resist.

"The soldiers escorted the Indians to camp and called for reinforcements. All through the ensuing restless night, more troopers arrived, and by morning, more than five hundred men with four

Hotchkiss guns surrounded the camped warriors. Colonel James Forsythe arrived and assumed command. At first light, reportedly drunk, he assembled the Indian braves and ordered his nervous men to disarm them. Fatigue and mutual animosity led to an alarm. A shot rang out, and Big Foot died. Chaos and a riot ensued. The Hotchkiss guns did the most damage. They were five-barreled cannon that could fire fifty exploding shells a minute. Ordered to fire at will, they quickly leveled the Indian tents, killing many women and children and wounding several of their own men. The Seventh Cavalry troopers went wild, pursuing and killing the fleeing Indians. The carnage lasted three hours.

"When the slaughter was over, only six warriors and forty others of Big Foot's people had survived. The soldiers lost twenty-five dead and thirty-nine wounded, the majority hit by friendly fire. When the tragedy occurred, my father and I were less than twenty miles away near Fort Robinson on the Pine Ridge Reservation. Upon receiving reports of the massacre, we assembled a force and rode to the site. Arriving the following day, we found the frozen and mutilated bodies of two hundred and fifty Sioux men, women, and children, strewn over a three-mile area as they attempted to flee. I was stunned, and I wandered the battlefield for hours, trying to comprehend the horror. For Joseph, watching the Seventh Cavalry bury the horribly twisted and frozen corpses of the Indians in a mass grave was worse than finding Fetterman's ambush site. It was a scene straight out of Dante's *Inferno*, and it sickened Joseph so much that except for his testimony at the subsequent investigation and court-martial, he would never speak of it until just before his own death many years later. I myself have never forgotten the bodies of the women and children.

"In the aftermath of Wounded Knee, representatives of the peace movement raised an outcry against the slaughter. Newspaper accounts and congressional pressure became intense, and finally the War Department ordered General Miles to appoint a board of inquiry. It quickly found that Colonel Forsythe had been derelict. The board recommended a court-martial be held. Reluctantly, over the strong objections of many hard-line conservatives, General Miles approved the recommendation and appointed a Board of Officers.

Thus, in 1891 at Fort Laramie, Colonel Forsythe was tried by general court-martial for his role in the slaughter of Wounded Knee.

"Emotions on both sides ran high, and witnesses for the prosecution testified that Big Foot's band had been decimated by disease and starvation. They had surrendered, turned in most of their arms, and camped peacefully for the night. Outnumbered and outgunned, they were not a threat to the overwhelming forces surrounding them. Testimony also revealed that during the night preceding the slaughter, Colonel Forsythe and his soldiers had consumed large quantities of whiskey and fed their hatred with frenzied talk of avenging Custer. Cries of 'Remember the Big Horn' were heard all during the carnage.

"On the other hand, the defense insisted that the Sioux had given up only their oldest weapons and had conspired to conceal their best Winchester rifles under their blankets. According to the defense, when the Indians assembled in the morning, they created considerable confusion. Then, a Sioux medicine man gave a prearranged signal, and the warriors threw off their blankets, raised their rifles, and fired into the surrounding soldiers.

"Joseph was summoned as an expert witness who had fought the Sioux for twenty-five years. He made the following points: The brave men of the Seventh Cavalry were not on trial, only its commander. Over five hundred well-armed soldiers supported with emplaced artillery faced about one hundred poorly-armed warriors whose leader was sick with pneumonia. Under those circumstances, Colonel Forsythe should have been able to control the situation and prevent the deaths of his soldiers and the slaughter of two hundred women and children. Wounded Knee was a leadership failure.

"Reasonable doubt apparently existed in the minds of the members of the court-martial board. So it was that when the verdict was announced, Forsythe was acquitted of all charges, and no one was ever punished for what happened at Wounded Knee. Would you want to be a part of such a travesty?"

"Surely Wounded Knee was an exception," Andy said. "We were fighting primitive people who raped women, tortured captives, and mutilated the dead. The rest of the Army is not guilty for what a poor leader permitted in one extreme situation."

"I hasten to agree that the Army is full of fine men who have served their country well," Junior said. "I would only point out that leadership again failed and that the initial reaction to such a horror was to cover it up. I know that emotions ran high on both sides, and I grant you that the Indians frequently resorted to extreme measures. I don't seek to justify what either side did. I simply want you to understand what leadership in war is all about. Let me continue.

"When we were in the Philippines in July of 1901, General Chaffee took command. He was also a veteran of the wars against the Plains Indians. At the time we met, he was fresh from the Boxer Rebellion, and he had been frequently denounced by the Anti-Imperialist League as a man of uncompromising brutality. His new mission was to bring about an end to the remaining fighting in the islands. The Filipino rebels on Samar planned an appropriate welcome for him. In September the town of Balangiga invited seventy-six men of the Ninth Infantry to visit, men from the same unit Joseph had commanded at the battle of the Rosebud. Once in the town square, the soldiers were suddenly ambushed. Fifty were massacred. The rest fled to their boats and made their way back to Luzon. Returning with reinforcements several days later, they discovered dead Americans still lying in the streets with their throats cut and stomachs slashed open. The senior American sergeant with the unit was upside down in a water barrel with his feet cut off.

"Teddy Roosevelt, then President since McKinley had been shot, angrily directed that the rebellion be crushed. General Chaffee established a separate command for Samar and appointed Brigadier General Jakob R. Smith, an old Indian-fighting buddy, as commander. Standing orders were to burn and kill, anything to subdue the rebels and avenge the Ninth. Smith in turn appointed a Marine Colonel Waller, as the task force commander. Waller was to take no prisoners and to kill any male ten years or older, the same order General Connor had given his men in the Powder River Valley near the Bozeman Trail the year before Joseph and Ida went west from Fort Leavenworth.

"For the next four months, Waller did as he was told. In the process of searching and destroying, his forces burned whole cities and herded the natives into fortified villages. Soldiers then fired on anyone found outside the walls. Soon the isolated guerillas had nowhere to turn for help. Alone in the jungles, they could not survive. At great cost, Waller accomplished his mission and pacified the island of Samar. In the process, one of his officers, a Lieutenant Day, went wild in an orgy of pillage and indiscriminate murder of prisoners.

"Upon receiving reports of mass killings, General Smith ordered Waller and Day back to Luzon for court-martial. It was a repeat of Colonel Forsythe's trial after Wounded Knee, and the military board quickly acquitted them, without prejudice. Day went on to serve a full career, and Waller eventually was a strong candidate to become Commandant of the Marine Corps.

"When the results of Day's and Waller's trials reached Washington, however, even the conservative Congress joined the public clamor for justice and peace. The pressure eventually forced General Chaffee to order the trial of his old friend, Jakob Smith. Again, the charge was war crimes, in this case the killing of prisoners and orders to shoot all males ten years or older. The court had finally learned its lesson, and it convicted General Smith. As his sentence, however, he was simply asked to retire a year early. He did so without prejudice, reduction in rank, or forfeiture of pay and the governments first instinct was to cover it up.

"Again the Anti-Imperialist League went berserk over the mild sentence given the General. The author Mark Twain was the League's most ardent spokesman. Just a few years before, Twain had visited Fort Laramie on a promotional tour, and he and Joseph had become fast friends. At that time, he professed to be a great supporter of the military. Acquisition of foreign territories in the Spanish-American War had changed him. As the conscience of America, he wrote savage articles castigating our government for the bloodshed in the Far East, and he gave frequent, angry lectures about our imperialistic behavior. He wanted to change the American flag from white stripes to black, as a sign of mourning over the killings, and to alter the white stars to skulls and crossbones to mark our piracy. He had great popular support. Yale even awarded him an honorary degree, as the students and faculty wildly cheered."

"These incidents must be exceptions," Andy said. "You and grandfather are not like those people. Men like General Pershing are good officers. They can rid the service of the bad."

"Of course the Army is full of decent men who do their duty and defend their country, but atrocities continue to occur. What does a soldier do when his best friend is killed and the body desecrated? He retaliates. Wounded Knee was no exception. In 1906, three years after President Roosevelt proclaimed that war to be over, a similar tragedy occurred. At a place we called The Crater, near Jolo on the Island of Mindanao, forces under General Leonard Wood trapped nine hundred of the Moros' men, women, and children at the bottom of an extinct volcano. Those Moros were ferocious fighters, and they had killed many a good man. Now the surviving soldiers wanted revenge. Like Forsythe's men with those Hotchkiss guns at Wounded Knee, Wood's soldiers placed artillery on the volcano's rim and fired for a day and a half into its center until all the Moros in the crater were dead.

"Mark Twain and the Anti-Imperialists went crazy. Nine hundred natives were dead, with the loss of but fifteen American soldiers. It was worse than Wounded Knee. They demanded justice, but nobody listened, and as at Wounded Knee, no one was ever punished for the massacre of those women and children. General Wood went on to become the Army Chief of Staff."

"But why are you telling me these things?" Andy asked.

"Because your grandfather objected strongly to what Smith and Waller stood for. He secured his sector of the Philippines without using such extreme measures, and he wanted Washington to learn a positive lesson from the difference. He was ignored. Before you become a part of such ignorance, you should know it exists."

"But only a year ago, you accepted General Pershing's call and went to Washington to become a General. You looked so fine, and now you seem so changed, so tired. What has happened? Where are the stars they promised you?"

"The stars were offered," Junior said, "but I turned them down and requested retirement instead. For you to understand, I must tell you one final story.

"In Washington, my office had mobilized over a million men, and they were trained and on the way to France when the first hint of trouble surfaced. A friend of mine, Colonel Charles Young, asked for a combat command in France. He was the second colored graduate of West Point, a member of the class of 1889. Like us, he was from Ohio and had served many times with the Buffalo Soldiers. He had had a brilliant career and received many early promotions. As a lieutenant colonel, he had been a regimental commander with Pershing chasing Pancho Villa. Now he was the highest-ranking colored officer in the United States Army, and he wanted a colonel's command. I knew that General Pershing had always supported Young's career, and I was positive the request would be granted. I was wrong. Colonel Young was ordered to retire for disability. When that answer arrived in Ohio, Young got on his horse and rode alone to Washington to prove his fitness. The effort was wasted. He was sent instead to Liberia as Military Attaché, where he died of jungle fever.

"If I was shocked at the degrading treatment given Charles Young, I was stunned at what happened to the Ninety-Second and Ninety- Third Divisions. We formed them when 400,000 coloreds answered the call of the NAACP for their members to volunteer for military service. Most selected support duty, but forty thousand wanted to serve in combat units. Thus we formed eight regiments and began their training. Soon, we began to receive reports of racial unrest. In communities around the training camps, we heard reports of fights, police brutality, and hate editorials. Then the Sergeant Major of one regiment was assaulted in Spartanburg, South Carolina. He was a fine man, widely respected in the Division and the Army. His beating by local whites threatened to ignite a rebellion, and race riots were starting. Washington's response was what stunned me.

"The Army made the colored regiments into two Divisions and sent the half-trained Ninety-Second Division to the British and the Ninety- Third to the French. You must know that for years the French and British had been waging a war of attrition, and they desperately needed men to replace staggering losses. They put great pressure on General Pershing to send them soldiers for the trenches. The matter escalated until British Prime Minister Lloyd George and French

Prime Minister Clemenceau personally asked Pershing for men. He then announced that he would not be coerced, and he dictated a policy statement that Americans would serve only under American command. No sooner had that been announced, than the Army sent the two colored divisions to the French and British.

"The coloreds objected to serving under foreign flags. The commanding officer of a regiment of the Ninety-Third, Colonel William Hayward, was especially irate. Upon receipt of his orders, he went to the American Expeditionary Force headquarters in Paris to confront General Pershing personally, and then he publicly criticized the General for sending his regiment to static warfare in the trenches. His protest made no difference. The French eagerly welcomed the Ninety-Third with a parade. The British Attaché in Washington was not as grateful. He wrote a prejudiced letter objecting to the Ninety-Second's being sent to England.

"These were the famed Harlem Hell Fighters, who served one hundred and ninety-one consecutive days in combat, never giving up ground nor losing a prisoner of war. The first American to receive the French Croix de Guerre with Star and Palm was their Sergeant Henry Johnson, who was out of ammunition yet rescued a soldier by charging the Germans with a knife. Fifty-seven men of one regiment received the Distinguished Service Cross. Another lost nearly half of its men, and still another was the first Allied unit to reach the Rhine. One hundred and seventy-one colored soldiers received the French Legion of Honor, and the Ninety-Third was the most highly decorated unit in the American Expeditionary Force. Altogether, these Divisions suffered over six thousand casualties, killed or wounded in action. I tell you these things only to demonstrate that these men served their country well in spite of being shuffled aside.

"After serving in the trenches and shedding blood for this country, the colored soldiers felt that they had earned respect. That has not been the case. None has been permitted to join the American Foreign Legion, and every time they object to this or push for their rights, angry whites react. More often than not, confrontations escalate into mob violence. Riots have taken place in Long View, Washington, St. Louis, Chicago, Knoxville, and Omaha, to name a few. Omaha was the worst, for in that city whites dragged a colored soldier through the streets, riddled his body with bullets, and hanged the corpse on Main Street.

"What I've told you about the fate of the colored Divisions is bad enough, but it's nothing compared to what happened to our old comrades, the Buffalo Soldiers, in the summer of 1917. After they ended their two-year chase of Pancho Villa, they returned to New Mexico. When Congress declared war on Germany in the spring, however, it didn't want the Buffalo Soldiers in Europe. Instead, it had the Army disperse the regiment as guards on the Mexican border. One battalion went to Houston, where the local citizens received it with a storm of overt racial hostility.

"Houston was on a fresh temperance crusade, and they were energetically cracking down on alcohol and prostitution. The Houston police had a long-established reputation for treating coloreds badly, and the city had a new Chief of Police. With the arrival of the Buffalo Soldiers, he sent his cops after them while ignoring similar violations by whites. Adding to the problem, the people of Houston demanded that the posted Jim Crow laws be strictly enforced. The veteran soldiers would not back down. They wanted their rights as American citizens who had fought for freedom. Demanding respect, they tore down every segregation sign they saw. It was a volcano about to erupt.

"After a month of confrontation, the inevitable happened. On a sultry, hot evening in August, over one hundred soldiers mutinied against their officers, seized rifles and ammunition, and staged a three-hour rampage through the streets of Houston. Before they could be stopped, they had killed twenty white citizens. The police arrested 156 soldiers, and Washington directed the Army to investigate.

"The Department of the Army ordered Colonel George O. Cress, Inspector General of the Southern Department, to conduct the preliminary hearings. Colonel Cress had served several years with the Buffalo Soldiers, and he was aware of their record of service. After investigating all sides of the Houston story, he concluded that racial animosity in that city was the primary factor that had incited the coloreds to hate the whites and demand their rights. He recommended clemency. In Washington, the Inspector General of the

Army, General John L. Chamberlain, disagreed. In his view, the riot-ing soldiers had shown contempt for the very laws they had sworn to uphold. Chamberlain was a conservative officer who had never served with colored troops, and there is some evidence he may have been responding to pressure from someone higher up. At any rate, he recommended prosecution.

"The first trial convened on November 1st. Presiding was Brigadier General George K. Hunter. His board was diversified geo-graphically, with a mix of both northerners and southerners. It was comprised entirely of line officers, the majority of whom were West Point graduates. The testimony took a month. Then, on November 29th, after the longest mass trial in Army history, General Hunter announced the verdict. Citing wartime necessity, he immediately sentenced thirteen Buffalo Soldiers to be hanged and gave forty-one more life at hard labor.

"Immediately and without judicial review, the executions were carried out, and a second court was convened. Fifteen more soldiers were tried. After brief testimony, five were sentenced to death, and the rest were given hard labor. Responding to public outcry, however, this time the executions were held up to permit judicial review, although a third trial immediately went forward. Forty more were tried. Eleven were sentenced to be hanged, twelve got life, and fourteen were given hard labor. After brief review, President Wilson commuted ten death sentences to life and reduced several of the hard-labor verdicts. To close the subject, the Army dropped charges of dereliction of duty against the white officers who had been in command when the regi-ment went wild. The colored community was outraged.

"I tell you all this to show that some part of the system is sick. Disgust over poor leadership on the part of men like Smith and Forsythe was one reason that after I returned from the Philippine Insurrection, I left the Army. I subsequently took the job in Washington because I had great faith in General Pershing. I now wonder if even that trust may have been misplaced.

"Why was Colonel Young not given command? Probably because no one wanted a colored colonel commanding whites in combat. But Pershing had always supported Colonel Young in the past. Why not now? And when he sent the colored divisions to the French and British, it was a violation of his own policy, and I find it inexplicable. And after Colonel Cress recommended clemency for the coloreds in Houston, Pershing clearly could have intervened, yet he did not. His silence is what is the most damaging. He had served many times with the Buffalo Soldiers—in Arizona, Cuba, the Philippines, and Mexico—and they had always supported him. When they found themselves in peril, however, he would not intercede. Loyalty must go down, Andy, and my faith in General Pershing and the Army's basic fairness has been shaken.

"In his defense, it has been said that General Pershing is a fine officer who believes that no soldier should have anything to do with politics. For him, much of what happened to Colonel Young and the colored soldiers was just that: pure politics, and he may have believed that for him to have intervened in those trials or postings to the French and British would have been inappropriate. While I agree that soldiers should remain above politics, I now believe General Pershing could have done more to defend the men he had commanded.

"So I refused promotion and took retirement. To remain on active duty would be to accept this sordid business. Racial hatred and distrust are deeply engrained in the Army, and I find that disgusting. And thus I am asking you if you want to be a party to such prejudice?"

"I don't think going to the Academy would mean I was a party to any such hatred," Andy said. "From what I have seen, the Army is far better than the country at large in its treatment of the coloreds. Maybe I could have a positive impact, maybe even change things for the better. I want to try."

"You are an idealistic young man, and I am proud of you. But I must warn you that this evil is deeply entrenched."

CHAPTER FOUR

Andy had to use the next two years well, for experience had shown that more than half of the applicants who took the West Point entrance examination would not qualify for the Academy. He was determined not to fail. More than anything else, he wanted to win a competitive appointment, as Junior had done. On the other hand, if he did not score high enough to win a slot, but simply passed the test, he might also receive a direct appointment to the Academy from a Senator or Congressman. So Kate approached all three of those men to remind them that Andy was the son of a successful officer who had served with General Pershing. She also pointed out that Teddy Roosevelt himself had served with Andy's grandfather and made him a Brigadier General.

She quickly secured a competitive appointment from their congressman and a promise from one of the senators. Both were more than anxious to do a favor for the son of a constituent who was also a prominent banker. Neither knew that Junior was ignoring Andy's ambitions and Kate's maneuverings. Instead, he was immersed in his work. Almost a different person, he took no vacations and neglected his health. He told no more stories, and he seemed to want to distance himself from family and friends. He had other matters on his mind, and he was aging rapidly.

Junior had had a difficult time qualifying for the Academy, but Andy had an excellent academic background. He now studied so hard that in May of 1920, he was selected valedictorian of his graduating class. Nor did he neglect preparation for the arduous physical side of Academy life he was sure would come. He gave up baseball as not being rugged enough, and he took up football because it was physically demanding and growing in popularity. For want of experience in that game, he played in the interior line where the going was rough and the primary requirement was the ability to slug it out with the opposing lineman. In that regard, he also went out for boxing in anticipation of being "called out" as Junior had been. Six feet in height and weighing over two hundred pounds, he was a formidable force in both sports.

After graduation from high school, he moved to Washington, as Junior had, to Mallard's preparatory school to cram for the entrance examination the following February. The scholastic discipline there was much easier for him than it had been for his father, and he found plenty of opportunity to continue his physical training. By the time he reported to Walter Reed General Hospital, where he was to take the mental and physical tests, he felt ready.

After the first two days of the examinations, he was sure he had passed both the physical and mental tests. The third day was an unknown, since it involved individual questioning by a board of officers. Now, Andy waited with other nervous aspirants outside the conference room where the interviews were being held. He was not really tired, but this was the final hurdle. He was positive that the first two days had gone well. He had crammed so hard for the mental part of the examination that when he opened the test, it appeared routine and his answers came easily. The physical too had seemed a snap, because he was in top shape, and apparently no problems had arisen. But the officers inside the room before him were going to ask him questions. What kind? When his name was called, it was just like the recruiting station back home. He squared his shoulders, took a deep breath, and entered.

The board was headed by a Colonel, who was seated in the center of a long table on some sort of dais. Three officers sat at each side, and the seven of them seemed to peer down at Andy. He was seated at a smaller table beside a Captain of the Medical Corps who had a file about Andy's application. At first, the questions concerned the results of the academic tests and the physical examination, but then the Captain changed tack.

"You say you fight a lot?"

"No, I box," Andy said. "There's a difference." "Do you ever lose?"

"Everybody does now and then."

"And how do you feel when you lose?"

"Mostly angry at myself," Andy said. "Usually during the fight I've made a mistake or moved poorly. I know better, so I'm mad at myself."

"Do you consider quitting?" "No. I never think of quitting."

"So you would never quit, never give up?" "I'm not sure what you mean, give up."

"I mean that if you were ever faced with insurmountable odds and could see no way out, what would you do? Would you consider quitting then?"

"Okay, Captain," the Colonel said. "What point are you trying to make with this quitting business?"

"Well, this man has a family history. His father and... ."

"And nothing," the Colonel said. "Both his father and grandfather were fine officers, not quitters as far as I'm concerned. And this boy doesn't look like a quitter to me. I suggest you move on."

That was all there was to it, but Andy could not fathom what the Captain had been trying to say, or why the head of the board seemed to interrupt the younger officer's attempt to explain. Then, after a few additional exchanges, the Captain closed his file, and the Colonel dismissed Andy. The interview was over. Andy was free to return home and await results.

Kate gave him a copy of what she called a "Plebe Bible," a source of information for first year cadets, and she told him the upperclassmen would ask him questions about everything in it. She called it "Plebe Poop" and said he would be required to recall its data instantaneously. He worked at it so as to be ready for what she called "Beast Barracks," an initial period when the beastly civilians like Andy changed into new cadets.

As enthusiastic as Kate was about his going to the Academy, and as much as Andy wanted to talk about what life would be like when he arrived, Junior remained silent on the subject. He was up early and gone most of each day at work, and when he came home, he was withdrawn and uncommunicative. He was different from before the war, even neglecting the horses he had always loved to ride. Andy really missed the rapport he had shared with his father, but try as he would, he could find no way to break into the shell Junior had thrown up around himself. It was a discouraging time for Andy. Not only did he face the uncertainty of waiting for the results of the examination, but he also had apparently lost the father he loved.

And his peers were not helpful. Horrible memories of the terrible war so recently concluded had turned the nation inward, and pacification was sweeping the country. Andy's high school classmates made no effort to understand why a buddy with Andy's apparent potential would even consider a military career. And worst of all, the high school girls refused even to discuss it, much less go out with him. For a boy who had always dated the most attractive among them, their neglect was painful. He forced himself to shrug off their slights, however, putting all his energy into daily physical workouts.

In May, the news came. Apparently, the board of officers must have listened to its Colonel, for Andy had his appointment. He also had his choice. He had won a competitive, at-large slot, and in addition, his congressman was offering the Cincinnati district vacancy. No matter which opportunity Andy selected, he had just a month remaining, for he was to enter West Point at the end of June, a member of the class of 1925.

The Walkers gave a lawn party to send him off. Half of Cincinnati seemed to be there. A string quartet played in the gazebo, and the champagne and caviar flowed freely. Junior's associates confided that they had a position reserved for Andy in banking after graduation and a brief period of obligatory service. When he answered that he wanted to be a combat engineer, Jeanette said he could always build bridges with Walter in the family construction business. Even a smattering of his high school chums showed up to say goodbye, although most of the girls remained noticeably distant. Those who were friendly seemed more interested in attending the West Point fancy balls than in Andy. Paul did repeat the offer of a job in his shipping firm, and Rose urged him to consider it. Andy said he would. All in all, it was a fine party, except that Junior remained with them only a short time before he pled fatigue and went inside. And when Kate and his sisters took Andy to the train station the following day, Junior did not accompany them.

Andy had a Pullman compartment to himself, and the trip took a day and a half. The droning click of the rails combined with the roar of the engines and the lonesome sound of the train's whistle to induce a hypnotic drowsiness. Andy slept when he was not daydreaming of home or wondering about his immediate future. A current popular song was Al Jolson's "The One I Love Belongs to Somebody Else," and thoughts of a full moon and that starry night with Honey kept repeating in his mind. Would he ever find her again? On the morning of the second day, the train pulled into New York's Grand Central Station, and he took a bus and ferry to Weehawken on the New Jersey side. There, he boarded the New York Central railroad for the short trip up to the Academy.

The three passenger cars were filled with young men like him. Most were dressed casually in short-sleeved shirts, slacks, and comfortable shoes. All were traveling light, anticipating the stress- filled reception awaiting them at West Point. Andy threw himself into a coach seat next to a stocky boy with short blond hair and direct, blue eyes.

"Andy Walker," he said, and held out his hand. "Ken Link," the other replied. "Where're you from?" "Ohio, you?"

"Virginia," Link said. "You know anything about West Point?"

"Yeah, my father was class of '90. He fought the Indians and the Filipinos, and in World War One."

"My grandfather was an officer too," Link said, his voice hard, "in the war of northern aggression."

"Well my grandfather was with Grant at Fort Henry and Stones River. That was before he got wounded by your daddy's artillery at Shiloh and limped for the rest of his life. You have a problem with guys from Ohio?"

The other paused and looked Andy up and down.

"No," Link finally said, holding out his hand again. "I guess I can live with that."

"Good," Andy said, shaking with a strong grip. "Where we're going, we have to hang together."

"You got a deal," the other said. "Now tell me what to expect when we get there."

"Well remember, more than anything else, for the first year, it is us against them. We need to hang together and help each other out all we can. They are going to test us from the very beginning. When we arrive, the first thing that's going to happen is some upperclassman will yell at each one of us to 'drop that bag.' When he yells at you, drop it. Don't bend over and set it down. Drop it."

They began to discuss the welcome awaiting them and what Beast Barracks would be like. Other young men joined them, and a lively discussion followed until they arrived at West Point. By then, Andy was established as a leader in the class of 1925.

The Academy rail station was down by the Hudson River, and several signs directed new arrivals to head up the hill to the reception area. The grade was steep, and by the time their group reached the grim upperclassmen waiting at the sallyports of Beast Barracks, several of the prospective plebes were out of breath. Andy was not one of those. His heart was pounding but his step was firm as he walked toward the opening in the great granite walls.

"Drop that bag," a firm voice barked, and it all began.

This was the fourth and final year of Douglas MacArthur's reign as Superintendent of West Point, and he had made drastic changes in the Academy Junior had described to Andy. MacArthur, class of '03, was a war hero with two distinguished service crosses, seven silver stars, and various other medals. In spite of his superb combat record and Pershing's support, he had been reduced to the rank of Colonel after the war. Pershing had revived his prospects by appointing him Superintendent and returning him to the rank of Brigadier General. Two years later, Congress made him a Major General and endorsed the many changes he had made.

Always a casual dresser, especially in combat, MacArthur had neglected traditional spit and polish and relaxed the purely martinet aspects of discipline, alienating some of the senior cadets in the process. But most of all, he had brought about momentous changes in the academy's athletic program. For when MacArthur had arrived, West Point was competing in only three sports: football, baseball, and basketball. He loved athletics, attending all games and most practices. He once even stopped a varsity scrimmage to show the All-American end, Earl Blaik, how to run a pass pattern. More than that, MacArthur wanted every cadet to compete, so he started intramural sports, requiring everyone to play. He told them that "Upon the fields of friendly strife are sown the seed that on other fields and in other days will bear the fruits of victory."

Gradually, MacArthur won the respect of the cadets, so he could turn to the problem of hazing. Because of several hazing scandals when he was a cadet, in one of which he was physically tortured, he had almost been forced from the Academy, and he had never forgotten. Thus, one of his goals was to eliminate the last remaining vestiges of the worst aspects of hazing, and that included the practice of "calling out" a plebe to beat him up. Life for a plebe was still arduous, and the upperclass cadets could be very cruel, but those practices that had resulted in serious injuries to plebes in the past had been eliminated by the time Andy arrived.

Now in his last year at the academy, MacArthur had turned the majority of his attention to the woman he was about to marry. Back when he was a cadet, he had once been engaged to seven women at a single time. Now, he wanted just one. Her name was Louise Brooks, and she was recently divorced with two children. Immensely rich as a result of the settlement, she was experienced, aggressive, and attractive. In a strange coincidence, she had been General Pershing's mistress in Paris while MacArthur was in the trenches as Chief of Staff of the Rainbow Division. Louise and Black Jack had parted as friends, but she remained attracted to military men, and she had set her sights on war hero MacArthur. She told reporters that he might be a General in the Army, but he was a Private in the bedroom. He took that as a compliment, and preparations were well underway for a gala wedding at Palm Beach on Valentine's day of Andy Walker's Plebe Year. It would be the celebration of the year. The New York headlines would read "Mars Marries Millions." After the marriage,

Pershing must have resented losing Louise after all, for he banished MacArthur to the Philippines hoping to end his career.

"What's your name?" the cadet in front of Andy demanded. "Andrew Walker, sir," Andy said.

"Sound off, mister. You're not in church." "Andrew Walker, sir," Andy yelled. "That's better. Now listen up… ."

At that moment another cadet came up and spoke quietly to Andy's tormentor, who shrugged and went on to another plebe. The new inquisitor turned to Andy. A cadet officer, attired in dress whites with a red sash, he fixed Andy with steady eyes.

"New Cadet Walker, I have been waiting for you" he said, in a southern drawl. "I am Cadet Robert Harrison, your worst nightmare. I don't like damn Yankees and cowards who can't finish what they start. You look like a soft version of both, and I'm here to make sure you don't embarrass the Academy by lasting a year. Do you understand?"

"Yes sir," Andy shouted.

"Now dumbsmack, when I talk to you, I want you to pull your neck back so far that I see five wrinkles in your neck. I want to see the pain in your eyes."

Andy jammed his chin in.

"And suck up that big gut," Harrison demanded. Andy pulled in his stomach.

"Pop up that puny chest," Harrison said. "Stay there and keep your eyes straight front. That, dumbsmack, is a brace."

Harrison then proceeded to indoctrinate Andy into the rituals of Beast Barracks, never letting up on the brace or permitting Andy to rest. The physical demands of that first two months were intense. Plebes ran everywhere. Up at five a.m. to prepare for reveille formation, they flattened against the wall in a brace every time an upperclassman passed. When they were not running, they were marching, shining brass, or polishing shoes. They took bayonet drill, hiked in the woods, camped in the hills, and spent hours on the rifle range. They ate "square" meals while sitting at attention. Bob Harrison was everywhere, yelling in Andy's face, inspecting his tent, and forcing him to change uniforms time and time again, just to see how fast

Andy could do it. Andy's legs cramped at night and the pain woke him up, so he could not rest.

In all his life, he had never been so tired, hungry, and thirsty. He began to doubt if he could make it through Beast Barracks, much less the entire plebe year. In short, Harrison was making Beast Barracks a hell, and he was doing a good job of living up to his promise to drum Andy out of the Corps.

None of Andy's classmates seemed to be under such pressure. Kenny Link was breezing along with no special problems. They tried to figure out why Harrison wanted Andy out. Kenny thought it was a southern thing. Harrison was from Georgia, and he hated the memory of General Sherman's march from Atlanta to Savannah. Confirmation of that idea came from Kate. In one of his letters home, Andy had mentioned Harrison, and Kate was quick to reply. The Harrison family was old southern military. In the past, the men had gone to the Citadel, but because of the great popularity of Pershing and MacArthur, Robert had chosen West Point instead. The Harrison antipathy for the Walkers dated from the Civil War. Joseph had fought Harrison's grandfather at Shiloh, and Junior had competed with the father on Mindanao. In these clashes, the Walkers had won far more than their share, and Harrison was using Andy to settle a longtime family grudge.

Once Andy knew that the reputation of his family was at stake, that knowledge made enough difference to pull him through. Thereafter, when Harrison yelled at him, Andy pictured Joseph chasing the man's grandfather through Georgia to Savannah. Whenever Harrison started to haze him, Andy visualized Junior whipping the man's father in the Philippine provinces of the Far East. The thought of his family stiffened his spine, and when September came, Andy was fifteen pounds lighter, but he was still at West Point.

Good things began to happen almost at once. Academics took precedence over the harasment, and the Corps turned its attention to studies. Even Harrison had to knuckle down and study, and that left less time for hazing Andy. The curriculum was primarily mathematics, chemistry, and physics, and Andy was well grounded in those subjects. West Point was an engineering college, and he had prepared for an engineering education. He wanted to follow Uncle Walter and build bridges, and he had the aptitude for it. Harrison still singled him out when their paths happened to cross, but that became less and less frequent. And the more Harrison hazed him, the more the rest of the upperclassmen left Andy alone. The men in Andy's company were especially protective, for they wanted him to play football and box for their unit. And so there was a trade off, and Andy was able to take occasional encounters with Harrison in stride.

Along with other requirements, the Academy insisted that each cadet meet minimum social standards, and every plebe had to learn to dance. Andy was thus required to attend Saturday afternoon group music sessions taught by the Cadet Hostess. She was fifty years old, and not his type, so he had to dance with fellow cadets until he could show proficiency in movement. Once he passed the scrutiny of the cadet hostess, he graduated to the next level: a Sunday afternoon tea dance arranged by said lady. For such occasions she contacted one of several nearby women's colleges, each of which had agreed to send young ladies to the Military Academy whenever the hostess scheduled a dance. Thus, late in September, Andy's examination in dance theory was with fifty beauties supplied by Marymount College of Tarrytown, New York. He did not look forward to the occasion, and he later discovered that the nervous young ladies from Marymount dreaded the session as much as did the cadets.

The arrangement was as follows. The Cadet Hostess and her counterpart from Marymount stood side by side at a table in the middle of a large room. From doors on the opposite sides of this room, a single file of cadets and young ladies approached the matrons at the center table. The cadets were in white uniforms with red sashes, while the ladies wore tea dance gowns. The hostesses introduced each arriving cadet to his dance-by-chance partner, and the newly paired twosome proceeded to the dance floor to demonstrate proficiency. This random selection process was stately, efficient, impersonal, and filled with tension. Each young person in that room dreaded being paired for the hour with a clumsy bore who might embarrass them both into having to attend a second session. Andy was no exception.

He need not have worried. His partner turned out to be Penny Boone, and she was a knockout. With auburn hair and blue twinkling eyes, she was tall enough in heels to look him right in the eye. He was tall himself, with the dark eyes and black hair of the Walker men, and they were a striking pair. They took to each other from the very start.

He made her laugh by describing how apprehensive he had been until he saw her. Then he made her nervous by telling her that when they met, she was so beautiful he could hardly speak. They both relaxed when they discovered that both could dance well and that conversation came easily for them. Andy loved it. When he discovered that Penny's father was a prominent banker in New York, he could not believe his good fortune. He resolved to apologize immediately to the cadet hostess for speaking ill of her dance program. Needless to say, he passed the test.

Deciding they wanted to see more of each other, Penny and Andy found that she could take the train up the east side of the Hudson from Tarrytown to the town of Garrison. There, she could cross the river on the West Point ferry in time for him to meet her at the dock after Saturday inspection and parade. They would walk the mile to the Hotel Thayer where she could stay in the women's dormitory. On Saturday evenings, they went to a movie or danced at a rare plebe "hop." On fair Sunday afternoons, they wandered around Trophy Point as Andy described how Junior and Kate had met. On some days, they took a picnic blanket and explored Fort Putnam on the battlements above Lusk Reservoir. Just before dusk on Sunday, they walked back to the dock, and she took the last ferry to Garrison.

During the week, Andy's afternoons were devoted to football practice. He tried out for the plebe team to represent Army at the freshman level. Their primary duty, however, was to prepare the varsity for its weekly game. After two weeks of tryouts in the trenches of the line, Andy made first-string guard, and more formal workouts began. West Point was a single wing team in those days, and Harrison was a varsity fullback. Once a week, when the plebes adopted the tactics of that week's opposing teams to scrimmage the varsity, Harrison delighted in running his plays at Andy, ducking his head and driving his greater weight at the younger man. Andy frequently found himself at the receiving end of a double-team block just as Harrison slammed into him, but he stubbornly held his ground, looking for a chance to put his helmet in Harrison's face. It was a war. By the end of football season, Andy had learned to stay low with arms and legs spread wide so he had a platform to drive at the charging back. In spite of many cuts and bruises on both men, neither gave an inch. Once MacArthur attended such a scrimmage, and he shook both men's hands after practice. He called them warriors and congratulated them by saying he had never seen such hard-nosed football. Few upperclassmen dared haze Andy after that.

Early on a bright Sunday afternoon in late fall, after Army had beaten Navy in football, Andy and Penny were walking near the Superintendent's quarters, when Harrison emerged from a nearby sallyport. He must have been watching from the barracks, for he immediately came up to them. He was an imposing sight in chapel dress gray with a red sash and a cadet captain's gold stripes. Ignoring Andy, he spoke directly to Penny.

"I am Cadet Harrison," he said. "This kid is not enough man for you. He is a quitter. I have a leave coming next weekend. Let me call you."

"No thank you, sir," she said. "I am quite content to be with Cadet Walker."

"You may not realize," Harrison said, putting his hand on her arm, "this kid is a wimp. You need a man."

Penny pulled away from him, and Andy stepped between them. "You, sir, have crossed the line," Andy said, "and I demand immediate satisfaction."

Harrison paused for a moment studying the two of them.

"You aren't worth the effort," he said to Andy. "Some day she will find that out."

Then he turned and left them.

Andy started to go after him, but Penny held him back.

"He is the one who is not worth it," she said. "And if you hit him, we might not be able to see each other for a very long time. I don't think I could stand that, so right now I want you to take me somewhere and kiss me very hard."

They walked across the Plain and onto Trophy Point, where Junior had met Kate. In a secluded spot overlooking the Hudson valley splashed with the last remnants of the red, yellow, and orange, changing leaves, he took off his jacket and placed it on the ground for her to sit upon. Then he lay down beside her and pulled her to him. A hot spring night amidst the scent of new mown hay came to his mind. He was transported back home to a late spring baseball game, but he did not need the barbecue or white lightning to produce a warm glow. And he did not hesitate. This time, he was the teacher, and she was the willing student.

Their romance flourished at Plebe Christmas. The Academy granted leave to the three upper classes, but the plebes had to remain on campus. West Point was their responsibility for two weeks, and they took full advantage of the opportunity to rid themselves of bracing and square meals. They held dances each evening and almost completely ignored the prohibition against "public display of affection." Penny stayed at the Thayer Hotel for the entire time. West Point was snowbound, so the two of them found sleds and played like kids, rolling together in the snow and pelting each other with snowballs. Flirtation Walk was open to them, so they talked for hours by Kissing Rock, taking full advantage of its name and exploring the new sensations their first experiments at love offered them. At the end of that Christmas break, they were convinced they were meant for each other.

When the ladies left and the upper classes returned, Gloom Period descended upon Andy and his classmates. That was when winter took its greatest toll. Everything seemed gray to them, the weather, the uniforms, and even the cadet faces. Only the onset of intramural athletics broke the monotony of the season.

Andy was the heavyweight boxing candidate from his company, and Bob Harrison represented his mates as the returning champion. The two were sure to meet. The inevitable bout took place at the end of Gloom Period. Andy's roommate, Kenny Link, was in his corner, and the stands were filled. The cadets all knew about the feud between Walker and Harrison, and the word was that one of the two would suffer a knockout. Kenny was worried, because the judge was to be a tactical officer from Harrison's regiment. On the other hand, Andy simply wanted a way to repay Harrison for six months of hazing and the assault on Penny.

The matches were three rounds, two minutes each. Harrison was taller by an inch or so, and about fifteen pounds heavier, but he was not as quick as Andy. When the bell rang for the first round, Harrison charged, but Andy kept him away with a series of strong jabs and elusive moves. Harrison tried to end it quickly with an overhand right, but Andy saw it coming and ducked under it. Once, Harrison draped himself over Andy and attempted unsuccessfully to push the smaller man to the canvas. Andy broke free and continued to jab and duck Harrison's haymakers. At the end of the round, Kenny said it must have been a draw, but the judge might have given it to Harrison for aggressiveness. Kenny told Andy to find a way to punish Harrison.

In the second round, therefore, when Harrison swung another wild right lead, Andy did not duck. Instead, he moved to his left and countered with a hard left hook. Harrison blinked and swung again, and this time Andy repeated his left hook and followed it with a hard right to Harrison's stomach. The bigger man staggered for a second and covered up for the rest of the round, so Andy could not find an opening. At the break, Kenny told him he won the round, but he had to find a way to take the offense. Andy started the third round with quick jabs, and Harrison moved cautiously. Then Andy jabbed hard, doubling up immediately with another left hook. The blow brought blood in Harrison's mouth, and he wildly chased Andy around the ring until the final bell. Kenny was confident Andy had won, but the judge awarded the bout to Harrison. Then he came over to Andy and said, "Nobody ever won a battle running away. You never tried to finish him."

That was the end of Harrison's hazing. Plebe year was soon over, and Harrison graduated. Andy had won. He was free, an upperclassman, one they called a "yearling."

Andy's final three years were spent with Penny. He never considered another woman, but pictured himself as an officer of the Army Engineers with Penny at his side. This was what F. Scott Fitzgerald called the Jazz Age. Women wore their dresses and hair short. Their hairdo was the "Bob," and for the first time, their skirts generously showed their legs. They drove men crazy as they danced the Charleston in high heels and flapper skirts. Millions of them became criminals by drinking prohibited whiskey. Penny was no exception. She had romance in her heart and stars in her eyes. She loved West Point. Her favorite song was Ira Gershwin's "Fascination." For both of them, it was great to be alive and in love. Andy coasted through football and studies, daydreaming of her and their life together. Though they saw each other only on the weekends and not at all when the Hudson was frozen, they were convinced their union was meant to be. At the start of his first class year, after two years of dating, he proposed to her by Kissing Rock. They informed their parents that they intended to marry after Andy's graduation in June of 1925, and both families were delighted.

Andy was saddened by his father's sickly appearance at that June Week. Kate had tried to prepare him in her letters, but he was nevertheless shocked that Junior was so obviously ill. He had lost much weight and his complexion was sallow. Most of his thick black hair had gone, and the little that remained was white. He seemed in a daze, and for most of the week, he was silent. When he did speak, moreover, his words were tentative and halting. He seemed confused at his surroundings and the changes he found at West Point. Even when Kate took him out to Trophy Point where they had met on that gorgeous summer day twenty-seven years before, he was lost.

Junior's illness dampened Andy's enthusiasm at successfully finishing the Academy and winning Penny's hand in marriage, and June Week did not turn out to be the festive occasion he had anticipated for such a long time. Instead, the days dragged slowly by until Graduation Day finally arrived and Andy marched with his classmates to their last ceremony in Cullum Hall. With a full heart and with great expectations, he took his place in that hallowed chamber and looked around, trying to memorize the great portraits, red velvet tapestries, and brass railings. His family was there: lovely Penny, his glowing mother, and his pale father. Andy was to graduate tenth in a class of seventy. With his classmates, he listened impatiently to the unimpressive graduation speaker, and then the culminating moment came. He felt as if he were back at the recruiting station in Cincinnati, but he took a deep breath, squared his shoulders, stood with his classmates, and moved across the platform to receive his diploma. As he did so, Junior rose suddenly from his front row seat, staggered toward the podium muttering incoherently, and fell to the ground, the victim of a massive stroke.

CHAPTER FIVE

A week after Junior's stroke and Andy's graduation, Penny and Andy were married in a simple ceremony at the West Point chapel overlooking Trophy Point where Junior and Kate had met. Because of his father's illness, they called off the reception and deferred their honeymoon. Andy applied for and received special leave to take care of his father. The rumor was that General Pershing personally approved the request.

When Junior was sufficiently stabilized to travel, the family took him by train back home to Cincinnati. For three months, Andy was at his bedside each day. This was a difficult time for both of them, for Junior was agitated and he struggled to talk. His words were barely audible and sometimes incoherent, and Andy had to concentrate intently to make out the story that Junior seemed desperate to tell. With considerable difficulty, Andy pieced together the details and made sense out of Junior's rambling fragments.

The story began with an account of the three meetings between Joseph and the Sioux medicine man, Sitting Bull. The first of these was on Yellowstone in August of 1873. There the Sioux had been killing railroad surveyors, ranchers, and travelers. And soldiers sent to protect citizens had to remain on constant alert to deal with Indian harassment that often turned into pitched battles. Thus Fort Leavenworth decided to conduct a campaign to subjugate the savages. By the summer of 1873, a General Stanley had assembled a significant force at Fort Laramie. His mission was to lead an expedition of one thousand infantry and cavalry soldiers that would escort a survey party from the Northern Pacific along the north bank of the Yellowstone River. Stanley's selection to lead the force was puzzling, however, for every officer in the Army of the West knew that Stanley was a drunk. Rank and politics seem to have dictated the choice. To compensate for his commander's weakness, the Department Commander at Fort Leavenworth appointed good men to lead the soldiers and do the fighting for him.

Thus Colonel George Armstrong Custer commanded the cavalry, and Major (Brevet Lieutenant Colonel) Joseph Walker led the infantry. By the first of August, the soldiers and surveyors had made good progress along the Yellowstone River. Warriors were evident every day and all around the expedition, sniping at workers and attacking stragglers. They carefully avoided contact with the main body of soldiers, however, for the surveying force was clearly strong and ready. Stanley's order of battle each day positioned Colonel Custer and his cavalry in front and to each side as a screening force for the main body. In addition, Stanley always put Colonel Walker in the forefront with the lead cavalry elements, for Joseph now spoke the Crow dialect, knew sign language, and had the most experience in fighting the Sioux.

At mid-morning on August 4th, Crow scouts reported Hunkpapa Sioux ahead. The warriors apparently wanted to talk, so Joseph and five escorts rode ahead with the Crow to meet them. As they neared a small group of Sioux warriors waiting on the trail before them, Joseph dismounted and limped toward the savages, accompanied only by his Crow interpreter. Slowly, a chief in full war regalia then left his horse and moved toward Joseph, also noticeably limping. It was a scene straight out of a very bad melodrama. Angrily, Joseph stopped, thinking that the Indian was mimicking him, but his interpreter whispered that this was the great medicine man, Sitting Bull, who was limping because he had been shot in the foot by a Crow bullet many years ago. With him was the ever dangerous warrior, Whitefeathers.

Sitting Bull held his hands out in a sign of parley. He obviously had no weapon, but Whitefeathers concealed his hands beneath a blanket, possibly holding a rifle. Joseph was finally face to face with the treacherous savages who had murdered and mutilated Captain Fetterman and his men at Fort Phil Kearny six and a half years before. And Whitefeathers may have been with the savages who had almost killed Joseph's wife and unborn son in that attack on the Tongue River.

Joseph studied the famous medicine man. The Sioux was about forty years old. He was tall for an Indian, slender of hip and broad shouldered, and he radiated authority and confidence. On the other hand, the warrior with him was smaller, darker, and more evil looking. The man reminded Joseph of a rattlesnake about to strike, and Joseph readied himself to react if the brave showed a weapon. The group glared at each other in stony silence, the leaders thin lipped, each waiting for the other to break the tension. Electricity was in the air. Finally the Indian took the offensive.

"Why are you invading Sioux lands?" he asked.

"We are not invading," Joseph said. "We're surveying, but you are off the reservation."

"The Lakota are not squaw men," Sitting Bull said. "We will never live like prisoners behind fences in one place under the White Man's rules. The universe is our home. We will die before we submit."

"My soldiers will protect the railroad surveyors."

On hearing those words, Sitting Bull was visibly angry. He seemed about to explode. Snorting and stamping his foot like a wounded buffalo, he continued.

"A large Hunkpapa village is ahead," he said, his voice thundering like a buffalo stampede. "We are not on the warpath, but if your soldiers attack our women and children, we will fight to the death, and many Long Noses will also suffer and die. Leave us alone."

He paused to gauge the impact of his words. Then he turned and moved as vigorously as he could back to his horse. Watching Sitting Bull ride away, the Crow with Joseph said that the warriors who were with him were Cheyenne. Their presence meant that more than a thousand braves were lurking nearby.

Returning to Custer's advance party, Joseph thought about the Lakota medicine man. Sitting Bull was the tallest and most impressive Indian he had ever seen. The man had not harangued with the bombast and hyperbole Joseph had heard before from many Indians. Instead, he had spoken with a deadly conviction that would most certainly lead to future conflict. For his part, Sitting Bull also pondered his first meeting with this long-knife, paleface officer who was rapidly gaining fame among the Sioux as a formidable warrior. The medicine man had a reputation for being able to see into the future. He predicted birth and death, success and failure, victory and defeat, and even the exact day the drought would end. As he rode with Whitefeathers back to the thousand Cheyenne and Sioux warriors waiting and hoping for battle, he forecast again:

"That long-nosed officer will do great harm to the Sioux," he said. "He and I will both die by the bullet."

When Joseph told Custer about Sitting Bull, the village, and the Cheyenne warriors, the cavalryman dismissed Joseph's concerns. Hidden under canvas, Custer had powerful artillery the Sioux and Cheyenne had never before experienced. In addition his troops were now armed with Spencer repeating carbines, and they were veteran Indian fighters. With initiative working in his favor, he intended to attack all villages, because they were the places where he could find enough Indians to kill. He recalled his victory in Kansas on the Washita, when, greatly outnumbered, he had attacked and killed Chief Black Kettle. And so he scoffed at Joseph and sent word back to the main body to hurry and bring up the artillery. As he prepared to move forward, he told his officers that he hoped that Major Walker was correct and that the Sioux and Cheyenne really had a thousand warriors.

"The more the merrier," he said. "We will overcome all of them, and a great victory will be ours."

When the cavalry moved forward, the fight was not long in coming and it lasted six hours. During that tine, the Indians gave a good account of themselves, but the devastating artillery canister shells shocked them and wreaked havoc among their warriors. Joseph led his well-trained "walk-a-heap" infantry in a steady advance, and Custer led his cavalry in charge after charge. The result was never really in doubt, and finally the Indians broke off contact, dispersed into small bands, and scattered in the hills, the women and children having earlier made for the ravines and forests to hide. The soldiers suffered surprisingly few casualties and then moved methodically through the teepees and lodges of the abandoned village, shooting at anything they thought moved, burning everything that would accept the torch, and searching for any souvenirs worth taking. As he assembled his men to set up defensive positions for the night ahead, Joseph took grim satisfaction at the vengeance he had again exacted upon those who had assaulted his family. At the same time, in the hills and ravines surrounding the battlefield, Custer's cavalry continued for hours to exploit their success until darkness and fatigue finally forced them to return to camp.

Then the victory celebration began. Custer ordered extra whiskey for the men, and the more they drank, the more they boasted of their conquests, including the rapes of women and the killing of children they had found in the woods. Joseph objected to such atrocities, but Custer shrugged off the challenge. He reminded Joseph that young Indian boys were known to roam the battlefields killing wounded soldiers and that squaws frequently mutilated bodies left on the field after a fight. In war, he said, no one was innocent.

"All Indians are cowards," he said, "who attack women and children. They deserve the humiliation our valiant cavalry has inflicted upon them."

"The infantry and artillery fought too," Joseph said. "They might have played at least some part in the victory."

Custer paused to take a long drink of whiskey before he raised his hand for silence. Then he stood and proclaimed:

"A hard cavalry charge will wipe out any Indian village that ever existed."

Custer's officers sprang to their feet and cheered, but in less than three years, Custer would lead them in a hopeless charge against another Sioux village, and the Seventh Calvary would regret those foolhardy words.

For two years after that first meeting between Joseph and Sitting Bull along the Yellowstone River, the Sioux and Cheyenne debated their response to the new railroads and the great flood of white people pouring into the sacred Black Hills. In those often-fiery arguments, Red Cloud represented the conservative warriors. They were pessimistic about their chances against the White Man's many new weapons, and they knew that many more settlers might soon be headed their way. They wanted to compromise while they still could, and they called for immediate negotiations with the Great White Father in Washington.

On the other hand, Crazy Horse led the younger men, who hated the White fools who were invading lands that had been promised to the Sioux forever by that same Great White Father. Why should the Lakota trust those who had always lied to them? With their new repeating rifles and terrible, exploding artillery shells, the crazy soldiers were wantonly attacking villages, and the Indians had to do something before all their women and children were dead. They wanted to fight before more White reinforcements arrived. Supporting that argument, Chief Whitefeathers argued heatedly that the Sioux and Cheyenne should band together, swarm over the land in one large body, and destroy Fort Laramie, killing so many Long Noses that the rest would flee.

The debates were many, long, and heated, but the warriors could not decide. Thus, in the winter of 1875-76, they traveled to Grand Butte to seek the guidance of Sitting Bull, the great medicine man who could see far into the future. He listened to their arguments and pondered the implications. At the end, he ordered that ceremonial preparations be made at Wolf Mountain in the Rosebud valley. In June, under a full moon, the Sioux would seek a vision from the Sun Dance.

When six thousand Indians had assembled in the valley and the grass was green along the flowing stream, Sitting Bull had made his preparations. In semi-darkness before the first day, two hundred warriors mounted their ponies to await the sun. As the great red ball broke the hills to the east, Sitting Bull, silhouetted by the sun on the rise above them, gave the signal. Released, the warriors charged a great cottonwood tree he had chosen. Yelling and shouting, they circled around it, firing arrow after arrow into its trunk. Then they cut it down and moved it to be a sun-pole at the site of the ceremony, where they sank it into the earth, to be secured by a vast circle of hundred-foot lines. When it resembled a great maypole, they threw blankets and buffalo hides over the ropes to provide some degree of shading. Then they painted the sacred pole red, white, yellow, and black to represent the four directions of the wind and the four races of men. When they were finished, Sitting Bull blessed their work.

On the second day, one hundred of the finest warriors began their dance. Having fasted since the previous day, ten men at a time faced the sun and jumped up and down to the beat of great drums. Each group danced about ten minutes and then sought the shade as another ten took their place. The dancing continued all day, many of the fasting warriors participating often. Sitting Bull danced seven times before night fell.

On dawn of the third day, self-torture began. Fifty young warriors seeking ritually enhanced stature presented themselves to their chanting shaman. One by one, he seized and raised their skin between the breast and shoulder. Then lifting it up, he pierced enough flesh so that he could thread a thong through the wound. Whereupon, he tied the thong to a rope attached to the top of the sun pole. As the others circled him and great drums beat, the impaled warrior attempted to hurl himself back and break free from his tether by ripping it from his flesh. The torture took hours.

Sitting Bull was the last to dance. He pierced his own flesh and tied the thong to a line connecting him to the sacred center pole. His face raised to the sun and arms spread wide, he swayed and chanted, praying for the vision that would lead the Lakotas out of bondage. At dusk, he lunged backward, ripped free from his bonds, and collapsed. The thongs tore great wounds, and he lay twitching and moaning on the ground while the exhausted warriors gathered anxiously around him.

Until full darkness, he lay there as the others treated his wounds. Then he rose, ate, and rested. At dawn, with all the great chiefs and warriors seated before him—Crazy Horse, Dull Knife, Gall, Two Knife, Lame, White Man, Low Dog, Big Foot—Sitting Bull rose to say that the Great Spirit had spoken. The path was clear. The Lakota must no longer count coup. In the past, the Sioux had always demonstrated their valor in battle by fearlessly charging close enough to their enemies to be able to touch them. No attack was necessary, simply a touching. Each touch counted as a coup. This ceremonious touching was to be abandoned.

From that day on, the Sioux's goal was simply to kill as many White soldiers as possible. None was to be spared. No longer would Sioux warriors risk death by counting coup or attacking alone. All the tribes would mass together as a great, united army and kill every single soldier. And after the Indians had eliminated the long-nose armies, the White settlers would have to flee, and the Lakotas would regain their sacred lands. Then Sitting Bull raised his voice, and spoke even more eloquently. He told the warriors that the Sun Dance vision had revealed that within the year, only the Sioux and the buffalo would be left to enjoy the bounty of the Great Plains. They were now to prepare for a final battle, in which Crazy Horse would lead them, and victory would be theirs before the summer was gone. When Sitting Bull had finished his vision, the listeners' hearts were full. As one body, they rose to begin a massive War Dance.

This was the ceremony that led to the battle of the Rosebud and the defeat of Custer's Seventh Cavalry at the place of the grassy grass on the Little Big Horn. Just as inevitably, as an unintended consequence, it aroused the White nation to make available the men, money, and material that would create the forces that relentlessly pursued Sitting Bull and Crazy Horse until the Lakotas were finally defeated.

After their losses at The Crazy Woman's Fork and Wolf Mountain, Sitting Bull and Gall fled north with four hundred followers to sanctuary in Canada, and Crazy Horse took his depleted forces south to surrender at Fort Robinson. The departure of Sitting Bull from the Dakotas and the surrender of Crazy Horse ended the major battles of the Great Plains.

The second meeting between Joseph and Sitting Bull took place four years later. For up in Canada, the government would not give Sitting Bull and his followers the lands they wanted, and soon relations between the Indians and the Canadians became testy. Finally Canada tired of the Sioux, and the Royal Mounted Police forced Sitting Bull and his people to return to the United States. With two hundred followers, he surrendered to American forces at Fort Buford, just below the Canadian border where the Missouri and Yellowstone Rivers meet. Then Sitting Bull announced that he had become a man of peace who would never take to the warpath again. He refused to join the rest of his tribe at the Standing Rock Indian Reservation, however, saying that he feared he would be murdered as Crazy Horse had been after he surrendered. He declined to leave Fort Buford without some guarantee of safety. Finally, he changed his mind when the Army promised that Colonel Walker would personally escort him to the reservation.

The journey turned out to be the second opportunity the old foes would have to parley. They rode for three days, arguing as they traveled and camped together.

"Your soldiers are killing women and children," Sitting Bull said. "Why do you attack peaceful villages?"

"We attack only warriors," Joseph said. "But don't forget that your squaws and children roam the battlefields mutilating the bodies of our dead."

"The Indian Agents are stealing the Lakotas' land." "Indians sell their land," Joseph answered.

"No one can own the land," Sitting Bull said. "Besides, your Agents take the few supplies the Great White Father in Washington sends us."

"We prosecute those Agents we catch doing that."

"My dreams show me nothing but death and destruction in the Dakotas until all the Sioux are dead," Sitting Bull said. "And you are the one I hold responsible."

"Your people bring this upon themselves," Joseph said,"by committing atrocities and not negotiating."

"Nothing ever promised by the Long Knives has ever been delivered to us," Sitting Bull said. "Look at what happened with your Treaty of Laramie. No white man was ever to enter the Black Hills. Then you sent the soldiers back into those sacred lands. Why should any warrior ever believe you again?"

As they talked, Joseph became more and more uncomfortable in defending confusing policies made in Washington and carried out by corrupt Indian Agents. Sitting Bull could sense this, and he pressed for some solution to what had become a catastrophe for the Indians. The logic of Sitting Bull's arguments finally began to make sense to Joseph. Maybe the old medicine man was hypnotic or casting some sort of a spell, but Joseph began to reconsider his own views. Washington's policies were indeed confusing, and the Indian Agents were obviously corrupt. At the end of their journey, therefore, Joseph gave in to the other's arguments. He promised to intervene with his commanding general to assist the Sioux. That was in 1881, nine years before the final meeting between the two.

The intervening years were difficult for the Indians. The reservations were firmly under the control of corrupt Indian Agents. These men were dictators who paid no attention to what Colonel Walker or any other Army officer might request. And when Joseph visited the Dakota reservations, he found increasingly deplorable conditions. The food, clothing, and other supplies were never what had been promised by the treaties, and the Agents were stealing Indian lands and robbing them at every opportunity. Congress was trying to convert traditional nomads into farmers, and social engineers were attempting to convert the Indians to Christianity, taking their children and sending them east to live in foster homes and be raised as Whites. The Carlisle Indian school in particular gained a wide reputation for converting these savages into model citizens. It was a fraud. The attempt was doomed to fail, for the Sioux clung to their traditional ways and rebuffed every attempt at change.

Washington searched for something that would force the Sioux and Cheyenne to submit, and it determined upon one final blow: the Great White Father decreed that the Plains Indians would no longer be permitted to leave the reservations for their annual buffalo hunt. Evidently, the sight of all those armed savages thundering over the open prairies was too unsettling to the ranchers and settlers, who voted and paid taxes. When thoughtful men pointed out that the buffalo hunt provided the Indians with clothing, food, shelter, and an entire social system, wiser men in Washington replied that Congress would henceforth provide whatever the Indians might need. The decision was firm: the savages were not to leave their reservations. The situation seemed hopeless.

During the summer of Junior's graduation from West Point and subsequent return to Fort Laramie, however, the Sioux received fresh inspiration. A messiah had come. He was a Paiute shaman, a priest named Wovoka who had appeared a year earlier in Nevada and was now preaching the Ghost Dance, a religion that was a mixture of Christianity and the Great Spirit. He gave his audiences a vision of a promised land that was inhabited only by Indians, whose dead would rise in countless numbers from their graves to join the Sioux in hunting great herds of buffalo on wide-open plains amidst bountiful game and in never-ending summers. The shaman also preached that the Indians would achieve that promised millennium by dancing this new Ghost Dance, living peacefully, and doing right.

Many tribes were eagerly embracing that message, but not the warlike Lakotas. For them, the apostle Kicking Bear was the preacher of truth about this new dance, and he had made two changes to what Wovoka said. Kicking Bear's vision was that the promised millennium would be achieved only if the Sioux first killed all the White soldiers. In addition, he furnished each of the warriors a sacred "ghost shirt" that would protect them by deflecting paleface bullets. Kicking Bear's changes were a blueprint for war.

By August of 1890, Agent James McLaughlin, at the Standing Rock reservation, was worried. He had received intelligence that Sitting Bull was about to take up this new Ghost Dance, and he wanted the Army to negotiate with the old warrior before it was too late. General Miles ordered his most experienced Indian fighter and linguist, Joseph Walker, to perform that task, and that order led to a final meeting between the two.

In anger and contempt over the treatment of his people, Sitting Bull had refused to see Joseph since returning to the Standing Rock reservation. When he received a message that Colonel Walker was coming with his son to Hump Butte, up the Grand River, west of Little Eagle, on September 5th, 1890, however, he changed his mind and agreed to negotiate. On the thirteenth anniversary of the murder of Crazy Horse at Fort Robinson, the two met for the third and final time. The chosen place was Sitting Bull's small cabin in the remote Black Hills near the sacred butte that the old medicine man treasured.

The famous chief was then fifty-six years old, and he was show-ing his years. The White man's ways had taken their toll on him. He had tasted the firewater and fed at the trough of fame. He tired easily and he had put on weight. There were streaks of white in his hair, but he had not mellowed.

"Your Agents continue to cheat us," he said. "My people are dying like locusts in the fields, and you have done nothing."

"I've worked hard to help you," Joseph said.

"Your promises are like those of all White men—shifting peb-bles in the running streams," Sitting Bull retorted.

"You hurt your own cause with this Ghost Dance."

"The Ghost Dance is a religion, nothing more. Like your Christianity, it preaches salvation and life after death. You need not fear it."

"Then why do the Sioux speak of war?"

They talked for two hours, but as always they remained far apart.

Sitting Bull then rose and pointed at Joseph and Junior.

"You will die by the gun," he said. "Your sons will do evil against the red, yellow, and black peoples of the earth, who will rise and destroy your male children and give them no rest."

At this point in his narrative, Junior became extremely agitated. He raved about the curse and the danger it meant to Andy. In spite of Andy's attempts to quiet him, he ranted on about the slaughter of women and children at Wounded Knee, on Samar, and in the Crater. Finally, he slept. When Junior awoke, Andy tried to draw him out and persuade him to continue his story.

"Whatever happened to Sitting Bull?" he asked.

Junior paused as if considering a great question. Then he seemed to recall.

"Sitting Bull must have decided that the Ghost Dance was the Sioux's only hope, for after cursing us, he announced that he would parley no more. Then, he limped from the cabin. Our visit had nei-ther stopped the Ghost Dance nor persuaded the chief to remain neutral. Indeed, the meeting almost seemed to have been the deciding factor that persuaded Sitting Bull to join the new religion. Father and I left the reservation frustrated and concerned for the future."

Subsequent events occurred rapidly. In October, Kicking Bear made a clandestine visit to Sitting Bull, and the great medicine man signified his approval of the Sioux version of the Ghost Dance. In November, when he heard of Sitting Bull's secret meeting with Kicking Bear, Nelson Miles, now a General, ordered a vast troop movement that eventually would place over five thousand men, including the Walkers and Lieutenant Pershing, in a great circle around the Sioux reservations in the Dakotas. While that was happening, two thousand Indians assembled and began a Ghost Dance on a remote fortified plateau in the Black Hills called The Stronghold.

When General Miles received word that the Sioux had indeed assembled at The Stronghold for a Ghost Dance, he knew that war lay ahead, and he ordered his forces to tighten their circle. In the first week of December, the General also directed Agent McLaughlin to arrest Sitting Bull and prevent him from reaching The Stronghold. Thus, on December 15th, acting in compliance with the general's order, McLaughlin sent forty-three Indian police at dawn to surround the old warrior's cabin. When the police attempted to take Sitting Bull from his home, however, Indians living nearby stopped them, confusion ensued, and shoving began. Suddenly a young brave fired his rifle into the air, whereupon two of the Indian police, Bull Head and Red Tomahawk, each shot Sitting Bull. He died instantly, and the Indians rioted. The agent police barely escaped being captured and killed, and another great Lakota leader was dead at the hands of government agents who had been charged with protecting him. Agent McLaughlin reported the killing to General Miles, adding that angry Indians from the Standing Rock reservation were rushing to join the Ghost Dance and their brethren already at The Stronghold. This was the series of events that led to Wounded Knee.

At this point, Junior became agitated again. He repeated the curse and harangued Andy.

"Do you understand what it means?" he asked.

"What can the nonsense of an old Indian mean?" Andy asked.

"It means death to us all," Junior replied. "It led to the horror of Wounded Knee. And the slaughter at Balangiga, and the burning of villages on Samar. And those nine hundred Moros who died in the Crater on Mindanao."

"I know many died on both sides in wars Joseph fought," Andy said, "but that doesn't mean he was cursed."

"It led to his suicide," Junior said.

Andy had never heard that his grandfather had committed suicide, and he was shocked in disbelief.

"Is that really true?" he asked.

"Yes," Junior said. "He was cursed and he could not live with those horrible memories and the knowledge that he had been a part of them."

Then Junior gave Andy the diary Ida had kept for forty years, from the Civil War until Joseph's departure for the Philippine Insurrection.

"Read what your grandmother says," Junior said. "You will see that we are all doomed."

"Why are we doomed?" Andy asked. "What have you done?"

"I was at Wounded Knee, and I fought the Filipinos in the Insurrection. Always against people of color."

"You fought for your country," Andy said. "Are you doomed to die because of an old Indian's curse?"

"I have no hope because I brought about the hanging of the Buffalo Soldiers, men who had fought for me, good men whom I let down. For that, I must pay."

"But you didn't hang them."

"It was as if I did," Junior said. "To build up Pershing's expeditionary force, I took away the Buffalo Soldiers' leaders and sent them to France. I left those men alone to their fate in Houston, when I could have intervened. You must always remember that evil will triumph if good men remain silent, and I said nothing. I deserve whatever that curse has waiting for me."

Junior became weaker every day. He took no interest in food, and soon he did not have the strength to continue. Each morning, he asked for the date. Finally, with Kate, Penny, and Andy by his bedside, they told him it was September 5, 1925, and he closed his eyes a final time. It was forty-eight years from the day that Crazy Horse was killed at Fort Robinson, and Andy felt that Junior had almost seemed to select that same date for his own death.

Like his father before him, he gave up the struggle, too soon as far as Andy was concerned. The manner of his passing was a puzzle that haunted Andy. Then the words of the young medical officer during Andy's entrance examination at Walter Reed came back to him.

"Are you a quitter?"

He knew he was not, but he now knew why that Captain had started to cite for the medical board the example of Junior's early resignation from Pershing's staff. And he had been about to refer to Joseph's suicide before the Colonel had stopped him. Andy had not quit in the face of Harrison's hazing during Plebe Year at West Point, but why had Joseph committed suicide? And why had Junior given up so easily?

And what was this nonsense about an Indian curse?

CHAPTER SIX

Ida's diary consisted of three books, each more than four hundred pages long, written intermittently over a period of more than thirty-five years. Her handwriting was ornate and old fashioned, and occasionally almost impossible to decipher, but Andy stuck with it and gradually became accustomed to her script. Her allusions to contemporary events confused him at first, but visits to the library helped, and after several weeks of what amounted almost to translation, he had a fairly clear picture.

The Sanford family in America dated back a hundred years before the Revolutionary War, when Ida's forefathers had immigrated to America from Essex County, England, and settled in Milford, Connecticut. Captain Thomas Sanford served in the Revolution, and afterwards, he moved to the Ohio frontier. His son fought with distinction in the War of 1812, and President Monroe rewarded that young man with an appointment as an Indian Agent in the vicinity of present day Cincinnati. Politics caused President Jackson to revoke that appointment, and so the Sanfords shifted their considerable energies to the acquisition of land in and around that city. Their immense energy and enviable skill in land dealings resulted in real estate becoming the primary source of their considerable wealth.

Ida's father and brother were members of the Society of Cincinnatus, a patriotic organization open only to the sons who were descendents of men who had fought in the war for independence from England. Ida objected to the fact that the society was closed to her because of her sex, and she made it known early on that she was as patriotic as any male member of the society. Her father barely dissuaded her from enlisting as an army nurse in the Civil War, and her diary made it clear that Joseph's immediate patriotic response to the nation's call for volunteers was the beginning of her affection for him.

When Joseph was decorated and then commissioned because of his valor in the war, Ida noted on several occasions her ever-deepening feelings. When he returned home to recover, moreover, she knew he was the man for her. She devoted every possible moment to his healing, and her heart thrilled to see his loving response. When he told her he wanted to remain in the Army and he asked her to join him, she was overjoyed, and she replied that she wanted nothing more than to share his life in service to their country.

After marrying in 1865, they moved to Fort Leavenworth to join the infantry and prepare for its march to the Indian Wars. Joseph was a company commander, and the mission of his soldiers was to protect railroad construction workers as they laid out and built the rail line north of old Fort Kearney in Nebraska to Old Julesburg in northern Colorado. The regiment assigned Joseph and his company the task of protecting the advance survey parties. As they moved out in the spring, Ida was the only white woman with the company wagon train, and her home until October of that year was a tent and a covered wagon. In her diary, she described the journey:

"Transportation was limited to one wagon per company, and that was for supplies. Because I was the wife of the company commander, the wagon was mine. We had a cow for milk and a rooster and ten hens for eggs. Every day except Sunday, we rose before the sun. The soldiers brought me eggs the hens had laid overnight, and we were underway at dawn. The men marched in battle formation about three miles each fifty minutes, and then they rested for ten. A normal day's march was about eighteen miles before the company needed to halt in order to prepare its defenses for the night. Pickets had to be set out, tents to be pitched, horses fed, and the evening meal prepared. With only the camp fires for light, we retired soon after supper with guards posted against the constant threat of attack."

The route they were following was that of the Oregon Trail through what is now southern Nebraska and northern Colorado, and there the Sioux and Cheyenne were on the warpath. Thus, to Ida these Great Plains were dangerous and desolate places, void of trees, wildlife, and population, except for savage Indians, a few ranchers, and the stations of the stage from Kansas City to Utah. Apparently, the stagecoaches impressed her greatly, and indeed, their journeys must have been incredible experiences. Her diary noted that the trip from Kansas to Fort Bridger, Utah, cost two hundred dollars a person, and it followed a route through what seemed to her a virgin wilderness. A fully loaded stagecoach could carry fifteen people, their baggage, the mail, and a large number of packages. On their lonely ways, the stagecoaches were often attacked by bandits or Indians, the latter mostly the Oglala Sioux or Cheyenne under Chief Red Cloud.

The Sioux of the Dakotas had been fighting our forces on and off since Lewis and Clark first traveled up the Missouri in 1804. Of all the Plains Indians, they were the most numerous, organized, and warlike, and from the very beginning, the United States had constantly broken its word to them. As a result, they were more inclined to fight than talk. Now, in the spring of 1866, as his infantry moved westward, Joseph warned her that the Sioux were seeking revenge for the Colorado militia's unprovoked attack and massacre of two hundred Cheyenne men, women, and children at Sand Creek two years before. In addition, the Sioux and Cheyenne were also especially angry over the increased use of the Bozeman Trail through their best hunting lands.

In response, Generals Grant and Sherman were searching for ways to subjugate the savages. The railroads would play a major part in that effort, for not only would the new lines bring many settlers, the trains would also travel directly through prime buffalo habitats. President Johnson authorized the Union Pacific to use the Oregon Trail to Utah and west to California. The Northern Pacific was to pass through the Dakotas and Montana. To the Sioux, these new iron horses were more evidence of bad faith on the part of the white man, as well as forerunners of still more soldiers to come.

Ida was on the southern route, where the primary railroad construction camps were heavily guarded by main elements of her husband's regiment and were too strong to assault. Out in front, and away from the larger body, however, her small wagon train escorting isolated surveyors looked more like an easy target, and the Indians attacked them almost daily. That summer was the start of her education in the horrors of Indian warfare. Joseph tried to clarify it for her.

"Several years ago," he said, "Sitting Bull, Red Cloud, and Crazy Horse, the recognized great Dakota (or Lakota, depending on your dialect) Indian chiefs, were invited by the President (the Great White Father to them) to visit Washington and New York. From those visits, the Indians discovered that more new Long Noses arrived in the latter port each month than were members of all seven Sioux tribes and the Cheyenne put together. The Indians could not defeat the masses of invaders in pitched battles, so they adopted hit-and-run tactics, committing horrible atrocities designed to frighten the new arrivals. Now they habitually torture captives painfully and cruelly to slow deaths, leaving the mutilated corpses for others to find and report. They hack apart bodies, castrating males and stuffing genitals into their dead mouths. White women captured alive are repeatedly raped by entire war parties each night at camp sites on the way back to the Indian villages, where they are then made slaves. The Army has just now rescued several white women from the Indians, and the poor women have confirmed the worst stories about repeated rapes. We have standing orders within my regiment to shoot our women and kill ourselves rather than allow any to be taken alive."

Ida was shocked but she realized that much of the Indian savagery was in response to similar atrocities committed against the Indians by the whites. Captured Indian women were frequently taken by white men as mistresses or forced into prostitution. Ida recorded gossip that General Custer had once introduced his Indian concubine, Monahseetah, to his wife, Libby. He insisted the strikingly beautiful girl was his translator, even though she could not speak a single word of English. Many whispered that she had shared his field quarters for more than two years. That arrangement was not unusual, for Indians often offered their squaws to powerful soldiers and officers in the belief that the generous braves would later receive the strangers' great powers and strength through subsequent intercourse with these women. Newspapers also carried frequent stories about Indians cutting off the heads of the conquered and eating the bodies, and the mistreatment of female captives was a repeated theme.

Andy found many entries in Ida's diary that showed she was painfully aware of these frightening stories, and he could understand how lonely and dangerous that summer had been for Ida. Occasionally, she might be able to visit a lonely ranch or stagecoach station along their route to bathe and refresh herself, but most of that dreadful time she lived surrounded by violent men, in the midst of the stench, heat, dirt, and mosquitoes of those empty Great Plains. She put it this way:

"Now and then, we passed occasional ranches where we bought a little butter and fresh beef. We had visits from the inhabitants, who gathered with great curiosity to see so many soldiers. The streams abounded with trout, and sage hens were plentiful. Once, some Indian squaws traded fur blankets and rugs with us for trinkets. Occasionally for a few minutes in some evenings, we shared a song or a story. But most of the time we were unable to relax for fear of the ever-present threat of attack."

Andy marveled at her courage and tenacity. Not only did she survive that dreadful summer, but by its end, Joseph's regiment had also accomplished its mission. With very few losses, they had advanced the Union Pacific railroad line about one hundred miles west of old Fort Kearney. The survey parties had completed their maps even farther west, and the task of Joseph's regiment along the Platte River was finished. It needed a new mission.

Headquarters at Fort Leavenworth thus ordered the regiment north. Their first stop was Fort Laramie at the junction of the Laramie and North Platte Rivers. Forty years before, St. Louis traders had camped there, and because of its notoriety, the American Fur Company had subsequently built a post on the site. The Oregon Trail passed nearby, and the Mormons used it on their way to Utah. Then 25,000 gold seekers swarmed through on their way to California. It was thus an historic spot, but Joseph's regiment could not pause for long. They had to move west to the embattled Bozeman Trail. By October, they were at Fort Phil Kearny, newly constructed at the base of the Big Horn Mountains. The bad news was that they then were deep in hostile Sioux territory on the contested trail. The good news was that Ida could move from her wagon into a regular house.

Three families had to share those single quarters with the Walkers, but the arrangement was better than living in a tent along the Platte River. In that recently constructed, well-protected, frontier military community, she was safe, happy, and pregnant.

The massacre of Fetterman's force only two miles from the fort just six weeks later must have come as a shock to her, for from then on, Ida's diary contained many more comments about the dangers she and Joseph shared. The loss of those eighty fighting men also left Fort Kearny seriously undermanned, and defensive preparations immediately became deadly earnest. Had the Indians chosen to attack the fort that Christmas, her survival would have been in doubt, but fortunately, harsh weather drove the warriors back to their own winter teepees. Noteworthy too was Joseph's grim account of finding the Fetterman battlefield, for it revealed his hatred of the Indians had increased. More and more Ida wrote of her fears for the safety of her family, the danger of renewed Indian attack, and her complaints about the extreme hardships of the severe winters of the Dakota Territory.

When the harsh weather broke in March, however, and Fort Laramie ordered Joseph's regiment to Fort Smith, ninety miles further up the Bozeman Trail, Ida insisted on going with him. Joseph told her it was too dangerous and arduous. She recorded his objections:

"If you were well enough," he said, "I would willingly take you with me, but the weather will be bitter cold, and our quarters will not be warm. Furthermore, the Indians will be on the warpath. And after the birthing, it would be better if you were to go back East to your family as soon as the doctor pronounces you and the baby well enough to travel."

"My heart was heavy at the prospect of a long separation," she wrote, "but there was no time to hold my hands and weep. I resolved to send my petition to the Department Commander for permission to go up the Bozeman Trail. He had the reputation for being a most efficient and just officer, and he won my heart with his reasoned response."

"I do not see, Mrs. Walker," the General answered, "how it would be possible for you and your child to undertake that dangerous trip to Montana. Think seriously of it. My advice would be for you to stay at Fort Laramie under General Gibbons' care until you are well enough to go home to be with your mother, but I will not be the one to separate a family. I leave the decision to you alone. If it is to be with your husband at Fort Smith, then I wish you well."

And so she went. Joseph's regiment was to complete a new fort on the Bighorn River in southern Montana, deep in Sioux territory. It was named after General C. F. Smith, who had been Commandant of Cadets at West Point when Grant was a cadet. Joseph and General Smith had both been wounded at Shiloh, where Smith died of gangrene, and Joseph was proud to be a part of preserving the brave man's name. Fort Smith was being built adobe-style on good ground, and it was barely completed in time, for spring and the irate Sioux arrived together. Red Cloud's braves soon were attacking woodcutters, hay foragers, and any others who ventured forth from Fort Smith's walls. Every supply train had to fight its way through the hostiles, and any group leaving the confines of the fort had to be well armed. The mission of the soldiers was to protect citizens on their way to and from Virginia City, but the men were hard pressed just to defend themselves and the women and civilian workers inside the fort.

In June, Ida decided that the safety of her child dictated that she return to Fort Laramie for the birth. When they camped along the trail that night near the Tongue River, she knew something was wrong. The soldiers were nervous, and the horses were restless. She was extremely uncomfortable, and she dozed fitfully if at all. She was shocked from slumber by the horrible screams of savage attackers and the volleys of answering fire from the soldiers. In the moonlight, she could see tumbling bodies and hear cries of agony. As she jumped to her feet, a painted Indian seized and threw her to the ground, and she collapsed in pain. Joseph's quick reaction saved her.

Ida recorded the difficulty of Junior's birth, as well as her happiness at his safe delivery. On the other hand, she was not happy that Joseph left them so soon to return to Fort Smith, and in 1868 she was grateful to note the Treaty of Laramie that ended Red Cloud's War. The forts along the Bozeman Trail were to be abandoned and left to the Indians.

Joseph received recognition for his success at Fort Smith, and he was brevetted a major. This meant he and Ida would enjoy the privileges of higher rank, but no increased pay. As usual, federal money was tight, and after the end of the Civil War, the defense budget was the easiest place to cut. As far as Andy could tell, the army of 1868 was very much like the one into which he had just graduated. As Kipling said, it was "Tommy this and Tommy that, and chuck him out, the brute, but it's 'savior of his country' when the guns begin to shoot."

The Treaty of Laramie embittered Joseph. Fetterman had died in vain. Countless other sacrifices had been wasted. Because the peace movement in Washington wanted to save money and reduce the size of the Army, gains won with soldiers' blood and sweat were to be abandoned. Forts Kearny and Smith could no longer be manned, and thus the infantry was ordered to return to Fort Laramie. Angry and frustrated, Joseph prepared for the retreat, his mission along the Bozeman aborted. Immediately after the Army abandoned the forts along the Bozeman that summer, Red Cloud's braves burned them to the ground.

Ida recorded that neither side respected the truce. The Sioux acquired their own repeating rifles and resumed their attacks on the few travelers that dared move through Indian hunting lands. Joseph seethed in anger and frustration at every report of Sioux treaty violations. Again and again, he volunteered to apprehend the perpetrators. His commander at Fort Laramie disapproved most of the requests, not because of any particular respect for the terms of the Laramie Treaty, but because the Army had no money for such excursions. And thus the renegades went free.

Frustrated, the Walkers took some consolation in the quiet routine of garrison duty and the increasing pleasures of family life. For three years, Ida found a measure of happiness in watching Junior grow. He learned how to sit well in the saddle and to take good care of his horse. These were good years, for her son showed promise of being a strong man who would stand tall. With olive skin and dark hair, he was a striking child. Ida noted the reaction of a particular Shoshone chief when he saw her son:

"One of the chiefs made us an astounding proposition to buy our boy. It took time for us to realize he was in earnest. 'Take ten ponies?' he said. 'Certainly not,' I replied. We began to feel he really meant this monstrous idea. 'Twenty ponies?' When we refused once more, he then offered to trade his squaw for the boy, evidently thinking that after the exchange, she could sneak away from us, and he would still have our son. At that, I took our dear boy into our quarters, and a terrible fear seized me that the Indian might seek to steal him. After that, we guarded him more closely than ever."

Joseph used this brief interruption in Plains Warfare to study Indian sign language and the Crow dialect, although he never passed up an opportunity to chase warriors who violated the treaty or disturbed the peace. Most got away, and Joseph remained obsessed with the injustice of it all. The Indians had killed his men and mutilated their bodies. Savages had assaulted his wife and unborn child, and still they escaped without paying for their transgressions.

Reports came to Fort Laramie that hard-liners in Washington had found a way to come to Joseph's aid. In 1871, President Grant persuaded Congress to address the Indian question, and it decided to abrogate the treaties. Henceforth, the Indians would not be treated as nations. Instead, they were to become wards of the State. They would be given land that would be reserved for them, and they were to stay there. Those that obeyed would be provided with food, clothing, and education by the government. Those who disobeyed were to be hunted down and killed. It was a terrible decision, for it destroyed the Indians' way of life.

Joseph was promoted to Lieutenant Colonel and regimental command at Laramie. That meant his family could move from the barracks-like building occupied by the junior officers and their families (they called it Bedlam) into a separate house, one of three reserved for the commanders. The Walkers' new home was a two-story, wooden cube, with a living room, dining room, and kitchen on the ground floor and two bedrooms on the second. Ida now had a porch, a fireplace, a well, a wood-burning stove, and her own outhouse, all of which were great improvements over the wagon and tent she had used ten years before along the Oregon Trail. Junior had his own bedroom, and the family shared a life filled with routine. Joseph drilled his men, Junior studied for college, and Ida recorded her observations of Indian life.

"My first impression of domestic life among the Indians was intensely disagreeable and prejudiced me greatly against the chiefs. I saw one of them walking in front of a squaw, whose back was bent under a heavy sack of flour, while he, with his strong body wrapped in a gaily colored blanket, carried nothing but a walking stick. Did he offer to help her carry the load? No indeed. On the contrary, he would use the stick to poke her in the back if she fell behind his pace. The brute. How I wished for a good strong soldier to knock him down. When I poured out my tale of outrage to my husband, he said that if the chief had treated the squaw differently, trouble would have resulted in his tribe. My indignation was wasted.

"Another chief before parting with his wife to go on a hunting trip told her to move camp and meet him in five days at a particular place. When he arrived at the appointed location, however, she was not there. Instead of a smiling wife and clean clothes, he found nothing. Returning home to his disobedient bride, he found that she had been advised by her mother not to move. He immediately took his gun and killed the mother-in-law so that he would not be disobeyed in the future."

In 1873, their peace was interrupted by General Stanley's campaign along the Yellowstone River, the time when Joseph first met Sitting Bull. Upon his return, Joseph told Ida about that meeting, his concerns about George Custer, and his fears for the Indian women and children in the village the cavalry had burned. When two years later, Custer stirred up a hornets' nest in the Black Hills with reports of gold, Joseph told her no good would come of it. The battles on the Rosebud and Little Big Horn confirmed his fears. As the Army pursued and punished Custer's killers, however, Ida noted Joseph's growing disenchantment over the treatment of Indian women and children. As he led Sitting Bull home from Canada and the old warrior urged better treatment for the defeated tribes, he therefore agreed to help.

Joseph was in a difficult position. He told Ida he had but three awkward choices. He could resign his commission and hold press conferences, give speeches, and write articles telling all who would listen about the evil Agents and the injustices they were perpetrating against the Indians we had promised to care for. If he did that, he would be granted momentary fame and then forgotten, having really done nothing to solve the problem. On the other hand, he could keep his commission, but use it as a pulpit of protest. If he did that, he ran the risk of being transferred and banished to some place where he could no longer influence the situation.

He decided on a third course. He conducted a low key, but constant campaign for reform from within the Army. The danger was the risk of being corrupted by the system he was trying to change. It was a risk he would take. Whenever his soldiers tracked down a brave who had left a reservation, therefore, his report contained a section on the abuses of power by the Indian Agents and a compendium of substandard conditions on the reservations that might have caused any reasonable person to attempt escape. Whenever a scientific or cultural expedition came to Fort Laramie, he joined it and entertained the group with vivid stories of the Indian Wars and descriptions of poor treatment of the tribes on the reservations. He wrote articles for eastern newspapers about mistreatment of Indian women and children. If a traveling writer or humorist like Mark Twain visited, and many did, Ida entertained them, and Joseph treated the man to a parade, all the while using the opportunity to regale his guest with tales of the Indians' plight. His efforts were wasted, for Indian atrocities were too fresh in people's minds and Custer's death was too recent for the public to forgive. Nothing changed except that Joseph earned a reputation as a peace activist.

For the next seven years, Ida recorded many incidents of maltreatment of the reservation Indians, who lost more than two- thirds of their land. Treaties had granted them 150 million acres forever, but by 1890 they retained less than a third of that. Land speculators and the Agents had taken the rest, while giving nothing of real value in return. The railroads compounded the Indians' problems, for while Junior was studying back east, the most important factor in changing the northern plains was the iron horse. As the warrior chiefs had foreseen, the Northern Pacific, now the Great Northern, completed its rail and spur lines across the plains, and the area was thrown open to massive inroads of settlement, ranching, and construction. By the time Junior brought Kate to Fort Laramie, three million Americans had settled in Kansas, Nebraska, and the Dakotas. On the other hand, the Indians, who had numbered about 225,000 on those prairies when Ida and Joseph had first gone west after the Civil War, were now reduced to half that number. Poverty, war, and the white man's diseases, especially smallpox, for which the Indians had built up no immunity, had taken a severe toll on the rest. Those who survived had no future. The odds were stacked against them. This was the situation that led to the Paiute shaman and the Ghost Dance after Junior returned from West Point.

Ida had not been able to travel east for Junior's graduation and wedding. She had been far too sick. Never a robust woman, she had been hard hit by twenty-five severe Dakota winters in poorly heated homes, and the cold had gradually taken its toll on her. She was not disappointed, therefore, when Joseph was relieved of his command and sent back east after his controversial testimony in the Wounded Knee court-martial. Winters at Fort Totten in New York were nowhere near as harsh and cold as those in the Dakota Territory, and her new quarters had much better insulation.

When Ida recorded Joseph's account of Sitting Bull's curse on the Walker family, she treated it as unimportant. Her only concern was the fact that Joseph seemed to see a correlation between the curse and the massacre of Wounded Knee. He felt he had failed in his promise to help Sitting Bull, and the old man's murder weighed heavily on his mind. Whenever he brought up the horrors of that battlefield, therefore, she would comfort him and change the subject. By the time General Miles recalled Joseph from exile for the Spanish-American War, she had dismissed the Walker curse as a joke. She was too busy helping Kate take care of Jeanette and Rose during the three years Joseph and Junior were fighting in the Philippine Islands. In fact, she was so busy taking care of the girls that she neglected her own health, and she was easy prey for the flu epidemic that killed her.

Ida's last recorded words in her diary were her hope that Joseph would return from the Philippines to be with her. The next entries were written by Junior four years later.

"On September 5, 1890, in that remote cabin when Sitting Bull told Joseph and me that our family would be cursed by conflict with people of color, I did not take him seriously. He seemed senile and less than lucid. Subsequent events have raised doubts in my mind. Sitting Bull's death shortly thereafter shook my confidence, and the horrors of the battlefield at Wounded Knee implanted a visual image I cannot forget. As the curse had forecast, neither Joseph nor I slept easily after that. I am convinced that the old chief's words and death, as well as the images of frozen Indian bodies were the reasons Joseph testified at Colonel Forsythe's trial. He was trying to justify himself in the eyes of a dead man. I am positive that ten years later, the memory of Wounded Knee and the subsequent court-martial influenced him to deal fairly with the Filipinos in Zambales Province. The excesses committed by some military leaders on Samar and Mindanao sickened him, and the laughable courts-martial of Glenn, Day, Walker, and Smith convinced him of the need for change. How could we expect our troops to control themselves if their leaders did not show the way?

"Joseph's failure to reach Ida before her death saddened him so that he could not continue, and he asked to be retired. His promotion to Brigadier General upon leaving the service after forty-one years gave him hope that he might be successful in bringing about changes in Army doctrine and attitude. Alas, that was not to be. After three years of letter writing, newspaper interviews, and pleas to congressmen, he was shocked beyond comprehension by the slaughter of the Moro women and children in the Crater on Jolo. His old friend, Mark Twain, seemed to be correct: the pressures of combat could lead the Army Joseph loved to extreme excess. Depressed by that conviction and lost without Ida's support and love, on the twenty-ninth anniversary of Crazy Horse's murder, Joseph killed himself.

"I do not believe that an old Indian's curse killed Joseph, On the other hand, I am convinced that after hearing Sitting Bull's final words and then learning about the medicine man's murder just three months later, Joseph became obsessed with the Army's treatment of people of a different color. When he heard about continuing atrocities in the Philippines, his obsession only deepened. The news of the slaughter in that crater led to his final desperate act.

"How could I possibly sum up the life of this man? I urge the reader not to think harshly of him, for I believe he had a good heart. Initially, he may have been obsessed with hatred for the Sioux, largely because of his experiences along the Bozeman Trail, especially the attack on Ida at the Tongue River. Over the course of the years, however, that hatred slowly changed to respect for the Indians and compassion for their plight. In changing and acting on their behalf, he grew as he learned, for he was a wise and thoughtful person. He served his country with considerable skill and dedication, attaining great merit, but even as he pursued the violent and aggressive life of a soldier at war, he was always considerate of others. He urged his men to live by a higher code. In spite of occasional reports of atrocities in combat and resultant attacks on his calling by the newspapers, he considered the profession of arms to be honorable. He loved ardently: his family, his country, and even his enemies. The manner of his going was evidence of his great compassion and sadness over the plight of the unfortunate peoples of the world, especially that of the Plains Indians.

"One measure of a man is the number of people who love him, and many people loved Joseph Walker deeply. The men who served under him seemed universally to honor and venerate him. I never found even a hint of rancor directed by subordinates against him. When you consider that he led soldiers for forty years, from the Civil War, through the Indian campaigns, to the Spanish American War and Philippine Insurrection, often under the most dangerous of circumstances, that is a powerful testimony to his ultimate worth.

"Joseph Walker could not live with his memories, and so he died by his own hand. What forces caused that act, I can only surmise. At first I thought it must have been Ida's death. Then I realized that the hundreds of dead Moros in that crater on Mindanao were related in his mind to the frozen bodies at Wounded Knee. I do not mean to dismiss the possibility of an act of vengeance by the Great Spirit. If that is true, it makes no difference, for in my case, I am overwhelmed by the manner in which the government treated those fine men I served with, the Buffalo Soldiers. My role in separating them from their leaders at such an important time continues to sadden me, and over these last few years, the knowledge that I played even a small part in their executions fills me with overwhelming guilt.

"Pray for us."

CHAPTER SEVEN

Andy finished Ida's diary shortly after Junior's death. This was the mid-twenties, and our peacetime Army had neither money for training nor equipment to train on. For the time being, it did not need Lieutenant Andy Walker. He therefore requested and received sixty days leave to settle family affairs. After they had interred Junior in the cemetery overlooking the Hudson River at West Point, Andy's concern was for his mother, but Kate told him she was happy where she was. She certainly did not wish to return to Boston, from which she had been gone for more than thirty-five years. Cincinnati was home now. Back east was the past; Jeanette, Rose, and their families were the future. She was a grandmother four times over, and she elected to stay put.

His family responsibilities in order for the moment, Andy finally had time to take Penny on their delayed honeymoon. They had more than a month before he would be required to report to Fort Belvoir for engineer training, and they decided to use the time to visit some of the places mentioned in Ida's diary. They wanted to see for themselves the Great Plains and famous Indian battlefields Ida had described, and the excursion would clear their minds from the immediate impact of Junior's sad funeral. So they stuffed Andy's 1918 Model T with provisions and set out for Wyoming. Knowing that the roads would be terrible and maps scarce, they figured that the best route would be between the biggest cities, where gas and hotels could also be found. They planned therefore to stop at St. Louis, Kansas City, St. Joseph, and Lincoln. This last was a little north of the most direct path, but it would put them close to the start of the old Oregon Trail, which they wanted to follow. The biggest gap between cities of any size would be along that trail through

North Platte to Cheyenne, so they decided to make an adventure out of it, taking sleeping gear and extra gas just in case.

"The first wagon trains along the trail started in the spring of 1842," Andy told her, "the year that Joseph was born. Their goal was free land on the Columbia River in Oregon."

"And this was where Ida went?" she asked.

"Only out to the Wyoming border," he said. "The full trail to Oregon was a little over two thousand miles long. And the wagon trains went only about fifteen or twenty miles a day. They set out in the early spring, most of them loaded too heavily, and they needed to make it through the South Pass of the Rocky Mountains in Wyoming before winter set in or they risked death in the snow and cold. To make better time, they quickly jettisoned excess weight as they went. Even so, many didn't make it. Some thirty thousand died along the trail before the coming of the railroads rendered it obsolete."

"I'm not sure I like the sound of that," she said. "We'll be safely back before the end of the month."

And they encountered no real problems as they spent their first real moments together since marriage. As it turned out, they passed a delightful week along the country roads and Main Streets of the mid-West. In small hotels and cafes, they got to know each other, and after two flat tires, they spent one crisp night under the clear October stars along the Oregon Trail. Once under the full moon that night, he called her Honey, but it was a mistake easily covered up.

When they reached Cheyenne, the Chamber of Commerce produced fairly good directions north to Fort Laramie. At that site, however, they were disappointed to find nothing but waste, rubble, and abandoned buildings. By the end of the Indian Wars, Fort Laramie had grown into a large installation of some fifty buildings and a grand parade field, but when those wars were over, it had been sold. Its new owners had gone bankrupt and left it to rot. The barracks deteriorated, the battlements collapsed, and the decaying houses bore little resemblance to the grand trading post and vital headquarters Ida had described in her diary. They could not visualize thousands of Indians gathered around the fort for months to negotiate with the representatives of the Great White Father. Joseph was there too, back in 1868, and out of those contentious meetings came the great Treaty of Laramie, still in effect fifty-seven years later and the subject of continuing controversy. How could this dry, desolate spot before them have had such a profound effect on their family, the Sioux, and the nation?

"Sorry Penny," Andy said. "A trip for nothing."

"It was pretty good in that bedroll under the stars." "You want to go on?"

"Of course," she said. "Let's make more memories."

And so they went on to Casper to spend the night and seek directions to Fort Phil Kearny. Between Buffalo and Sheridan to the east of the highway, it was still not easy to locate. Only seventeen acres, it had burned to the ground when the Cheyenne torched it after the soldiers were ordered to abandon the forts on the Bozeman. When Penny and Junior finally found it, little remained. Ida had described the place as rectangular, with twenty-foot, vertical- log walls. Only small mounds of earth remained to indicate the fort's bare outlines. From those mounds, Andy peered north where Fetterman's tragic force had sallied forth in its doomed quest for glory. The distance to the hills over which the hapless force disappeared seemed far too short, and the fields of fire were extremely limited. To Andy, an enemy unexpectedly charging over the rise would overrun the Fort's defenders before an alarm could be raised.

"Ida said she felt safe here," he said. "I don't see how. And after Fetterman's massacre, there were very few soldiers left in the fort."

"It was still better than a covered wagon," Penny said. "Just barely," he said. "Let's find the Rosebud."

That battlefield was even more remote. Far from the main routes, the place was supposedly out in a farmer's field, off an unimproved road, and nothing existed to mark its exact location. When they finally found the man who owned the lands, he claimed to know exactly where the battle had been fought, but the place was not what Andy had expected. In grandiloquent terms, Junior had described Joseph's life and death battle, yet the Rosebud was just a trickle of a stream, and strategic hills that had been keys to control of the fields of fire were but small knobs. Nothing remained to hint at the great Indian charge that almost overran Joseph's battalion. Andy was discouraged.

"Almost a thousand Indians came over that hill," he said.

"And Joseph had only three hundred men down there." He pointed out what he thought Junior had described. "The Indians circled round and round the trapped infantry. The battle was almost lost before it started."

"What saved them?" she asked.

"Discipline, training, organization, rocks they took cover behind, ditches they dug, and the timely charge of friendly Crow and Shoshone Indians. As it was, they suffered many dead and wounded. It was a bad scene."

"And this was just before the Little Big Horn?"

"A week before. General Crook called it a victory. Then he went over to the Yellowstone to lick his wounds and fish. While he was camping on that lake, Custer died."

The Big Horn battlefield was just north, on the other side of a Cheyenne Indian Reservation. It was such a short distance away that General Crook could easily have joined with and saved Custer. The failure to do so was incomprehensible. On the field itself, enough had been preserved for them to visualize the fight. As he stood on the hill where Custer had died, Andy could not believe how close they were to the great village that the General had attempted to take by storm. The distances were so short and the terrain so open that anyone but Custer would have been overwhelmed at the sight of thousands of teepees below him just an easy mile away. How could anybody in his right mind have charged so many Indians with a force of just two hundred and fifty cavalrymen, and without infantry or artillery to support them? Yellowhair, as the Sioux called him, must have been deceived by his easy successes on the Washita and Yellowstone Rivers.

"What a waste," he said. "And Joseph might have been lost in exactly the same way."

"What do you mean?" she asked.

"Commanders like Custer and Crook who have big egos do not care enough about their men."

Both Penny and Andy were beginning to understand the harsh conditions under which his grandfather had fought. The trip was starting to be worthwhile after all. After they had spent just an hour wandering the battlefield, shadows began to lengthen, and they had to drive to Hardin for the night.

The next morning, they rose early and set out to find Fort Smith. According to their sources, it was about fifty miles up State Route 313 toward the north end of Bighorn Lake. They were headed for the town of Yellowtail, near which was a crossroad that some maps identified as C. F. Smith. There, a sign on the single, run-down store was the only indication that the site of the old fort might also be near. A white-haired lady was rocking on the front porch.

"Sure, I know the fort," she said. "It's in a field about a half mile back where you came, but there ain't no way to get to it. An old Indian owns the place, and he won't let no white man past his gate. I'd stay away if I was you."

"But my folks spent two winters there fifty years ago," Andy said. "We just want to see where they lived."

"I don't think he'll let you," she said. "Says he hates whites. He's got guns and bad dogs, and everybody there goes around armed. It might even be dangerous. A smart man would leave well enough alone."

"We'd still like to give it a try," Andy said. "How can we find it?" "Curiosity killed the cat, but like I done said, it's about a half mile on the left. They's a brown fence and a gate. Sign on the mailbox is Whitefeathers."

Andy was amazed and delighted. From what Junior had said, Whitefeathers had been born about the same year as Joseph, and if this was the same person, he would be almost eighty years old. He had seen everything back then, and if he could remember anything, he would be an invaluable source and a treasure of information. They had to try.

Almost exactly a half-mile back toward Hardin and the Big Horn battlefield, they found the gate. It was set back in a brown slat-board fence so that Andy could pull off the dirt road to open it. And as the old storekeeper had said, the name on the mailbox was

Whitefeathers. The gate was locked with a strong chain and covered by signs reading "Keep out," "No trespassing," and "Private." About two hundred feet from the gate up an ill-kept gravel driveway was a dark sprawling wooden house that needed paint. Behind the house was a large orchard where Junior could see a dozen people working, but they gave no indication they had noticed him. No one glanced up or paid any attention whatsoever to Andy, Penny, or their car.

Beside the lock on the gate was a bell hanging on a chain. When Andy rang it, a satisfying clanging sounded over the silent fields, but nobody in the field looked up or reacted in any way, and Andy could see no activity behind the closed windows at the house. After a few minutes without a response, he rang again, this time as loudly as he could. After that, he went to the Model T and tooted the horn. Then he took out a picnic basket and set it on the car's bonnet. He and Penny spread out a lunch and settled down to eat. Occasionally, he tooted the horn or rang the bell.

After an hour of this, a man appeared on the porch of the house, descended the steps, and walked slowly toward them. He was wearing jeans, a denim jacket, and a black cowboy hat, under which Andy could make out long, straight, black hair and a round, brown, beardless face. He wore beat-up cowboy boots and carried a double-barreled shotgun, over and under. With a scowl on his face, he looked as mean as he obviously intended to. Andy had to stop himself from raising his right hand and grunting "How?" The man paused about ten feet short of the gate, shifted the shotgun so that it could be quickly raised to point at Andy, stared at them, and snorted.

"My name is Andy Walker," Andy said. "I would like to see the remains of Fort Smith."

"Nothin' to see." the man said. "Go away."

"My grandfather was Joseph Walker," Andy went on. "He commanded soldiers at the fort for a year. I just want to walk that ground."

"Can't. It's private land."

"Is Chief Whitefeathers still alive?" Andy asked. "I want to meet him. Then I'll go away."

The Indian glared at Andy as if he were a rattlesnake needing to be killed. Then, without a word, he turned and went back to the house. Andy consoled himself that the shotgun was no longer pointed at them, and that was progress of a sort. Soon, the front door of the house opened, and their interrogator walked slowly back to the gate.

"You said Joseph Walker?" he asked. Andy nodded.

The Indian grunted again and then slowly and deliberately unlocked the gate, reluctantly opened it, stood aside so they could enter, and then just as carefully locked them inside.

"This way," he said and turned toward the house.

They trailed him to the front door and into the darkened house. Andy was beginning to think this was not such a good idea. Only the old lady back at the crossroads knew they had headed for Whitefeathers' place, and she had not appeared to care one way or the other. They entered a dark room in which the only light was from shaded windows and a small fire burning in an open fireplace at its center. Smoke rose toward an opening overhead. On the walls were shields, headdresses, and hide blankets. It looked and smelled like the stale inside of a large teepee in the winter. On the floor facing them on a pillow lay an Indian wrapped in a buffalo robe, the oldest man Andy had ever seen. Behind him stood two large, armed Indian males. The man who had led them to the house pointed to pillows across the fire from the old man. Penny and Andy were obviously meant to sit there.

"Chief Whitefeathers," the escort said and then joined the others, who seemed to be bodyguards. Before Andy could say anything, the old man spoke, without looking up, in a whisper that Andy had to lean forward to hear.

"What do you know of Joseph Walker?"

"He was the angry white chief who fights the Sioux," Andy said in the Crow dialect. Junior had taught him the words in the native language. It was the only Crow he knew.

The answer seemed to startle Whitefeathers. "Who was your father?" he asked.

"Junior Walker," Andy answered. "He said you attacked his mother at the Tongue River Ford in 1867, just before he was born. Joseph shot the man who did it. Were you there?"

Whitefeathers considered the question.

"I was with Red Cloud against Fetterman," he said. "Do you know of that battle?"

"I know it was more a massacre than a battle." Whitefeathers almost smiled at that.

"I also know about the Hayfield and Wagon Box fights," Andy said. "Were you there also?"

The semblance of a smile vanished.

"I was born the same year as Chief Crazy Horse," the old man said, his voice faint, as if he was trying to remember. "For years, we battled side by side against the White Men who were invading our lands. We defeated Old Yellow Hair. So after Crazy Horse surrendered, you murdered that great chief. He was as great as the Medicine Man, Sitting Bull, and you killed him too. You betrayed us so many times. Why should I believe you? No White Man keeps his word."

"My grandfather met Sitting Bull three times," Andy said, "once before the Yellowstone battle and twice more after that."

"And your father?"

"He went with Joseph to see Sitting Bull at his cabin before the great Ghost Dance at The Stronghold."

"Were they at Wounded Knee?" Whitefeathers asked. "Did they kill Big Foot and his children?"

"No, they arrived the day after," Andy said. "They took no part in the battle."

Satisfied that Andy was a Walker, Whitefeathers raised his voice. He closed his eyes as if he were in a trance and began a rambling soliloquy about the forts along the Bozeman Trail, the Long Noses' cannons and their attacks on Sioux villages, and the soldiers breaking the promises of the Treaty of Laramie by invading the sacred Black Hills. His voice turned to glee when he recalled Fetterman's death, Crook's Rosebud defeat, and the Lakota's Grassy Grass triumph. He droned on in contempt as he recalled attacks on helpless women and children at Slim Buttes, Wolf Mountain, and Wounded Knee. He spoke bitterly about the murders of Crazy Horse and Sitting Bull, and his voice filled with sorrow as he recalled the imprisonment of the Lakota on the Standing Rock Reservation. Finally he ended his monologue in triumph: he owned Fort Smith, and no white man would ever regain that land. His voice was hypnotic, and while he was speaking, Andy lost track of time. Then the old man paused as if trying to recall something very important. After a moment, he seemed satisfied. With great effort, he straightened himself, raised his eyes and pointed at Andy. Speaking deliberately, he repeated Sitting Bull's curse, the one Junior had told Andy about:

"Your family has sinned. For those sins, people of red, yellow, and black will kill your every soldier child and grant you no rest."

With that, exhausted, Whitefeathers closed his eyes and fell back against his cushion. Andy knew he was dismissed, but he still tried to ask a question. It was no use; the old Indian was asleep. The three bodyguards then stepped between the chief and Andy, indicating it was time to go. Two escorted Andy as if he was dangerous, and the third walked with Penny. Together, the group marched out to the car.

"You won't get in here again," one said as he closed the gate behind them. In the chill and the gathering dusk of that October evening, they were alone.

For the next week, as they drove home to Cincinnati, they analyzed Whitefeathers' performance.

"Why do you think he let us in?" she asked.

"Certainly not to discuss anything," he said. "I barely said a word." "I have a theory," she said.

"Let's have it."

"He wanted to repeat the curse." "Possible," he said.

"No, probable," she said. "You saw how he took great pains to make sure you were Joseph's grandson."

"Maybe. It sure wasn't just a friendly chat."

"Do you believe anyone has the power to curse another?" "Not for a minute," he said.

"Then Joseph killed himself and Junior died from a stroke, both on the same day, September 5th, the day Crazy Horse died, and it was just a coincidence?"

"Joseph consciously chose that day and Junior may have inadvertently caused his own death in obsession over the date. No person of color killed them."

"Maybe not," she said and lapsed into silence.

They had little opportunity to ponder the question, for Sanford was born in 1926 and Kathleen a year later. During the next ten years, the Depression wore both them and the nation down. In the Army, this was a time of forced leave without pay, slow promotion, and a discouraging future. Even so, Penny and Andy were better off than most. Many people lost their homes, and some went without food. At least Andy and his family had the necessities of life and a job, and they were grateful for those. But the military had little money, and they lived in dry and ugly places: Fort Sill, Fort Leonard Wood, and Fort Polk, the dust bowl of America. Andy built sewers, showers, and latrines instead of bridges, and Penny forgot the romantic dreams of formal balls and afternoon teas she had visualized during their West Point courtship years. All they could do was endure until better times came, if ever. She grew discouraged and said she wanted to go back to New York, and he wanted to be a real engineer, but disappointments piled up, and the struggle embittered them and drew them apart.

Some relief appeared in 1937 when Andy received orders to report to Pensacola for river and harbor duty with the District Engineer. Federal money was beginning to become available, and Andy worked on waterways, locks, and bridges. The family lived in a rented house on the outskirts of Pensacola. Sparse though it was, they thought it better than the Army forts they were used to. Sandy was eleven years old, and he loved the gulf beaches; he wanted the family to make a day trip to the water every summer weekend. So, when Penny's mother died and left her a little money, they decided to buy a small cottage near Destin, a quiet Gulf beachfront community across the bay from Pensacola. The place became a family refuge from the city. For more than a year, they found a modicum of happiness there, but in 1941 that changed, for Andy was ordered to Hawaii. Kathleen and Sandy didn't want to go, but Penny told them the beaches and the weather were better in the islands, and they gave in.

The Army sent them by rail to New York where they were to board the luxury liner *USS Washington*. Andy took leave so that Penny had a week to visit her father in Westchester and revel in the pleasures of the great city where she had grown up. She was so happy that she momentarily considered staying there with the children while Andy went to the Pacific alone. But she and Andy had done too good a job in talking up Hawaii, and the kids were looking forward to the islands. So they talked her out of staying in New York, and in the late spring, they embarked.

London was under the blitz, German U-boats silently prowled the Atlantic, the United States had occupied Iceland, and the Nazis had just invaded the Soviet Union, but on board ship, the Walkers relaxed in splendor. What a grand trip it was! Our country was emerging from the Depression, and federal money was flowing again. After fifteen years of sewer duty in dust traps the Army called bases, Andy finally felt like an engineer officer. The Walker cabin was small but comfortable, and the *Washington's* food was plentiful. Penny did not have to cook, and her spirits revived. Sandy and Kathleen raced through the great ship's mahogany and brass halls, making friends and exploring the many hiding places. Their favorite spot turned out to be the top deck at night, where they sprawled in deck chairs and listened to music from the latest superheterodyne portable radios. Thousands of stars pressed down on them as they tuned in Tommy Dorsey, Glenn Miller, Artie Shaw, and the Ink Spots, playing songs like "Star Dust," "Dancing in the Dark," and "Tonight We Love." As they dreamed, they forgot the stories of lurking submarines.

The *Washington* took two days to sail majestically down the East Coast to the Panama Canal. The canal normally permitted two-way travel, but their liner was so big it had to make a daylight, one-way transit. The engineer within Andy was in heaven. He buttonholed Kathleen and Sandy.

"The locks take us up eighty-five feet," he explained. "And a ship this size uses fifty million gallons of water as it rises six stories high."

"Where does the water come from?" Sandy asked. "The Army built a 163 square mile lake."

"The Army?" Kathleen asked.

"Yes. The whole thing was built about twenty-five years ago by two Army colonels. One was an engineer named Goethals who did the actual construction by moving enough dirt to build seven Great Pyramids. But first, the other colonel, named Gorgas, had to rid the place of malaria and yellow fever so his buddy could get the work done without killing all his men. You see, the French tried to build the same canal here earlier. They lost 22,000 men and went bankrupt in the process."

"The French?" Sandy asked.

"Yes, the same French engineer who had built the Suez Canal. He didn't know the mosquitoes carried the diseases, so his men died, and he gave up."

"Are the diseases still here?" Kathleen asked.

"No. Gorgas drained the swamps, cut the grasses, burned the trash, and screened the buildings. He made Panama a safe place in which to live."

"And Colonel Goethals built the locks?" Sandy asked.

"Those and the Gatun Dam," Andy said. "It is one and a half miles long and a half mile wide at its base."

"The Army owns it now?" Sandy asked.

"The Secretary of the Army is the only stockholder," Andy said. "Sailing through here makes me proud to be an engineer."

He stayed on deck the whole day, until the Miraflores Locks lowered them back to sea level and they docked at Balboa. Then they were underway at sea again, up the West Coast to San Francisco. Three days later, they entered the great bay, passing by the Presidio and under the recently-completed Golden Gate Bridge. The children escaped so Andy wouldn't give them another lecture, this time about that magnificent structure. He remained on deck nevertheless and gazed in wonder at the beautiful span.

After an overnight stay in the city by the bay, during which they rode a cable car and ate at Fisherman's Wharf, they boarded the *USS Washington* again, and this time she headed directly west. They sailed for five magnificent days into the setting sun. At night, in balmy seas under what now seemed to be millions of stars in a heaven that was closer than ever, they marveled at what wonders God had wrought. On the fifth day, Diamond Head appeared, and soon they were in Honolulu. Twenty-four hours later, they were in Army quarters on Bragg Boulevard at Schofield Barracks in the middle of the island of Oahu. Overwhelmed by the tropical beauty of the place and the balmy weather, they ignored the many ugly rumors of war.

CHAPTER EIGHT

When the Walkers arrived at Bragg Boulevard on Schofield Barracks in the spring of 1941, Andy had been an Army officer for sixteen years. He was a Captain with no combat experience, and promotion seemed remote. By the time MacArthur had reached sixteen years of service, he was a Brigadier General and a heavily decorated combat veteran on his way to becoming the Army's Chief of Staff. In Pershing's sixteenth year, Roosevelt had promoted him in one great leap from Captain to Brigadier General, and the General eventually commanded the American Expeditionary Force. No such great responsibilities apparently awaited Andy. He was neither a combat veteran, nor had he married the daughter of a Senator or come to the attention of a President.

Andy was not concerned about the future, however, he was simply happy to be in a combat battalion, although his commander did not authorize much combat training. For in spite of sporadic rumors about war with Germany and Japan, Army life in Hawaii remained quiet, relaxed and content. The entrenched older officers still thought in terms of a peacetime military force with no money to train and nobody to fight. Without a combat mission, they moved casually through their duties, waiting until they could retire with thirty years of service. En route, they had cocktails each day at five on the veranda of the Officers Club. Seldom wearing field gear, they preferred white gloves, polished riding boots, and silver spurs. They spoke just occasionally to an enlisted man, and then only to administer stern discipline, for after World War I, the senior noncommissioned officers had taken charge of the Army. Kipling put it well:

"The 'eathen in 'is blindness must end where 'e began, but the backbone of the Army is the Non-commissioned man!"

Not since the Civil War had an American General personally led his men from the front in combat. Teddy Roosevelt with his Rough Riders in Cuba and Douglas MacArthur with the Rainbow Division in World War I had ignored that rule, but Andy's seniors in Hawaii in 1941 showed no inclination to follow those leads.

Penny was happy. Putting the harsh years at Forts Sill, Polk, and Wood from her mind, she loved Hawaii and the leisurely life of an officer's wife. In the safety of Schofield Barracks and the serenity of the beautiful Hawaiian weather, Sandy and Kathleen required little supervision, so they roamed freely. She let Johnson, Andy's enlisted aide, do most of her housework, while she had coffee with the other ladies. She was especially fond of Saturday night dances at the officers club, for they reminded her of courtship days at West Point, and she looked forward to dressing up for each end-of-week party. In the beauty of Hawaii, she forgot the Depression and immersed herself in the excitement of the club bands, cheap booze, and generous slot machines. Her dreams were coming true.

On the other hand, Andy was in trouble almost from the moment he arrived. He was assigned as the operations officer of a combat engineer battalion, and his mission was to build emplacements for heavy coastal artillery on the north shore of Oahu. No more sewers and water lines for him, this was a combat requirement, and it was what he had been trained for. He was ready for the task, and he eagerly lined up the needed men and equipment. His seniors in the chain of command were not as enthusiastic. They wanted their engineers to build athletic facilities for their entertainment, especially boxing rings. For each regiment had a boxing team, and competition between units had taken on all the aspects of combat. Esprit de corps was at stake, not to mention some fairly heavy wagers. Every outfit wanted to own up-to-date fighting arenas, and all commanders petitioned the engineers to build them. Because of Andy's ring experience, the projects should have been easy for him. But with senior Majors and Colonels from sixteen regiments and other separate battalions all clamoring for priority, Andy faced difficult choices and a heavy schedule. In spite of his desire to build redoubts and train for war, his commander put coastal artillery emplacements on a low priority.

After a few weeks, in spite of the many obstacles put in his way, his project was ready, and one Monday Andy took his men to the north coast to begin work. They were off to a good start by early afternoon, but then his commanding officer appeared in a command car; the soldiers called it a "Peep." After a brief inspection of Andy's work in progress, the boss took Andy aside to educate him.

"The Wolfhounds want a boxing ring by Saturday," he said. "We need to help them out."

"But emplacements have priority," Andy protested. "The guns are exposed."

"Things look fairly peaceful out here. The guns can wait a little longer. Leave a few men, but get over to the 27th and build them a ring. We owe them."

His boss seemed to owe almost everybody, and during the following three months, this scene frequently recurred. Andy became more and more frustrated at the lack of progress with the artillery redoubts on the north shore. Although the Hawaiian military boxing league was having a popular and successful season, coastal artillery emplacements remained sadly lacking. The heavy guns sat out in open fields, long tubes trained on the empty ocean, but exposed to attack by ground, sea, or air. Worst of all, nobody but Andy seemed to care.

He worked hard every day, staying late at the shore with the few men he could manage to keep on the job there. He tried to change attitudes, urging his superiors to commit to his project and arguing with anyone who would listen about the need to complete the redoubts. He told them that his was a combat engineer battalion, and the artillery would need those emplacements in the event of an attack. Few paid him any heed, for war seemed far away, and he developed a reputation as a maverick. Worst of all, Penny upbraided him every time he arrived home late and dirty after a hard day's work.

"Where've you been? We have to be at the Bacons' at five. And look at you. You're a mess."

"Out at the shore digging."

"Why on earth? Nobody cares about the artillery."

"They'll care when the shooting starts."

"What shooting? Look around you. This is Hawaii. We're at peace, not war."

And so it went, with frustration on the job and more and more friction at home. Andy told himself that his situation could not get any worse, but it did, with the arrival of Lieutenant Colonel Robert Harrison. Newly returned from the Philippine Islands and several years of service there on MacArthur's staff with Major Eisenhower, Harrison was to be assigned as commander of the 35th Infantry Regiment. Over the years, he had stayed in touch with his former Superintendent at West Point, and it had paid off. As a result, he had many friends in high places, and he had been promoted before his contemporaries. Now he was to receive a command eagerly sought after by many, more senior, competitors. As a result, he had also become an odds-on favorite for stars.

Harrison's 35th Infantry, the Cacti, was a part of the 24th Infantry Division. That Division and the 25th had been formed out of the Hawaiian Rainbow Division. The numerical designations were those of the last two Buffalo Soldier regiments, so Andy felt right at home. His battalion was in general support of the Divisions. That meant the engineers were to lay mines and build bridges, roads, airfields, and revetments whenever the supported forces needed them. In combat, the roles were evident: the engineers responded to the current operational mission, but in peacetime, the relationship was not as easily defined. What was clear was that the 35th Infantry had at least a partial call on the services of the engineers. Thus, early on, Andy's boss sent him over to meet the new Cacti commander.

Andy reported as ordered to the 35th Infantry's regimental headquarters, and the Sergeant Major therein asked him to take a seat. Colonel Harrison was busy, but he knew of Andy's arrival and would be free in just a minute. That minute became an hour, and Andy felt the snub. Then the Sergeant Major came to escort him into Harrison's office.

"Well, well," Harrison said, after the sergeant had left them. "We meet again, Yankee. I never thought I'd see you a commissioned officer. I'm not entirely sure it's a pleasure." "The feeling's mutual," Andy said.

"Watch your tongue, Captain. Rank has its privileges, and that includes not listening to smart alecks like you."

"And I'm sure the infantry has its needs. If you'd make those known, I could be on my way, and we'd have no further need to communicate."

"Why aren't you building the 35th its boxing ring?" "Our mission is to build bunkers for the artillery." "Your boss tells me you can do both."

"He's correct, but it will take time. In my book, the guns come first."

"Build the ring, Dumbsmack, then we'll fight again. It would make a good exhibition."

"Nothing would give me greater pleasure," Andy said. "Maybe this time we could find an impartial judge. In the meantime, my priorities come from my chain of command; not yours."

"I beat you last time, and I could again."

"I'll oblige you anytime you wish," Andy said. "And I'll bet we won't even need that judge."

"You know I'd win again, Walker. You come from blood that always quits when the going gets tough, and everybody knows it too. You might as well resign your commission right now, because you're going nowhere in this man's army. I'll see to that. Now get out of my sight and tell your boss I want him to finish that arena, and I want it now."

Seething in anger and frustration, Andy wheeled and left without saluting. Although he immersed himself in his work for the rest of the week, he had barely calmed down by Saturday night at the Officer's Club. Penny was beautiful, food and drink were plentiful, and the music was good. When the sound of "Fascination" reached them through the crowd, Andy took her out on the floor. In her arms, he felt human again. They floated around the room, just as they had the first time they met. It was a beautiful moment he wanted to last, but then he felt a tap on his shoulder. Andy turned to see Harrison.

"May I cut in?" the man asked.

The meeting in Harrison's office was too fresh in Andy's mind to allow such an invasion.

"No, you may not," he said. "This dance is mine." "I take that as an insult," Harrison said.

"I mean it as such," Andy said. "Rank does not have every privilege you think. Now leave us, sir."

Harrison wheeled and left as Andy ignored him and led the startled Penny away to finish their dance. Andy did not see Harrison for the rest of the evening. Although Penny acted a bit annoyed, Andy thought the incident was over. When they arrived home, she had other ideas.

"What's the matter with you?" she asked. "He just wanted to dance, and he seemed rather nice this time, not at all like back at West Point. Why make a scene?"

"He started that scene in his office on Tuesday. The dancing thing was just another offer to fight."

"What are you fighting about?"

"He wants me to build toys for his boys." "And you do not?"

"I need to build positions for the artillery."

"You're obsessed with fighting and war," she said. "Obsessed?"

"Yes. Fighting's crazy. And that includes fighting with men like Harrison who are going places in the Army. And that reminds me, I hate you for teaching Sandy to shoot that pistol."

"Every boy needs to know how to handle a weapon," Andy said. "I'm just showing him the basics."

"You're making him a killer, and I want you to stop. I'll blame you if he hurts himself."

With that, she left the room and would not speak about it any more. Andy went to sleep bewildered at her attitude.

Early the following morning, he awoke to the sounds of repeated thumps and chattering woodpeckers. Suddenly he realized that woodpeckers did not make those kinds of noises. He jumped out of bed and called for Sandy. They raced out the front of the house and onto Bragg Boulevard. Fighter planes circled overhead.

"Red and Blue maneuvers," Sandy shouted. "Not scheduled," Andy called back.

Just then, a Japanese Zero swooped down with machine guns blazing as it strafed the length of the road. Andy pulled Sandy down beside their old Ford, too near its gas tank for comfort. The Zero's cannon were terrifying, but did little damage. Andy checked to see if Sandy was all right. Reassured, he lifted the boy from the ground, and they raced back into the house past the startled women. Penny and Kathleen stood frozen at the door beside Corporal Johnson, who had just arrived.

"A Japanese attack," Andy yelled. "I need to report to the battalion. Plans call for evacuation of dependents. Johnson will take care of you."

Moments later, as he said goodbye to the family and dashed out to throw his hastily assembled field gear into the waiting truck Johnson had brought, Andy gave Sandy the .45 caliber pistol they had trained on.

"Do what Johnson tells you," he said. "I'll be back soon. Use the pistol only as a last resort."

Then he had to go. As he drove away, his last view of his wife and children was that of Penny taking the pistol away from Sandy and giving it to Corporal Johnson. The day rapidly became a blur. The secondary mission of his battalion was to fight as infantry, and their field positions were around the artillery on the north shore. As the engineers manned their dugouts, they noted that the guns had been strafed, but not severely damaged. Cannon cockers were manning them, but thankfully there were no targets evident out at sea. In the absence of the battalion commander, Andy organized the few members of his outfit who had shown up and put them to work providing the protection that the artillery needed. Alert for attacking Zeros, they labored until dusk. Gradually, more and more soldiers reported to the field. After dark, Corporal Johnson joined them.

"What about the families?" Andy asked.

"We spent the day in concrete barracks for protection from attacks by Jap planes. Just before dusk we loaded everybody into a bunch of school buses, and the military police escorted them from Schofield toward Honolulu. The word is that even if the Japs attack again, they probably wouldn't hit downtown Honolulu. It didn't seem like such a good plan to me, because the infantry has set up roadblocks all along the highways. Everything is blacked out, and the guys on those night posts are scared. They are shooting at sounds and anything that moves. I almost didn't make it out here, and it must be hell for those kids on the school buses."

"Let's go find out," Andy said, running toward the truck.

"Not a good idea, sir," Johnson said, as he climbed into the driver's seat. "Better stay low."

Johnson was right. Andy heard small arms fire all around them. They had to stop at eight roadblocks in the thirty miles to Schofield Barracks. Nobody had had time to set up passwords, so they had to approach the roadblocks cautiously and talk their way through squad after squad of frightened infantry. Maybe it was his imagination, but it seemed to Andy that Harrison's Cacti regiment was the most disorganized of the bunch. When they finally made it to their battalion headquarters. Andy's commander was inside, safe behind its concrete walls. He had been there all day.

"Most of the men made it to our field positions," Andy said. "We are digging in. Do you have any orders for us?"

"Uh, no," the colonel said. "It's been hell here. I haven't been able to get a thing out of higher headquarters, and the shooting has been continuous. You send me a radio-telephone operator in the morning.

That way, I can let you know what's going on. If we have any change in mission, I'll radio you on the command net. Any men who report in from now on will stay here to guard the headquarters."

"Where did the women and children go?" Andy asked.

"To Pali High School in Honolulu. They'll be living with civilian families who have volunteered to take care of them."

"Were any dependents hurt?" Andy asked. "The men will want to know and to get in touch with their families. Who has an address list?"

"The Military Police have reported that nobody was hurt, but they don't have a roster of where the women and children went. I suppose headquarters will eventually develop a list of addresses. If and when they do, I'll get a copy out to you."

"I want to go to Honolulu," Andy said.

"Denied." The colonel said. "Go back to the field and take operational control."

For the next two weeks, Andy could not leave the north shore. A week after Congress declared war, Andy was promoted to Major, and he had many new responsibilities. His battalion commander never made it to the field, and rumor had it that he had resigned his commission. Andy was given temporary command of the battalion. A list of dependent addresses in Honolulu did come to Andy by messenger, but headquarters would not permit the men to leave the field.

They had all they could handle to finish the artillery emplacements. In addition, Andy had to prevent the men from roughing up the occasional native farmers they came across on patrols, for rumors of spy activity had replaced fear of Japanese attack. Finally it became clear that the Japanese were not going to invade Hawaii, and he could rotate the men in small groups back to Schofield, where they found that their wives and children had been allowed to return to their quarters. After a month, it was Andy's turn to take a break. Tired and dirty, he arrived at Bragg Boulevard, only to find an irate Penny.

"This is crazy," she said. "Nobody is telling us anything. What's going to happen to us?"

"You'll be okay. Our furniture will be packed up and sent home when the Navy has space. All the wives and children will go too, just as soon as transportation becomes available."

"When will that be?"

"My guess is not too long. We're bringing soldiers over here and don't want the ships to go back empty."

"Are you coming with us?"

"No. We're headed in the opposite direction." "Where?"

"Sorry, I can't tell you."

"This is absurd. Where'll we go?"

"I know it's tough on you, but that sneak Jap attack has started something it will take a long time to fix. Actually, you can go wherever you want, but I would suggest you use the cottage in Destin. The kids know the area, so it won't be so hard on them, and living there is a little easier to take. But be prepared for a slow trip, and the furniture may take a long time in coming. The railroads are full of soldiers and sailors who have priority."

"I didn't sign up for a war. Take us home."

"You know I want to, but I can't. I'm being promoted again next month, to Lieutenant Colonel and command of the battalion. We've been told we will move to the South Pacific as soon as we can assemble the men and equipment. We're hard at work preparing for the move."

"You care more about that battalion than me."

"We're at war, honey, all of us. It'll be up to you to get the kids home to safety and take care of them. There are lots of families just like ours. And all of you will be on your own for the time being."

"I hate this war, and you too. I'm sorry we ever married. Life with you has been a sorry mess."

And for the next month, she never let up. To her, their furniture was poorly packed for shipment, and their travel priority was too low. Then she protested that just to fill the cabins aboard their ship, the *USS Lurline*, families were broken up and unfairly segregated by sex, and she and Kathleen were crammed into a room filled with strangers. And to make matters worse, the cruiser escorting them to San Diego had been damaged in the attack on Pearl Harbor. As it could only make way slowly, they would be traveling at reduced speed, and they would therefore be more vulnerable to seasickness and attack by Japanese submarines. When the time came for them to embark, she was not anything like Ida or Kate, sending their men off to war with a brave smile. She barely said goodbye. As Andy hugged Kathleen and Sandy a final time, Penny ignored him. He stood there hurt and bewildered, and the last words he heard from her were complaints to the cabin steward about her deck assignment.

CHAPTER NINE

Two weeks after Penny stormed up the gangplank in Honolulu, the Transportation Command in San Diego wired a report to the Hawaiian Command of the safe arrival of the *USS Lurline* and its damaged cruiser escort. Since the transport full of dependents had had to reduce headway in order to stay with the laboring cruiser, the *Lurline* had zigged and zagged constantly, and most of its passengers had indeed become quite seasick. But now they were safe, and shortly thereafter, Andy received word that his family was on the Southern Pacific Railroad headed for their beachfront home in Destin, Florida. He was then able to turn his attention more completely to the needs of his battalion command and their upcoming combat assignment.

Throughout the Hawaiian Command he witnessed a new sense of urgency. Officers and men were working at top speed. Those not fully responsive were being sent home, including several senior officers who had cut dashing figures in peacetime Hawaiian society, but whose shaking hands now rendered them apparently unfit for the upcoming conflict. They were quickly being replaced with younger men ready and eager to exact revenge on the Japanese for the infamous, surprise attack on Pearl Harbor. Promotions came fast and often, as the stagnation of the last twenty years in the Army fell rapidly away. In spite of the terrible toll taken by the Japanese on December 7th, optimism abounded, and Andy had never seen such high morale.

In early February, Andy received urgent orders to move his battalion by sea to the Fiji Islands in the South Pacific. After a frantic month of preparation, he loaded his men, equipment, and their supplies onto two transports, and they headed at full steam for the Fiji Islands. There, he was to prepare an airfield at Nandi on the island of Viti Levu for the rigors of combat use by heavy military aircraft. To do that, he had to strengthen and lengthen the runway, as well as improve the approaches. That mission was the subject of great pressure caused by the rapid advance of the Japanese through the Solomon Islands, the Dutch East Indies, and into New Guinea, for the allies had to protect Australia, whose loss would dislodge them from the Southwest Pacific Theater. That need became even greater when the Japanese attacked Darwin, on the north coast of Australia, in their largest air raid since Pearl Harbor. Then in the Battle of the Java Sea, they sank the *USS Houston*, the largest United States warship in the Far East, and Washington panicked. Everything possible had to be done to stop the Japanese before they would be in a position to attack Port Moresby and thus cut the vital shipping and supply lanes from Hawaii to Australia. On that island continent, fear increased and panic spread as long range Zeros began to be seen more frequently over the northern coast and the seemingly invincible Imperial Japanese Army advanced ever nearer.

Andy's mission to improve the Fiji airfield became even more important. Nandi was becoming the busiest Pacific-island airfield south of the equator, and the Fijis' fine harbors were the best on the shipping lanes to Australia. In the battle of the Coral Sea in May of 1942, those harbors and the Nandi airfield would turn out to be essential to Allied victory. Subsequently, the August invasion of Guadalcanal by American marines to secure Henderson Field would have been much more difficult had the improvements to the Fiji harbors and airfield not been made. At the time, however, Andy did not know of those upcoming events. All he could do was work his battalion at that airfield night and day as word continued to reach them of repeated Allied defeats at the hands of the confident Japanese. Each report of bad news spurred them to greater efforts.

By April, in spite of tropical storms and heavy rains, the engineers had made substantial progress. The island's small landing strip would soon be able to accept heavier aircraft. Regardles of this, Headquarters Pacific Command was demanding faster progress to make the airfield longer and wider with a better approach apron. Andy's battalion had to ignore the rainy season and increase its efforts. Andy was living on six hours of sleep a night, and rapidly wearing himself out. He had been to the Red Cross first aid station several times for treatment of minor cuts and bruises, and he was taking sleeping pills to shut out the sound of the rain and the torment of the mosquitoes in his small pup tent.

One night in mid-April, his battalion Sergeant Major came to awaken him from a fitful sleep. Trouble was brewing at the landing strip. A crowd of native islanders was protesting at the engineer work site.

"What the hell are they protesting against?" Andy asked as he hurriedly dressed and rushed for the sergeant's truck.

"Damned if I know," the man said. "But they're armed, and I think they want us to stop digging and moving dirt on the approach runway."

"Stop digging? What the hell for?" "You got me, Colonel."

Driving hastily through the semi-darkness, they arrived at the area in question, where Andy made out a crowd of some thirty Fiji men surrounding one of his bulldozers. They were shouting at his soldiers, who were hunkered down behind concrete pilings. The burly natives were armed with clubs and what seemed to be ancient muskets, and they appeared to be formidable warriors. And his engineers had their rifles ready.

At Andy's direction, the Sergeant Major drove his truck to a point between the two groups and stopped. Andy jumped out, ran into the glare of the truck's headlights, and called for the officer in charge. The shouting gradually stopped, and a young lieutenant then slowly stood up.

"What's the problem, Lieutenant?" Andy asked. "Those guys are throwing things at our operators." "Why?" Andy asked.

"I think they want us to stop work."

"That's the only thing we can't do," Andy said. "Get me something white for a flag so I can talk to them."

Andy tied an undershirt to a rifle barrel and walked toward the islanders, several of whom stood up and came toward him. It reminded him of Joseph's first meeting with Sitting Bull on the Yellowstone River almost seventy years before, only now, no interpreter was needed. In excellent English, made possible because the Fiji Islands had been a British Crown colony since the nineteenth century, one of them said that the engineers must not dig there, because the site was a cemetery and the islanders considered the place holy land. The spokesman said his men would attack if the work continued. The islanders looked as if they meant it and were capable of stiff resistance, so Andy told his men to stand down and perform overdue maintenance on their equipment and get a little rest themselves while he located some assistance. Driving quickly to headquarters at Suva harbor, he made his way to the officer on duty. It turned out to be his old enemy, Colonel Bob Harrison, who was obviously upset at being rousted from his comfortable bed in the middle of the night. He represented the Twenty-Fourth Infantry Division, however, and he had to listen.

"What the hell do you want, Walker?" he demanded.

"Some natives are protesting down at the airfield," Andy said. "They say it's church land, and we have to stop work."

"You can't do that. Kick their butts."

"No can do," Andy said. "We've barely enough men to man the equipment, and I don't think the Division wants a fight over a religious site."

"You always were a wimp," the other said.

But Harrison knew how important the airfield was, so he woke up the Assistant Division Commander. In his bathrobe, the General listened quietly to Harrison's distorted version of Andy's report. Andy could barely stop himself from interrupting to clarify what Harrison was saying. Finally, the General then asked for Andy's assessment of the situation. It differed.

"The natives will resist," Andy said, "and somebody's going to be hurt if we continue to dig in that area. We should try to comply with their demands. It's their island."

"If it's a cemetery, how long would it take to dig up and transfer bodies?"

"Several weeks," Andy said. "But their problem might not be bodies. The site may simply have religious connotations, and a priest might diffuse the whole thing."

"And do we have a local cleric who can handle this?" he asked, turning to Harrison.

"Not to my knowledge," Harrison said. "We could find one tomorrow," Andy said.

The General sat back with his eyes closed as if he were going back to sleep. The sight of that resting officer with Harrison standing by transported Andy back to Fort Smith when he and Penny were in Whitefeather's smoky room in that Indian's dark farmhouse near the Little Big Horn. For a moment, Andy thought of the Indian's curse. Then the General spoke.

"Gentlemen, you may not yet have heard the news," he said, "but Bataan has fallen. The Japanese are transferring men to New Guinea. They intend to attack Port Moresby."

He paused as if measuring his words.

"Colonel," he said to Harrison, "we cannot allow saboteurs to delay our efforts. Take some military police and disperse them. Use any necessary force."

"As for you," he said to Andy, "push your men harder. A major battle is brewing, and we need that airfield now."

That was it. In an hour, Harrison arrived at the work site with a police force in full battle gear. When the islanders resisted, three were killed, and more were injured, but work on the airfield approaches began again at dawn. The delay did not really alter Andy's timetable, for his men got some much-needed rest, and the equipment received that overdue maintenance. News of the incident inevitably leaked, but the official line was that the protesting natives were actually saboteurs, and the soldiers were simply defending the airfield. The report added that two Americans had been killed while preventing the enemy from damaging the field. Far bigger stories were in the news, and this one got lost on the wires. The airfield at Nandi was ready in May for the battle of the Coral Sea. Then, the allies won a great victory at Midway, and the Marines could invade Guadalcanal in August. Andy's battalion was able to stand down for maintenance, and he slept for a week.

During the next three months, Andy's battalion received and trained replacements, put its equipment in shape, and prepared for combat operations in New Guinea. They were busy but not really overloaded. Andy moved out of his small pup tent and into quarters with a regular bed, a desk, and a refrigerator run by electricity supplied from a small generator. He had a wood floor, a bed, a lamp, screened siding, and a canvas roof. Soon rested and sleeping comfortably, with the battalion running smoothly, he even had time to attend a few nearby picnics organized by Red Cross volunteers in the area. On several of these occasions, he talked with one of them named Helen Vincent. She had treated him at the aid station for minor cuts, bruises, and headaches. At these picnics, they naturally fell into casual conversation. She was about his age and had attended college at Skidmore, so she was familiar with West Point and its cruel tea dances. They laughed a lot about that.

"What's a smart lady like you doing in a snake infested jungle like this?" he asked her.

"I wanted to help," she said. "And before I married, I had studied to be a nurse, so the Red Cross seemed better than some sort of factory job."

"You're married? I don't see a ring."

"Divorced, no children," she said. "That was another reason to sign up for overseas duty with the Red Cross. I wanted to leave the old home town."

"Which was?"

"Bellfontaine, Ohio. Ever heard of it?"

"Sure, it's famous because it has both the highest and lowest points in Ohio."

"I didn't know that. Are you sure?"

"There's a hill in town about five hundred feet high, and that's high for Ohio."

"But the lowest?" "The Ohio Caverns."

"You're stretching way too far, 'tho I'm curious how come you know so much about Bellfontaine?"

"I'm from Cincinnati. My father loved Ohio. He called it the Gateway to the West. But why would you want to leave your home town?"

"I felt lost there, without a future except to wait for my husband to come home drunk after beer-drinking with the guys. He would then want sex, and it wasn't my idea of either romance or a life. I don't miss it. How about you?"

"Married to a gal I met at West Point. Two fine kids who I miss, but I can understand your feeling about your ex. Penny and I have had some hard times. She doesn't write much."

"Do you?"

"I've been busy," he said.

The picnics were pretty relaxed affairs. Everybody brought some food and drink, and they all shared. Helen always made some cookies, and Andy's Sergeant Major had a source for sour mash bourbon that brought back memories of white lightning. In pick-up volleyball games, they let off steam. Even with cropped blond hair and no make-up, and in spite of combat boots and fatigues, Helen attracted Andy with a sort of vivacious intelligence. She was fun to be with, and she made him laugh, but more than that, she made him feel like a man again. It was the casual way she touched him as they talked, as if she wanted physical contact. Or how he would catch her looking at him. Some women do those things effortlessly, either because they have been taught or are naturally talented. With Helen, it was the latter. He was at ease with her and the war seemed far away.

Once, when a sudden tropical rainstorm broke up a late evening picnic, Helen and Andy ran hand in hand for his jeep. He intended to drive her back to her tent at the Red Cross bivouac area. When they passed his quarters, however, he suggested she come in for a nightcap. Safely inside, they took off their fatigues to dry. They were in volleyball shorts. Andy was bare chested, and he gave Helen a dry tee shirt. He opened a fresh bottle of bourbon, and they had that drink and relaxed. Then they turned on the short wave radio and found some music. When the newly popular song "You'll Never Know" came on, they rose without a word to dance. She put her hand on the back of his neck, and she gently moved from side to side against him. He put both arms around her, and she put hers around his neck. He moved his hands down to her buttocks and pulled her to him. Then he buried his head in her hair and the scent of Chanel perfume and Lifeboy soap overwhelmed him. The intimacy of the moment was too great for either to resist, and they became lovers.

Later that night after he had driven her back to the Red Cross area, Andy tormented himself with guilt at his infidelity. How had it happened? Was it some sort of mid-life crisis? After all, he was approaching forty, a time when such things seemed to happen. Perhaps. But it might also have been the nearness of death, the strange situation they found themselves in, or simply his separation from Penny after a miserable farewell. He was inclined to think it was all of the above, together with the rain falling on that canvas roof, sour mash whiskey, and quiet music in the jungle night. At any rate, it had been some sort of magic moment, and he became an unrepentant lover. For more than a month, they shared as many of those moments as they could, listening to "Sleepy Lagoon" on the radio and exchanging secrets. Andy forgot whatever doubts he might have had and found himself happier than he had ever been. For him, this was completely new. He had not known many women, but he discovered that Helen was different. She could arouse him just by touching his shirt collar and looking up into his eyes or standing on tiptoes to whisper in his ear. He wanted her with a driving obsession and physical passion that was different from his romance with Penny. He never once called her Honey, and thoughts of his other life with Penny were like the song, "Long Ago and Far Away."

One evening as they shared a drink at the end of a hot day, the subject of death came up.

"Are you afraid to die?" she asked.

"No, but I really fear losing even one of the men under my command," he said. "I know that will happen before the war is over, and I don't know how I'll handle it."

"But how did you handle it when those saboteurs killed your men trying to stop construction of the new runway?"

"We never lost any," he said.

"But the news reports said several were killed." "The reports were wrong."

"But I saw several bulletins," she insisted. "And the papers described hours of hard fighting. Islanders died. Why did the reports say soldiers were killed?"

"I suppose it was to cover up for killing those natives." "But weren't they saboteurs?" she asked.

"No, just angry men."

"Angry about what?" she asked. "They wanted us to stop digging." "Why on earth?"

"It may have been a cemetery," he said, "or some type of religious place they didn't want defiled."

"Why kill them?"

"I wouldn't have done that, but the Colonel leading the reaction force was more aggressive, and it happened. The General in charge wanted to keep the work going. We needed that runway badly. You saw what happened at the Coral Sea."

"But why not just move the bodies or find someone who could advise you about their religion?"

"That's what I wanted to do, but the General must have felt that he didn't have time. He had to keep the project going. He made a decision."

"But if all this is true, we killed innocent people." "Maybe so," he said. "But not me or my men."

"I can't believe you," she said. "This is a crime and a cover-up. You can't just ignore it. You have to report it and punish those who did it, or it will happen again."

"War is a terrible thing," he said. "And I guess I would plead combat necessity. Bad things happen in war all the time, worse ones if you lose. And we are fighting a vicious enemy. You saw what happened in the rape of Nanking. Surely you wouldn't want that in San Francisco. Three hundred and fifty thousand women were raped and killed in China."

Their discussions went on and on, but they always ended in an impasse. And when she brought up the subject, she seemed more concerned with his attitude than over the killings. Again and again, she emphasized she was not comfortable with the idea of covering up the incident. It was a fault that she kept returning to, and Andy could not answer her. At the end, he was just as uncomfortable with the discussions as Joseph had been with Sitting Bull as they rode from Fort Buford back to the Standing Rock Reservation. Like the old Indian, Helen had the better moral position, yet Andy could not bring himself to write a report of the killings. His country was at war, and that had top priority for him. Shortly after he made that position clear, she stopped coming to his bed, and he heard that she had applied for a commission in the newly formed Women's Army Auxiliary Corps. A month later, she was accepted and transferred to Australia.

From the time Helen left him until he boarded ship for Port Moresby a month later, he pondered the situation, worrying it over in his mind. Why did he miss her so badly? He had not felt that way when Penny left. Helen may have had a better figure, but with her hair cut short to accommodate field conditions and dressed in field gear, she was not that much more attractive. True, she was divorced and certainly was far more experienced than Penny. At first, he decided that was it. Their affair had simply been sexual passion made more poignant by the dangers of war and the intimacy of rain on a canvas roof in the jungle. But in the end, there was more. Of course he missed the sex, but she meant something else to him. She was really different, and he just wanted to be around her to share the casual moments. And without her, he was lost in the jungle. Finally, he realized he really needed her. He should have listened to her and filed a report. He had screwed up, and he felt bad about it.

The real problem was what he would do about Penny. What was his future with her? For the life of him, he could not answer. He was ashamed he had failed her. Was his inevitable, Puritan-based guilt part of his sense of loss? Certainly he felt guilty over having betrayed Penny, but was there more to his emptiness than that? He found an answer when he began to accept Helen's contempt of the cover-up of the islanders' deaths. She had won, and the knowledge was like a knife to his stomach. Why had he accepted the cover story? He started to wonder if race was involved? Did the demands of combat really make the killings necessary? Did the need justify those deaths? The ends can never be used to justify the means, he knew that. What could he do? Now that the deed was done, nothing he did would change the fact that those natives were dead. Better to concentrate on commanding his battalion and deal with Penny later.

Evil triumphs if good men remain silent, and he had taken that route. So he was reaping the consequences of that decision. Then one night as he tossed and turned without sleep, a crazy thought came to him: The Fiji native islanders were brown skinned. The words of Chief Whitefeathers began to echo in his mind. The Walkers would commit crimes against people of color and could never rest until they paid for their sins. And so he was paying now. But surely an incident like that at the airfield could not compare to the tragedy of Wounded Knee or the massacre at the Crater. Three men died, but not hundreds, like the Indians or the Moros. He knew that dumb Indian curse was nonsense, but he could not sleep for thinking about it. He told himself that in the jungles of New Guinea, he would have other things to worry about, so he made himself go on.

Every now and then, however, as he fitfully tossed late at night, too many memories returned. In his dreams, he relived those nights with Helen, savored the perspiration of her warm body, shared her passion, tasted the sour mash bourbon, and heard again the strains of "Sleepy Lagoon." Then he would awake drenched with perspiration himself, and he could not go back to sleep. As he lay on the bunk they had shared for just a month, he missed her desperately. It was then that a hollow ache in the pit of his stomach bent him over in pain, and he knew that the affair was not over. Then, the words of another popular song came back to him, the one by Jo Stafford. The song was written to give the doughboys and their sweethearts hope for the future, and it worked for him. Every time he heard it on the short wave, he listened intently to the words, and he told himself he did not know where or when, but he knew they would meet again some sunny day.

CHAPTER TEN

New Guinea is a terrible place in which to fight a war or build a road. It is mammoth, the second largest island in the world, and its geography varies from miasmatic, tropical marshes in the coastal lowlands, to mountain ranges with peaks rising above fourteen thousand feet in the interior. Andy's battalion had been ordered to build a military road from Port Moresby in the south to the Japanese occupied port of Buna on the northeast coast. His work would become the infamous Buna Road. To accomplish his mission, however, he would have to cut through the Owen Stanley Range near snow-capped Mount Victoria, over thirteen thousand feet high. Just to move a battalion of soldiers over that terrain would be a daunting challenge, but to build a road there in the face of Japanese resistance would be close to impossible. Yet that was Andy's task, and it would require all that he and his men could give. They began construction in the winter of 1942-43.

This was the same route the Japanese had chosen in early 1942 for their drive south toward Port Moresby, intending to seize that key port and then mount an invasion of Australia itself. Now, the Americans sought to free that vital facility from that threat by driving the invaders back north. It was dirty work, made more so by attacks of man and nature. Malaria and yellow fever were common diseases in the lowlands where Andy was going, and they would take a huge toll among his men. And the jungle was full of strange creatures, poisonous snakes, howling monkeys, and great leeches that covered a man's legs and sucked his blood. The jungle floor was a bottomless swamp. And the swamp was a sea of mud that made road building on it a nightmare. The natives built their houses on stilts that raised them above the treacherous morass, but Andy's road had to be built on ground that acted like quicksand. Logs cut and laid out as an initial roadbed simply sank into the earth and disappeared.

The Japanese compounded his problems by fighting every step of the way. The Twenty-Fourth Division spearheaded the advance, however, and the main body of the enemy was gradually forced back so that the engineers could inch the road northward. The Japanese knew how important the road was, however, and they left behind small groups of soldiers hidden deep in the jungle. These men harassed the engineers day and night, coming and going in the concealment of the thick vegetation and triple-canopy jungle. They left suicide snipers hidden high in the trees and booby traps everywhere on the trails. They ambushed survey parties by day and lobbed mortar shells into camps at night.

To make matters worse, the infantry regiment assigned to protect Andy's battalion was the Cacti, with Harrison still in command. He was a cruel, vicious commander, and his men responded in kind to his leadership. Violating the very laws they were defending, they cut off the ears of dead Japanese soldiers and wore them as trophies on their belts. Repeated rumors whispered that Harrison's men had been ordered to take no prisoners, and once when Andy had to report to Harrison's headquarters compound for coordination, he found Japanese heads mounted on stakes at the gate.

"What the hell is that?" Andy demanded.

"Payment for the rape and murder of 350,000 Chinese in Nanking," Harrison said. "And for that sneak attack on Pearl Harbor. And for beheading our marines they captured on Wake Island, for bayoneting U.S. airmen downed on Rabaul, and for killing five thousand Americans on a sixty mile death march without food or water after Bataan. Need I go any farther?"

"Two wrongs don't make a right," Andy said. "All you are doing is degrading yourself and your men, not to speak of committing war crimes."

"What makes you the judge of us?" Harrison said. "For my part, I know that our pilots captured after Doolittle's raid on Japan were beheaded, and it is a fact that after our invasion of Guadalcanal, Japanese soldiers hacked to death captured marines and mutilated

American dead on the battlefield. The Japanese are monsters not deserving of compassion. You build that road and leave the fighting to the men of the infantry. All you engineers are wimps anyway."

They parted as usual in disagreement.

The Japanese did not allow the luxury of a divided American Command. They fought so hard that they came close to bringing the project to an end. Harrison's infantrymen were supposed to take care of defending the engineers, but they could not possibly be every-where. The situation was similar to traveling the Bozeman Trail seventy-five years before. The soldiers protected the main fortification and mounted occasional forays in pursuit of hit and run attackers, but everyday security was up to those who traveled or worked along the road. Thus Andy and his Sergeant Major had to allocate scarce assets to defense, in addition to building their road. And that caused additional delays.

They put out a standing order that tasks were to be done in groups so that men could band together for protection. The best rifle shots were made bodyguards for the rest. No one attempted the trails alone, and engineers trained in mine warfare searched the roads before the battalion moved. Like Joseph and his men along the Oregon Trail, the work groups ceased operations early in the after-noon so they could prepare fighting positions for the night. From their defensive perimeter, they set up listening posts and sent out patrols. Andy and his Sergeant Major toured the battalion perimeter at dusk each evening to raise morale and ensure readiness. The primary danger remained the Japanese light mortars, because small bands of enemy could easily carry those weapons in close enough to launch a few rounds and then melt away in the darkness. Such an attack resulted in Andy's first combat death when, early in the campaign, the Japanese worked a combat patrol close enough to his perimeter to lob five rounds into a bivouac area before disappearing into the jungle. Andy had emphasized to his men that if a shell came in, everybody not under cover should throw himself to the dirt and remain prone until the shelling ceased. Most of the explosive force of a mortar's burst flew upward, and a soldier flat on the ground was fairly safe. This time when the first round came in, a Private Stone tried to run for a bunker, and the second round got him. Andy had to write that painful letter of condolence to the man's family. It was one of the saddest duties he ever had to perform, but he could not let the loss deter him. He drove his men and himself hard, taking no breaks, even when he received word of Kate's death. When that news came, he had been deep in the New Guinea highlands for over a year, and he was offered thirty days leave back to the States. He declined, because his mission had reached a critical juncture.

His efforts paid off. After struggling in the jungles and mountains for a year and half, Andy's battalion finished the Buna Road, and Japanese resistance ceased. In May of 1944, the allies captured Hollandia, and his battalion was given a break for maintenance and recuperation. Half of his men went on leave to Australia or the States, but Andy remained in New Guinea to receive replacements, supervise repairs, and begin planning for the next campaign.

The war in the Southwest Pacific also continued without a pause. Under MacArthur's strategic direction, General Krueger's Sixth Army continued island hopping north and west, bypassing Japanese soldiers on unimportant islands as the Americans worked their way toward the Philippines. Andy's engineers were soon back in combat. Roads were not as critical in that effort. So the battalion was given a new mission to build the crucial, temporary airfields needed to provide the vital land-based air support for that effort. As the fight moved inexorably westward, the return to the Philippines was on everyone's minds. Thus by the fall of 1944, preparations were well under way for an October invasion of Leyte.

The operation order called for several landings on the east coast of that island to be followed by a drive counterclockwise north and west around the interior mountains to the major port of Ormoc on the western coast. That port was the sole Japanese supply and reinforcement point, and its capture would mean the effective end of the battle for Leyte. The coastal landing went smoothly, but for the next three months, as the Allies drove north, they struggled against fierce Japanese resistance. The situation threatened to turn into a stalemate.

Finally the Allies drove the Japanese far enough north so that higher headquarters could give Andy's battalion the mission of building a road westward into the interior highlands. The infantry had to force the defenders back far enough for the road to reach deep into the rugged mountains, so that heavy artillery could then be brought far and high enough to fire more than fifteen miles over the mountains and interdict the Japanese at Ormoc. It would be tough fighting and difficult construction.

By this time, Bob Harrison had been promoted to Brigadier General and was the Assistant Division Commander. Once in that position, he seemed to have no other interest than to push Andy to finish that mountain road. In spite of the almost impossible winter weather, difficult terrain, and unending Japanese ground attacks, Harrison constantly harassed Andy and his men. Daily, he complained they were not working long or hard enough. His arrogance did nothing to improve the morale of Andy's battalion or help with the road building, but once it nearly drove Andy to fisticuffs. As on several previous occasions, while Andy's men slipped and slid in the muddy ravines, Harrison arrived in his Jeep to berate them. It was on one of those visits that Andy shoved his face in Harrison's.

"You want this job?" Andy said. "You can take over yourself right now, and I'll be out of here. Either that, or get the hell out of my way."

"Who do you think you're talking to?" Harrison asked. "You will pay for that insubordination." But he turned and left the area, as Andy's men cheered the departure.

By early 1945, the road was able to support heavy vehicles, and soon the long-range artillery was shelling the Japanese positions and port facilities in and around Ormoc. The fire must have been effective, for Japanese supplies rapidly dried up, and gradually the Allies gained the upper hand throughout the island. The battle for Leyte was over, and Andy never heard more about insubordination from Harrison. Andy's mountain road was clearly too instrumental in conquering the island to permit criticism of him or his battalion.

As soon as Leyte was secure, General MacArthur turned his attention to Luzon. In 1942, when the Japanese had forced him to leave by submarine from Corregidor, he had promised to return, and by March of 1945, his picture was in all the newspapers as he waded across the beach to keep that promise. Andy's battalion followed, landing in April.

The Japanese fought fiercely on Luzon, and the engineers had to repair many a road demolished by the retreating enemy, but gradually resistance ceased. Then word came of victory in Europe, and Penny finally wrote to announce that Sandy had successfully completed his Plebe Year at West Point as a member of the class of 1948. Andy had little time to rejoice, however, for he had to turn his attention to planning for the Sixth Army's invasion of Japan. It was to be a gigantic effort against what was anticipated to be fanatical resistance. No one doubted that the Imperial Japanese Command would fight to the death against the Allied invasion, and rumors circulated that half a million Americans would die in that effort. Every soldier in the Philippine Islands readied himself for a vicious struggle, and Andy's engineers were no exceptions.

The battalion had lost half of its original complement, and Andy needed time to prepare men and machinery for the terrible fight ahead. His mission was to go in with the fourth wave near the old capitol of Kyoto and repair destroyed roads to the interior of the island, so that the invasion could press inland. In three years of combat Andy had been scratched and cut, but not seriously hurt. He had complaints about occasional strange jungle fevers, but he anticipated far worse times ahead, and he tried to steel his men for the task. It was a daunting prospect, and morale was not high on Luzon. Thus when word came of the explosion of the first atomic bomb over Hiroshima on August 6th, Andy was stunned. When a second such bomb destroyed Nagasaki on August 9th, he dared hope that an invasion of Japan might be averted. His relief became complete when, shortly thereafter, the Emperor Hirohito ordered the Imperial Japanese armed forces to surrender.

Among the American soldiers in the Philippines, there was little compassion for the Japanese women and children in the cities destroyed by the atomic bombs. Andy and his men felt only relief at not having to fight their way across the heavily-defended Japanese beaches. They would be going home, apparently having survived a terrible war. Why was there so little sorrow at the deaths of so many in those cities? In Andy's view, the cruelty of the Japanese soldiers had created a monster. It was the ugly face of war. So at first, he thought of the atomic bombs as a deserved retribution, only partial payment for the Japanese attack on Pearl Harbor and many other atrocities.

After Japan surrendered, however, and Andy went to Kyoto as a part of the occupying force, he began to have doubts. As a part of the massive clean-up of cities leveled by American air raids, Andy visited Hiroshima and Nagasaki. The destruction was beyond belief, and he began to ponder the alternatives. He knew that President Truman's decision to use the atomic bombs was made to shorten the war and save many American lives, and he supported that decision, perhaps selfishly, but without reservation. But was the decision made easier by the brutality of the Japanese? Why were such bombs not used in Germany? Was it because the Germans were not as cruel as the Japanese? Or was it because the Germans were Caucasian and the Japanese were not? It was true that the war in the Pacific was deeply racial, but Andy could not believe that such bias might have been involved in the decision to use the bomb on inhabited cities. He began to wonder if instead of attacking those crowded places filled with women and children, we might have attempted something else, perhaps a demonstration drop of an atomic bomb on an uninhabited desert island. But would such an explosion have convinced the Imperial Army to surrender? These questions constantly recurred to Andy, often at night as he lay sleepless and pondered his own role in the terrible climax to the war in the Pacific. On one such occasion, an absurd idea came to him. Were the massive destruction of those cities and the deaths of so many women and children of color somehow a return of the Indian curse Junior had mentioned? He immediately rejected the idea.

He thought back to the Filipinos he had met on Luzon. They had shown him no animosity. Once, he had even gone to Zambales Province, where Joseph and Junior had led the Buffalo Soldiers for three years against the insurgents of General Aguinaldo. The people of that province were delighted to meet an American officer, and when they found out he was Joseph's grandson, they were overjoyed.

They gave him a warm reception and treated him like royalty. Their affection for him could not have been more sincere.

They showered him with attention, holding a feast in his honor each night he was there. They plied him with gifts and begged him to return when he could stay longer. He was overwhelmed. Those grateful people could not possibly harbor a curse against him, and so he dismissed the idea from his mind.

Andy was promoted to Colonel and assigned to MacArthur's staff in the Engineer section. As such, he dealt daily with the destruction caused by the atomic bombs. He toured whole cities of flimsy houses where neighborhoods had simply disappeared. Streets and utilities like water and sewers no longer existed. It was almost too much to bear, and he began to have doubts. He was not shy in voicing his opinions, moreover, and on one occasion, he talked to a reporter.

"Did we have to drop those bombs on crowded cities?" Andy asked. "Could we have done otherwise?"

"What would you suggest?" the man asked.

"How about treating the Japanese Imperial Command to a demonstration bomb on an isolated Pacific island?"

"Would that have persuaded them to surrender?"

"We won't know, will we?" Andy asked. "Because we went ahead and dropped those bombs on all those women and children. And why did we drop them on the Japanese and not the Germans even though they were available?"

"You tell me," the man said.

"Well the conventional wisdom is the Japanese were cruel barbarians, and the Germans were not as bad. But a cynic might think that the decision was based on race."

"How so?"

"The Germans were just too much like us, but the Japanese were people of color."

"That's pretty bad," the man said.

"I'll tell you something else that is pretty bad too," Andy said. "Before the war, President Roosevelt signed a League of Nations letter that condemned attacks on civilians in undefended cities. How could

President Truman have so blatantly turned that around in Hiroshima and Nagasaki?"

"To save American lives," the man said.

Andy had no answer for that, so they ended the discussion. But such questions coming from a senior combat veteran made for a different viewpoint, and the reporter subsequently quoted Andy in a "Stars And Stripes" editorial that was given wide circulation. As he had so obviously questioned the integrity and motives of the senior commanders who had decided to use the bomb, Andy became a figure to avoid around MacArthur's headquarters. No one openly challenged him, but everyone stayed out of his way, waiting for the axe.

One evening not long after the offending editorial was published, Andy was assigned the main entrance as night duty officer. Just before supper, General MacArthur stalked out of his office and headed with his usual entourage toward the front exit. Suddenly, he stopped and turned to Andy.

"Are you the Andy Walker who had that intramural fight with General Harrison back at West Point?" he asked.

"Yes sir," Andy replied.

"That was a hell of a battle," he said, staring intently at Andy. "You must enjoy a good fight."

"I don't go out of my way to find one," Andy said, "but if one shows up, I'm ready."

"And so you talked to that reporter about the decision to use those bombs against Japanese cities?"

"Yes sir," Andy said.

"You picked a bad fight," MacArthur said. "And you were dead wrong. The atomic bombing was even better for Japan than it was for the Allies. Those bombs killed less than three percent of the people the fire bombings of Tokyo did in March. Moreover our ability to develop and deliver atomic bombs firmly demonstrated our clear military and scientific superiority, and in doing so, we destroyed the prestige of the Japanese military. The bombs' obvious overwhelming power thus made it possible for the Imperial Army to finally admit defeat and surrender, instead of fighting to the death and killing hundreds of thousands of American and Japanese boys in the process.

More importantly, the early end of the conflict also prevented the Russians from joining the war in the Pacific and invading and occupying northern Japan. That would have resulted in far greater injury to the Japanese, both short and long term. You should think before you criticize those of us who must make difficult decisions."

The General then turned to an aide and said, "Send this officer home immediately. I want him out of my sight."

CHAPTER ELEVEN

When General MacArthur said immediately, he meant it. About an hour after the General departed the building, his deputy chief of staff arrived with a replacement duty officer and two military police sergeants.

"Return to your quarters and start packing," the deputy told Andy. "And give me your security pass. These men will run your errands and clear you from the headquarters."

"What's going on?" Andy asked.

"You heard the General. You're going home, and he doesn't want to see you around here before you leave."

"Do I have orders?" Andy asked.

"They're in the mill," the deputy answered. "Where am I going?"

"On thirty days leave while the Department of the Army decides what to do with you. You can choose where you want to spend your leave. We'll pack what you can't carry on the plane tomorrow and ship it to the destination of your choice."

"The plane tomorrow?" Andy asked.

"You have a ticket to Anchorage, and you'll be authorized space-available transportation from there to any place in the United States. Just tell us where."

Andy was being run out of town on a rail. They wouldn't tar and feather him, but he had no choice, even if he wanted one. Oh well, he thought, it was high time he faced Penny, and he really wanted to see the kids.

"Destin, Florida," he said.

By the evening of the following day, Andy had made it to Alaska, but there he remained stranded. What with thousands of Pacific war veterans all scrambling to get back to the States, it took him three days to find a seat on a flight to Seattle. Then he spent a week more on trains to San Francisco, San Diego, and finally across the country to Mobile. It was October 1945, however, and America still loved its war heroes, so milling passengers applauded as he embraced Penny and Kathleen at the station. His uniform was wrinkled and he had lost weight, but he was tanned and handsome, and he had all those medals. Once at home, the parties and his hero's welcome lasted about a week. Then the subject of his next duty station came up.

"I want to leave Florida," Penny said.

"That may not be possible," Andy said. "Although the job I'm most qualified for is at the Pentagon, they probably won't want me up there."

"Why not?" she asked. "You have a fine combat record." "Apparently I've offended General MacArthur," he said, "and I'm on everybody's avoid list."

"Offended MacArthur? What on earth?"

"I talked to a reporter and questioned the use of the atomic bombs against Japan, and the General didn't like it."

"What did you say?"

"I wondered about the decision to kill so many noncombatants at Hiroshima and Nagasaki. Most who died were women and children, and I asked if something else could have been done, maybe a demonstration explosion on an uninhabited island. I asked if race had been a factor in the decision to drop atomic bombs on Japan, but not Germany. I felt strongly about those questions, and I still do."

"And that offended MacArthur?"

"Seems so. He told me the atomic bombing of Japan was the best thing that could have happened to both us and them. His point was we saved the lives of as many as a million American and Japanese soldiers, by making it possible for the Imperial Army to accept surrender without losing face instead of fighting to the death. He also claimed that we kept the Russians from joining the war and occupying a third of Japan. That would have been the worst possible result for the Japanese. He pointed out that we killed fewer people with those atomic bombs than we did in the March fire bombing of

Tokyo. He said I should have kept my mouth shut, and he sent me home."

"And now what do you think?" she asked.

"I accept his criticism, but I also remember old people and children with scars from radiation and the massive devastation of those cities, and I still wonder if we could have done something differently."

"And MacArthur will keep you from the Pentagon?"

"He doesn't want to see me again, so I won't be anywhere near the seat of power. I know you want to leave here, but my guess is they'll assign me to the Engineer District at Pensacola again. I hear they need a Chief of Staff."

And it came to pass. Andy was offered that position in the District office. It was a pretty good job, with considerable authority and responsibility, and he had no choice. But Penny did not like the idea one bit. She badgered him until he agreed to take her north for a Christmas visit with her father in New York, when Sandy would be able to come down from West Point to join them.

Penny's father lived in an exclusive section of Westchester County, and his grand house was at great contrast with the less than opulent places Andy had taken her over the last twenty years. Penny was so obviously pleased at being home that Andy was discouraged, mostly because he recognized that he had not lived up to her expectations. He felt bad about that, but there was nothing he could do about it. When Sandy arrived, he brought Nancy with him.

"Nancy from Destin?" Andy asked.

"Yes, Nancy with the laughing face," Sandy said. "She's grown up," Andy said.

"You bet she has, and we're going to marry right after I graduate," Sandy said, "just like you and mom."

The announcement caused a celebration. For a little while Andy ceased worrying about Penny and enjoyed sharing in the love Nancy and Sandy so obviously felt for each other. It was hard for him to recall that he and Penny had once been that happy. By the end of Christmas week, however, doubts had worked on him to the point that he decided to have a man to man talk with Sandy about his career. He waited until the day before Sandy was to return to the Academy. Then after supper, he took the boy aside.

"You are so much like me and my father," Andy said, "that we need to have a talk about your future. Have you thought much about that?"

"Sure I have," Sandy said. "I'll graduate from West Point, marry Nancy, have a family, and serve my country for many years as an artillery officer."

"Serving your country and raising a family are fine goals, but there are many ways to serve, maybe politics or such. You know, when Junior graduated and married Kate, he felt just like you. But you may remember he left the service as soon as he could after fighting against the Philippine Insurrection."

"I've wondered about that."

"He wasn't comfortable with the way Washington handled the slaughter at Wounded Knee and similar incidents that took place in the Philippines. It was a tough decision for him, because he loved the Army, but he decided to leave the service."

"But he returned for the big war."

"Yes, because Pershing asked him to, and that's what I want you to think about. You remember the Buffalo Soldiers Pershing, Dad, and Joseph had served with so many times? Well, they were treated miserably in that war, and Junior felt guilty that he had a role, however small, in that miscarriage of justice. He told me that the system was so corrupt that even a man with as much power and prestige as General Pershing could do nothing about it."

"Dad, that was a long time ago," Sandy said. "It has nothing to do with the Army today or me."

"It had something to do with me," Andy said. "When I graduated, Junior tried to talk me out of taking a commission, just as I am talking to you now. He told me how discouraged Joseph was after the courts-martial of Colonel Forsythe at Wounded Knee and General Smith in the Philippines. He said the system was flawed, and I shouldn't be part of it."

"And did you find that to be true?" Sandy asked.

"I've found that some senior officers like Bob Harrison can be tyrants and tarnish the men they lead. You've heard how power might even corrupt strong men like MacArthur and Pershing. It takes an unusual person to avoid that fate, and the government can be very cruel. Life in the service can be difficult. Look at the contrast between your mother's life with us over the years and that of her father here. And military life was not good to Ida, nor to your mother. Nancy will have to be very strong just to survive constant changes and disruptions to her family, even without the outbreak of war."

"We've discussed that," Sandy said. "She's stronger than she appears."

"Joseph thought that about Ida, and he was wrong. Why would you submit Nancy to such a test? Even a man as strong as General MacArthur can be tempted. Look at how petty he was with me over the interview I gave. He ran me out of Japan and has put me on a blacklist, just because I disagreed with him."

"That has bothered me ever since Mom told me what General MacArthur said to you," Sandy interrupted. "I hate to tell you, Dad, but from what I have read and studied about the situation in Japan, I find myself agreeing with the General."

And that was the end of the discussion. Sandy and Nancy left the next day for West Point, their engagement and his plans for a lifetime career in the Army intact. Penny then announced that she wanted to stay for awhile with her father when Andy went back to duty at Pensacola. Thus, with Kathleen attending college at the University of Florida, Andy was alone.

In March, Penny came down for a visit. She started several conversations about their future, but he could not face the subject. He would make another drink and change the question. Most of the time, he turned to the testing of nuclear weapons. As the Chief of Staff of the Engineer District, he reviewed all the incoming messages, and he had seen several wires about such tests in the Pacific. He seemed obsessed with the subject, and his strong reaction confused her.

"They can't do that," he told her. "There are people living on those islands."

"But the newspaper says those places are remote," she said, "not near anything like shipping lanes, airways, or fishing grounds. They seem like the perfect places to test."

"Baloney," Andy said. "Hundreds of natives on Bikini Atoll will be displaced permanently, and three other islands will have to be evacuated for the duration of the tests. By relocating them to terrible places, we are treating them like the Japanese in California after Pearl Harbor."

"But if we have to test," she said, "the papers say Bikini has a large lagoon to anchor targets, and there apparently are no nearby islands that might be contaminated, just an empty ocean downwind."

"Wrong again," he said. "I know this area from the war. The wind direction is unpredictable, and the islanders will be in terrible danger from fallout. You should have seen what happened to the people at Hiroshima and Nagasaki as a result of fallout. It's horrible, and it should not happen to those poor natives."

She was puzzled. Why was he so concerned about those tests? He was not making much sense, and the more he drank, the worse he behaved.

"The islanders on Eniwetok may also have to be displaced," he said. "We are treating them like we did the Sioux, putting them on reservations where they can't survive. And the Bikini islanders are starving, so we are moving them again, this time to an island with no lagoon or anchorage. And all of them are in danger from radioactive fallout. We treat people of color badly."

The whole conversation bewildered her. He was acting very strangely, and she wanted no more of it or him.

"I no longer understand you," she said. "In some strange way, the war changed you, and I have not been comfortable around you since you came home. As sad as it is, I believe it would be best for both of us if I went back to New York. Father says he has a job for me."

Andy offered no comment.

She left the following morning. Her father gave her that job at his law firm. She returned to Destin once to collect some personal items. That was when she told Andy that she was happy in New York and was thinking of staying there. She said he could visit her if he wanted to. When he neither asked questions nor raised objections, she left again. At first, she wrote weekly, and he answered each letter. He never asked her to come back or offered to visit New York. Soon the letters began to come less frequently. Then they stopped altogether. She had a good job, and her father was well off, so she never asked for money, and he never sent any. They just seemed to drift apart and let the marriage drop. Sandy and Kathleen were almost grown, and the subject of divorce or formal separation never came up. Neither of them cared.

With Penny gone and Kathleen spending most of her time with a steady boyfriend, Dan Butler, at Florida, Andy was pretty much on his own. Now and then, Nancy would drop by, but her visits tended to be brief, and Andy had the feeling that she only came because Sandy asked her to. Left alone with his sour mash, Andy stared at the walls and brooded about continued atomic testing in the Pacific. Finally his anger became too much and he called a local reporter.

"If the bombs they are testing were ever used on a large city in the United States," he told the man, "millions would die immediately, but many more would be sickened from radiation and linger in pain for months or even years. I visited the hospitals in Japan after the war, and it was horrible."

"Then why are we testing such things?"

"For the sake of power," Andy said. "And we have more than enough of that already. And before the war, we agreed not to bomb undefended cities. Now, we are making such attacks integral parts of our plans. We call it massive retaliation."

"But these are just tests," the man said.

"And that's a crime too," Andy said. "These tests are exposing everybody out there to radioactive fallout. And the natives are in the greatest danger. Their islands are being contaminated, and their children are being exposed to a lifetime of tumors and cancers. We are trustees of those people and their land, and we are doing a criminal job of it."

Andy intended the interview to create a sensation, but he was far too extreme and technical, and the reporter was not skilled enough to write a coherent story that made sense. In a resulting Op. Ed. piece, Andy ended up sounding very strange, and the national press did not pick up the story. On the other hand, his boss subsequently warned him about the release of classified information, and he ordered Andy to clear all future news releases with the Pentagon.

Two years later, when Sandy graduated from West Point, Andy went up to attend the June Week and wedding. Penny drove up each day from New York. She was trim and efficient looking, really quite attractive, but Andy took little notice. Then, at a supper in the officers club for the four of them several days before graduation, he drank far too much, and after supper he began to harangue them.

"Three atomic tests are scheduled on Eniwetok Atoll in the Marshall Islands," he announced after still another drink. "The United States government is creating a radioactive catastrophe out there."

"Surely they know what they are doing," Nancy said.

"What they are doing is violating international law, and it's a war crime."

"How so?" Sandy asked.

"The United States signed a proclamation of the League of Nations in 1938," he said. "Roosevelt pushed for it. All of the member nations agreed not to bomb civilian populations from the air in case of war. We would not bomb cities or civilians. Once we were at war, however, he changed. He pressured General Arnold to fire-bomb Tokyo, and that led directly to Hiroshima and Nagasaki. Now we are exploiting Pacific islanders and trying to make even more destructive bombs to drop on women and children in undefended cities."

"You've had one too many," Sandy said. "And I don't see what this has to do with us."

"You're set on becoming an artillery officer," Andy said. "And your government is developing nuclear projectiles for you to use in your howitzers. It's insane, and I implore you not to be a part of it. Quit before it is too late."

"That's enough," Penny said. "You're drunk."

"I'm sober enough to remind you that both my father and grandfather felt as I do now. They found out too late that the system they served was corrupt. And you know full well that the Walker family is cursed with a burden of great guilt from the Indian Wars, the slaughter of the Moros in the Crater, the race riots of World War I, and now the exposure of native islanders in the Pacific."

"The Walkers aren't a part of that testing," Penny said. "And you never believed that curse before. Why now?"

"All this is beyond me," Nancy said, "and I don't want it to ruin our wedding." With that, she rose from the table and left the room.

"You're not making much sense to me either," Sandy said. "I'm going to grab that commission and serve my country in the United States Army." And he followed Nancy.

"You'd better sober up," Penny said, "or you're going to ruin Sandy's graduation just as your father did yours. And from the amount you've been drinking, a stroke might not be far behind."

With that, she too left the room, and Andy was alone. He poured another bourbon.

The confrontation must have affected him, however, for he behaved himself the rest of the week and did not make a scene at Sandy's graduation. At the wedding and reception, he was the picture of decorum. The family tentatively forgave him, although Penny kept her distance.

After graduation, Sandy went to Fort Sill for basic officer training. Walter was born in 1949 and Sara in 1950. In the spring of 1950, when Sandy was ordered to Japan, Nancy could not go with him, so she opted to stay near her family home in Pensacola. While Sandy was dropping her off, he came by to see Andy. They discussed Korea.

"We've taken all our Divisions out of Korea," Andy said. "And Secretary of State Dean Acheson has just announced that Korea is not in our sphere of influence. If that is really so, then why did we keep an advisory team there?"

"To train the South Koreans so they can defend themselves and stop the spread of Communism."

"That worries me." "Why?" Sandy asked.

"We have stripped the South Koreans of weapons and left them unable to defend themselves. It's as if we want to get involved if they are attacked. It would be that land war in Asia I've told you about," Andy said. "And that would be wrong. It is too big and has too many people."

"We have to stop them somewhere," Sandy said. "But in a racist war? Is that smart?"

Sandy was puzzled again. Andy had been obsessed about the United States' dropping the atomic bombs on Japan, and his obsession probably cost him a star. And then he spoke out too strongly about atomic testing in the Pacific. Now he was starting to act strangely about Korea.

"It's hard to follow you, Dad," he said. "I'm on my way. Maybe you should see a doctor. At least, cut down on the booze."

With Sandy gone, Andy repeatedly invited Nancy to bring the kids over to the Beach at Destin. She declined every invitation. And Kathleen did not come home from college for the summer. She went with Dan to visit his parents in Jacksonville, and Andy was very much alone again.

When war broke out in Korea that summer, Andy called Nancy to offer comfort, and he discovered that the War Department had reported Sandy missing. He frantically went to work to find out what had happened. Time and again, he requested information from the Pentagon, but he received nothing other than word that Sandy's unit, a battalion of the Seventh Cavalry, had been overrun. After weeks of frustration, Andy volunteered for duty in Korea. A week later, he received a call from Washington.

"Sorry, Andy," the man said. "You're staying put."

"But I'm a combat veteran. They need officers like me."

"Frankly, we agree. We are just now trying to fill several vacancies you'd be perfect for. But the word is that MacArthur personally must approve every Colonel or General assigned to his command. I'm told he lined out your name."

"Where'd you hear that?"

"A General named Harrison working for General Collins at Field Force Headquarters," the man said.

"Bob Harrison?"

"That's the one. Actually he was pretty obnoxious about it. Not only said you weren't wanted, but added the Army would be better off if you retired."

Andy's anger and frustration lasted two weeks longer, and then Sandy showed up in Pusan. He and several others had worked their way by night through the North Korean lines and showed up tired, hungry, and exhausted, but safe.

Then Andy received a message from the Pentagon that sent him on temporary duty to the Military Mission to the United Nations in New York. The Soviet Union had become a nuclear power, and the United Nations was debating the question of proliferation. Owing to newspaper articles about his opposition to nuclear testing, Andy had come to the attention of forces urging a ban, and they wanted him to testify before a committee of the General Assembly. He flew to New York and took a hotel room on the East Side. His orders were to report to the United States Military Mission to the United Nations for a briefing.

When Andy arrived, he discovered that Bob Harrison had been assigned to the Mission. As had happened in Hawaii, Harrison kept him waiting for a long time. And when Andy finally was ushered into his office, Harrison opened brusquely.

"You keep your mouth shut. You hear me?" "How can I testify if I keep my mouth shut?"

"Don't wise off to me, Walker," Harrison said. "I'll put you before a Board of Officers, and they'll run you out of the Army with reduced pay."

"Go ahead," Andy said. "You've already done far more damage than that. I'll bet you even had a hand in keeping me out of Korea. And now you've kept me waiting so long that I'm almost late for my testimony. Want to come?"

When Andy rose to leave, he did so without shaking hands or saluting. An officer from the mission accompanied him to the committee room overlooking the East River. They barely made it on time, only to find they had to wait while the previous witness finished.

"The General was pretty angry when he saw your name on the witness list," the officer said.

"How so?" Andy asked.

"He blew his stack, and then he called your ex. Guess you know they've been dating."

"Dating?"

"Yeah, he brings her to all the parties. They're a pretty steady thing. I thought you knew."

'Hell hath no fury like a woman scorned,' Andy thought, and she had come back to haunt him. But the more he thought about it, the more it upset him. When he rose to speak, he did so badly, and he stumbled awkwardly through his testimony. He left the committee a paper he had prepared, but his heart was not in the subject. All he wanted to do was to get out of there.

He was in a foul mood on the plane back to Florida. MacArthur had kicked him out of Japan and kept him out of Korea. He had no future in the Army. And now Penny had turned to Harrison. In spite of their situation, his stomach churned when he thought of them together. It was all his fault, and it was too much. As soon as he arrived at his office the next day, he began assembling the data needed to put in his retirement papers.

Harrison had won.

CHAPTER TWELVE

By the summer of 1952, Andy had left the service. Then Nancy called to say that Sandy was on his way home from Korea. She invited Andy to the celebration. Beer and barbecue she said, and Andy added a flask of bourbon. It was a festive occasion, with family and friends, kids and dogs. At the party, Sandy looked tired but happy. Most of all, he was home safe. He looks just like me after World War II, Andy mused. I'll drink to that, he thought, and he hoisted one.

"What the heck happened when you were missing?" he asked when they were alone for a moment.

"After the invasion," Sandy said, "the 24th Infantry Division was hastily assembled in Japan and thrown into combat to slow the North Koreans. In late July, I was attached to the Seventh Cavalry when we relieved them in the line. Our senior sergeants were veterans of World War II, but the rest of the unit was pretty green. We had been in combat just three days near No Gun Ri when the North Koreans overran our company, and our defense just melted away. After a couple of days of confusion and chaos, nobody knew what was going on. Five of us ended up separated from the rest. I had my radio operator, and a platoon leader with two sergeants joined us.

The North Koreans were all around, and we didn't have much ammo, so we headed up into the hills. We avoided contact by moving south only at night and sticking to the highest terrain. We ate field mice and drank from the streams. It took us more than a month, and I lost thirty pounds, but we stuck together and made it to the American lines at Pusan. If we hadn't been in top shape, we wouldn't have survived."

"And when you were overrun, did you say the unit you were supporting was part of the Seventh Cavalry?"

"That's right," Sandy said.

"Seems like they've been around forever, and our family keeps running into them in the damnedest places. Joseph was with them when he met Sitting Bull during Stanley's Yellowstone campaign, and Junior met them at Wounded Knee."

"Well Korea was almost one big Little Big Horn, and it happened more than once."

"I'll buy that," Andy said. "What now?"

"Fort Sill, to attend the Advanced Course. They tell me I'll probably stay on as an instructor and try to pass on some combat lessons."

"Like Dad did at Cuba Libre in the war with Spain," Andy said. "What would be your first lesson?"

"Don't send untrained troops into combat," Sandy said. "Some of our junior officers had been in the Army less than two months, and they hadn't gone through a Basic Course. They had the highest mortality rates of all, as high as fifty percent. To be a company-grade officer in the first weeks of the Korean War was to die. But what would you say was the best lesson?"

"Well, since you're going to be teaching at the Artillery School, my first rule would be something like if you are in front of your lines, friendly artillery will be short."

"Come on, Dad. Be serious."

"I'm serious. You know the second rule? The only thing more accurate than incoming enemy fire is incoming friendly fire."

"How 'bout an infantry lesson?" "Tracers work both ways."

"Okay, Dad, but on a more serious note, you look bad. You've gained some weight, and that hair on your face is scruffy."

"I'm just growing a beard."

"Growing a beard is one thing," Sandy said. "But what you're doing is forgetting to shave. There's a difference."

"Yeah, but think of the time I save."

Sandy gave up, and they rejoined the party. Andy had a few more drinks and then began to offer drunken toasts to the nuclear tests in the Pacific.

"We'll soon be able to fry a million people at a time," he proclaimed. "And we won't need light bulbs, because all of us will glow in the dark."

Nancy's friends edged away from him, and she ushered Walter and Sara to another room. Even Sandy began to think his father had become strange, and shortly thereafter, he drove Andy home. Two weeks later, when Sandy left Pensacola to take his family to Fort Sill, he did not come to Destin to say goodbye.

The small cottage closed in on Andy. Kathleen and Dan eloped to marry and then moved to Jacksonville to sell real estate. Andy pestered his Army contacts by letter and phone, and he searched the newspapers for any information about the Pacific tests. When the new television service became available in his area, he switched from radio to the grainy, black-and-white pictures and watched the little screen with fascination as over sixty nuclear explosions took place in the Marshall Islands. It became an obsession. He was fixated by any small tidbit of news from the test area, doing little other than monitor what was happening out there. He stayed at home, avoided exercise, drank too much, and his health suffered.

Three years later, Sandy visited on his way to Fort Bragg where he was to take part in Airborne, Ranger, and Special Forces training. Nancy and the kids were not with him.

"Why Fort Bragg?" Andy asked. "And what's all this about Airborne, Ranger, and Special Forces?"

"Southeast Asia is heating up," Sandy said. "All Regular Army officers have to improve individual, small-unit combat skills. And there is new emphasis on counter-insurgency warfare. So everybody has to be Airborne or Ranger qualified. Artillery officers can take Airborne training at Fort Bragg, and that's better because after jump school, they can take their Special Warfare training at the Center there."

"By Special Forces, you mean irregular warfare."

"Actually there is a little more to it than that. Nation building is involved."

"Nation building?"

"Yeah, everything from digging wells to taking care of the people.

Try to make the railroads run on time."

"Sounds like politics to me," Andy said. "Where does the soldiering part come in?"

"That's the Ranger and Airborne training," Sandy said. "A lot of it is small unit tactics."

"You must mean guerrilla warfare," Andy said. "Joseph and Dad did the same thing against the Indians and used those lessons against the Spanish and Filipinos."

"In a way, you're right," Sandy said. "There are a lot of similarities. But in Vietnam, politics and economics are mixed in with protecting the people."

"Now you're really starting to worry me," Andy said. "Politicians have no damn business getting us involved in a fight in Indochina. I've told you that before. The United States does not need a war in that place. It is just too damn big. And people over there are cheap commodities. Their leaders don't care how many soldiers they sacrifice. They have plenty more where they come from."

"But we have to contain Communism," Sandy said. "All over the world, they are trying to take over countries. In the Far East, the North Vietnamese will not only take over South Vietnam, they'll invade Laos, Cambodia, and Thailand before they're through."

"Read your history," Andy said. "Our real adversary in the Far East is China, and the Vietnamese have been fighting the Chinese for over a thousand years. If the enemy of my enemy is really my friend, we should be allied with the Vietnamese, not at war with them. And remember that in World War II, we were friends. Ho Chi Minh fought alongside the OSS against the Japanese. In those days, we were on the best of terms. After the war, Ho wrote Truman again and again asking for the independence he had been promised. Truman never gave him the courtesy of a single reply. Even then, when the Viets started their war with the French, Ho issued orders to avoid harming Americans. He still thought we would step in and help him against the French. A lot would be different if we had."

"But the French were… ." Sandy began.

"The French nothing. They gave up their rights to Indochina in World War II. The Vichy French actually assisted the Japanese in using their airfields to attack us in Nationalist China and in the Philippine Islands."

"But if that's true, why're we helping them now?"

"The State Department has persuaded the President to trade Vietnamese independence for French cooperation in Europe. It was the only way we could get them to join NATO. And you mark my words, someday we'll regret that tradeoff. Instead of using the Vietnamese as a buffer against Chinese expansion, we're forcing them into the Chinese camp."

The conversation went downhill when Sandy admitted he had studied the use of atomic artillery.

"Do you realize that we've just exploded a hydrogen bomb in the Pacific?" Andy asked. "It was a thousand times more powerful than the bombs we exploded over Japan. It vaporized an entire island. Four nearby islands were enveloped in radioactive fallout. Observers and natives on those islands had nausea, vomiting, and severe itching. We've not seen the last of that either. Why would you want to put one of those bombs in an artillery shell and explode it on a battlefield? Your own people would die from radiation. It is insanity."

"Okay, Dad, I won't argue with you," Sandy said. "But just once more I'll tell you that you really should take better care of yourself. I'll bet you've put on fifty pounds, and you look bad. Do you ever exercise."

"What for?"

Sandy had no answers so he said goodbye and left for Fort Bragg. Andy sat in his living room, drinking and watching the atomic tests unfold like a classic Greek drama moving inevitably toward a terrible climax. When the last of the scheduled tests took place in 1958, he called a Pensacola reporter.

"You have a reputation," the reporter said. "I found out you did an interview in Japan after the war that didn't go over well with Army Brass. You're on somebody's black list."

"That was then," Andy said. "This is now." "Okay," the man said, "Shoot."

"You know that the United States just exploded the last of six-ty-six atomic tests in the Marshall Islands?" Andy asked.

"That's apparently correct. Is there a story there?"

"Three stories and a question," Andy said. "The first story is that when the United Nations designated the United States the Administrator of Micronesia after the war, we were to protect the inhabitants from loss of their lands or resources. Yet in the atomic testing just completed, two islands we were to protect have been completely vaporized and the inhabitants moved to an island with no lagoon, anchorage, or food. They are now starving. That is how we carried out our mandate. I have many more examples, but if I had commanded my battalion in New Guinea the way the United States has carried out its Pacific mandate, I would have been relieved of command."

"Fair enough. What's the second story?"

"Incompetence," Andy said. "Four years ago, in the final twenty-four hours before we were about to explode a gigantic bomb, the wind direction changed to unfavorable. Yet the test was carried out anyway. Islanders and technicians on nearby islands were drenched with a volcanic ash that caused nausea, vomiting, and skin rashes. Shortly thereafter, they developed skin burns, and their hair fell out. Still, the Atomic Energy Commission announced that all those who had been exposed were well and without burns. That leads into the third story."

"Which is?"

"The United States has just announced that the islanders who had been evacuated from some nearby islands may now return."

"That's some shocking story."

"No, listen. The real story is that for some time, we have sus-pected that radiation causes cancer, leukemia, and thyroid dys-function. Up to now, we've had no empirical data. So, guess what? Immediately after that bungled test, we set up a secret medical com-mission to monitor islanders who had been exposed. Not to protect them, but to gather data so we would know more about the effects of radiation on human beings. Evidently this secret commission needs more information, so it is now letting the islanders go back to places where the lingering radiation is higher than anywhere else in the world. So that story is about experimenting on humans, just like the Nazis did during World War II in the concentration camps."

"Those are pretty strong words," the reporter said. "But you said you had a question."

"And I do," Andy said. "Here it is: Would we have done these things to the Marshall Islanders if they were white?"

"You think all this is some kind of a racial plot?"

"I think your readers should ask themselves if the racial mix of the islanders made it easier for us to risk their lives. Here's another example. One nearby island was not evacuated because to do so would have cost time and money, and someone decided to risk brown-skin lives rather than spend money. I have asked myself if we would have taken that risk with white skin and blue eyes. What do you think?"

Andy then produced facts and figures supporting what he had just alleged. The reporter took copious notes, made copies of Andy's fact sheets, and agreed to check out the data and find independent verification. When the man left, Andy poured a drink, convinced he was putting before the country a scandal that had bothered him for years. A month later, the reporter called to say that his editors had killed the story. It was too controversial, and they could not find supporting evidence. Andy himself was considered an unreliable source, a drunken bum, and a sloppy pig. And try as he would over the next several years, Andy could find no one who believed him enough to take the story and run with it. His despair deepened.

In 1961, Sandy came by for a visit. He was on his way to Vietnam to serve as an advisor to the South Vietnamese Army.

"Don't worry, Dad," Sandy said, "the emphasis is on building them up so they can fight for themselves."

"Are you going to carry a weapon?" Andy asked. "Of course. This is a war zone."

"And can you use it to defend yourself?" "Sure."

"And how many advisors are going?" "Five hundred for now."

"Then you're involved in a war in Asia."

"No we're not," Sandy said. "At least not in the sense of a conventional war. Nobody thinks we should do that. Our mission is to prevent war."

"Don't be too sure. Anything is possible. You may not know it, but back when the French were surrounded at Dienbienphu, the Chairman of our Joint Chiefs of Staff, Admiral Radford, proposed that we drop three atomic bombs on the attacking forces. Many supported him. Had not General Ridgeway objected, we might have done it. Ridgeway pointed out that China might come in and we'd have a full blown war, so they vetoed the idea."

"Well, evidently we've learned our lesson," Sandy said. "As you've always said, atomic warfare would be crazy, so President Kennedy wants us to have an alternative to nuclear war. We have to be able to oppose Communism in many ways. General Taylor calls it a flexible response to the challenge of World Communism. So we're going to teach South Vietnam how to defend itself."

"All I ask is that you return alive and in one piece," Andy said. "Come by here when you do, and tell me honestly what you think."

Sandy agreed to take precautions and report what he found. Before leaving for Southeast Asia, he took Nancy and the children to join Kathleen and Dan at a new resort development just starting to take off on Hilton Head Island in South Carolina. Andy realized that they had gone there to avoid him, but as much as he wanted to see Walter and Sara, he could think of no way to change their opinions of him. So, writing an occasional letter to the editor, he drank and monitored the television for news of Vietnam and atomic tests in the Pacific.

Sandy's year was up quickly. He came home in one piece and was sent to Fort Benning to report on his experiences in South Vietnam, and while he was there, he drove down to see Andy. He was clearly discouraged.

"Looks bad," he told Andy. "The South Vietnamese Army doesn't want to fight, and the Diem government is isolating itself from its own people."

"And what are we doing about it?" Andy asked.

"We're sending in more advisors and pouring money at the problem. Unfortunately, with a corrupt South Vietnamese regime, not much nation building going on."

"That's exactly what the French did. And do you realize they lost a hundred thousand men over there? When President Eisenhower asked General Ridgeway what the French needed in order to win their war with Ho, he said they would need the support of seven American combat Divisions. And now that the French are gone, it would take twice that number. It's madness."

"That's what I told them at Fort Benning." "And what did they say?"

"They told me to get out of Special Forces."

Sandy went to Fort Campbell to join the 101st Airborne Division, and then he was selected to attend the Staff College at Fort Leavenworth. All the while, the United States' military and political presence in Vietnam continued to increase, and so the North Vietnamese also built up their forces.

In 1963, the first leukemia cases began to appear among the Marshall Islanders, but the natives ignored that evidence and started to return to their islands because the United States authorities said the soil was safe. Andy called his reporter to point out what was happening and to ask that his story be revived. The reporter called back a day later to say that the consensus was that Andy was a drunk and a crackpot. No one wanted to revisit Andy's ideas.

In 1965, a hundred years after his great-grandfather had left Fort Leavenworth to survey the Oregon Trail, taking with him his bride and a company of infantry, Sandy too left Fort Leavenworth, for a second tour in Vietnam. This time, he would be in command of a field artillery battalion. When Sandy came to Destin to say goodbye, Andy warned that continued escalation in Vietnam would lead to a conventional war that would produce more American casualties than people would support.

"Now that Diem has been assassinated," he said, "would you want your son to die in Southeast Asia fighting yellow hordes in support of another obviously corrupt puppet regime? If I were you, I'd get out of the Army and educate America about what is really going on in South Vietnam."

Sandy ignored him. He and his battalion arrived at Tay Ninh by the following month. They were in their first major battle against a North Vietnamese regiment six weeks later.

When Walter was drafted in 1967, Andy called him to say that if Walter decided to go to Canada rather than serve in an unjust war, Andy would support him. Walter listened, but would not run. He married his fiancée, Cathy, and she was pregnant before he left for Vietnam in the summer of 1967. He was with the Americal Division at My Lai on March 16th, 1968, and his son, Paul, was born that same day. When Walter was sent to Fort Benning to take part in the Army's investigation of the My Lai massacre, Andy asked to see him.

"What the hell happened?" Andy asked.

"I had been wounded at Dak To," Walter said. "When I was well enough to go back to the lines, the Americal had arrived, and they needed fillers with combat experience. Four of us went to Charley Company. Our platoon leader, Lieutenant Calley, was damn near incompetent. The company moved without light or noise discipline, and suffered daily casualties without ever seeing an enemy. I was a machine-gunner, with Rastus as my assistant."

"That's a racist nickname," Andy said.

"No it wasn't," Walt said. "It was a term of friendship. In return, he called me Honky, and we were the best of friends. And we had two assigned Black bodyguards. We worked as a team and survived because we did."

"There is no prejudice in a shared foxhole," Andy said. "Now tell me about My Lai."

"We were told that every living being in Song Be was VC, NVA, or a supporter. Women were alleged to carry weapons under their dresses, and kids threw grenades. Two days before the incident, one of our best guys was captured at dusk. All night long, we heard him screaming off in the jungle. At dawn, we found his naked body on the trail ahead. All his small bones had been broken. His eyes had been gouged out, his ears had been cut off, and he had been castrated. We were mad as hell and ready to kill someone. Calley told us we would be attacking a fortified village, and we were to go in shooting. Before dawn that day, we loaded into choppers and flew to a clearing near the village. Just after daybreak, we landed and went toward My Lai as a line of skirmishers. When we received no return fire, most of us stopped shooting and simply searched the village. I came up to a group of villagers huddled in a ditch, and Calley ordered me to fire on them. When I refused, he took my M-60 and shot them himself. That was the end of it."

Walter was not indicted. Calley was convicted of murder and sent to Leavenworth. Walter left the Army to study law at the University of South Carolina. In 1973, the same year the first Marshall Islander died of leukemia and President Nixon decided to pardon Lieutenant Calley, Walter graduated from law school. Penny and Bob Harrison flew down to celebrate. Walter met them at the Columbia airport. They were making their way onto the Interstate to drive to Hilton Head, when a car crashed into them. The three of them died instantly. The date was September 5th. The driver of the other car was a Vietnamese immigrant.

CHAPTER THIRTEEN

As they had never formally dissolved their marriage, Andy was able to arrange for Penny to be buried beside Walter in the National Cemetery at Beaufort, South Carolina. Sandy and Nancy were living at nearby Fort Jackson in Columbia. Walter had bought a house in Hilton Head Plantation for Cathy and the children, Paul and Beth, who were now the youngest of the Walkers. Kathleen and Dan lived in Sea Pines. Even Sara had joined the real estate business there after she graduated from Clemson the previous year. So the family was able to come together for support. In the gathering shadows of the late afternoon, they and about fifty friends assembled for the double graveside service.

At the time, Sandy was working as an advisor to the South Carolina National Guard, and the Adjutant General agreed to provide an honors detail, a bugler, and a chaplain. After the cleric said a few appropriate words, the bugler sounded taps and the military guard fired three volleys for Walter. The shots rang over the cemetery as the final notes of taps echoed, and then silence took over. The caskets were draped with American flags that the military detail folded precisely and presented to Andy and Cathy after the service. It was a quiet, dignified occasion that helped to bring closure to the tragedy.

Andy did not drink a single drop of alcohol during his week in Beaufort, and he was on his best behavior in his dealings with family and friends, never mentioning the Vietnam War or atomic testing. He did not mix with the others when they were together, preferring to remain in the background. He was so pensive and quiet that they wondered at his grieving, thinking that he might be sick. In spite of the terrible circumstances that had produced the change in him, they were more comfortable with him that way, for at least he was not being disruptive.

Andy did not linger long in the low country, but hurried back to Florida. Shortly thereafter, having shaved off the beard, he went to a physician in Pensacola for a physical examination. After the usual probing, bleeding, listening, and draining, the doctor called Andy into his office for a consultation.

"How's it look?" Andy asked.

"Aside from the fact that you drink too much, you're out of shape, and you're overweight, it's not too bad."

"Am I salvageable?"

"Maybe if you lost thirty pounds, stopped drinking, ate better, and got some exercise," the doctor said.

"That's all?"

"No, you'd also need to take some aspirin and vitamin E. And if the exercise and diet didn't work, I'd recommend you go on something to control blood pressure and cholesterol."

"What if I really wanted to get back in shape?"

"Quite frankly, I'd advise against it," the doctor said. "You'd probably hurt yourself badly and end up in worse shape than you are now."

"Point well made," Andy said. "But if I really wanted to try, how would I go about it?"

"If I were you, I'd consult a nutritionist and find someone qualified to guide me through an exercise program. But above all, I would not overdo it. Remember you're seventy years old. You could kill yourself trying to do too much."

"Dying is not the objective," Andy said. "I'll remember."

The nutritionist looked at his physical examination report. Then she told him to eat three helpings of fruit daily and more vegetables. She prescribed lots of water and much less salt and sweets. She told him the only permitted breakfast was cereal and toast. No coffee at all.

"How 'bout booze?" he asked.

"You shouldn't drink," she said. "If you must, then limit it to a little wine."

"That's pretty tough. Is it necessary?"

"You were the one who asked how to get in shape," she said. "I'm only giving you the facts. You've lived for a long time with a lot of bad habits you need to change. It won't be easy, and I'd bet against you."

She was correct about the odds against him, but that was the program, and there was nothing he could do to change it. He began his diet right away, and immediately, from that first day, he knew how difficult it was going to be, for he was hungry all the time. Tough as the diet was, the fitness part was even harder. Nobody wanted responsibility for someone as old and out of shape as Andy; he was too much of a liability. On the other hand, many were willing to give free advice. Realizing that free counsel was worth what he paid for it, he talked to two Pensacola high school football coaches, three cross country and track specialists, and the swimming and weight instructors at the YMCA. Then he sat down and worked out a rough consensus of what he had learned.

Apparently, the most important requirement was intensive stretching before and after every workout. For his heart and circulatory system, he needed to perform some sort of aerobics and stomach exercises at least five times a week. To build strength and raise his metabolism, he needed to lift weights every other day. Most of all, he was to take it easy, rest, and never, ever exercise through pain.

Once his plan was clear, he started each day with aerobics, either at the high school track or in the YMCA swimming pool. For a month, all he did was walk, and even then he occasionally had leg pain. When the soreness finally stopped, he began to jog very slowly. Over time he gradually increased his speed and distance, but every increase resulted in either hip or ankle pain, and he frequently had to revert to brisk walking. When he felt better, he occasionally tried a short sprint, but he found that neither speed nor distance really made any difference. The only factor that counted was how long he kept at a session. The best results came if he could work on aerobic training for an hour without causing soreness. On inclement days and when he was aching, he swam laps. Every other day, he used the weight room at the Y, where the trainer instructed him to work with many repetitions of small dumbbell weights, and to continue each particular set of exercise to exhaustion, increasing the weight whenever he could do more than twenty repetitions at a time.

He started with the big muscles of his back and legs, and then gradually added the smaller muscles of his arms and shoulders. On the days between weight sessions, he put in a lot of time at his desk, working on investments or researching the problems of the Plains Indians and Fiji Islands.

It was a monotonous routine, filled with boredom, and he never stopped being hungry, but he stuck at it as if he were back in high school getting ready to try for an appointment to West Point. Frequently, he didn't want to get out of bed to run or swim, but when he felt discouraged, he just worked a little harder. The plateaus were the most difficult, for every now and then, he seemed stuck at a given level. No matter what he tried during those stretches, he couldn't lose more pounds or increase weights he was lifting. At those frustrating times, it took all the discipline he could muster to keep going, but he never quit or eased up. The routine paid off. After a year of abstinence, diet, and exercise, he was rewarded by the loss of more than twenty-five pounds. Over that year, he had to take in his trousers several times, and at the end, he felt great. He went back to see the doctor.

"Wow, what a difference!" the man said. "How on earth did you do it?"

"Exercise and diet," Andy said.

"Lots of people say that, but they don't get your results. What's the secret?"

"I have a goal in mind," Andy said. "It kept me going, but what's the verdict?"

"Your cholesterol is back to under 200, with the good kind between 45 and 50. That's acceptable for a man of your age. Your blood pressure is 120 over 75, and I wish mine was that good. Your body fat went from over thirty-five percent to well under twenty. I don't see a prostate problem, and your heart and lungs sound good. If you'll write up a copy of your program for me, I'll give you a twenty percent discount."

Penny had been gone just over a year when Andy asked around and located a good private detective in Pensacola. After a set of perfunctory questions, he made his request.

"I want you to find a woman for me," Andy said.

"I'm not in that business," the man said. "Try any local bar and flash a large bankroll."

"Not that kind of woman," Andy said. "A particular one." "An abused, missing wife?"

"No, this one is from thirty years ago."

"That I can do," the man said. "Give me details."

"She was a Red Cross volunteer in the Fiji Islands in 1942. Back then, her name was Helen Vincent. In 1943, she joined the Woman's Army Corps in Australia, I think as a Lieutenant."

"That may be enough, but tell me anything else you know, just in case."

"She was raised in Ohio and attended Skidmore College. She had been married, but I believe she was divorced. She's about my age, or maybe a bit younger."

"And how old are you?" "Seventy-one."

"I'd have said you were in your fifties. You must have had the right parents. Can you tell me why you want to find this woman? She owe you money, or something? I'd rather not find her if it's going to lead to problems."

"No, I give you my word that I wish her only the best," Andy said. "But I'd like to know if she's alive and if so where. Were there or are there men or some children in her life, and what are her circumstances?"

"No problem," the man said.

After two months, the detective called Andy to set up an appointment. He said he had a complete file on a Helen Vincent and could answer all of Andy's questions.

"Turns out she didn't join the WACs in 1943," he said. "She went into the prior version, the Women's Army Auxiliary Corps. And not as a Lieutenant. Seems as though they had strange ranks like First, Second, and Third Officers. She was a Second Officer in something called the Army Service Forces, and they assigned her to the

Transportation Corps. It looks like she tried to join the Army Nurse Corps, but it fell through. For a time, she was with a hospital on New Caldonia, but when the Women's Army Auxiliary Corps was converted to the Women's Army Corps in 1943, she got a commission as a First Lieutenant and was assigned to a hospital ship. They evacuated our casualties from places like New Guinea and Leyte back to that hospital in New Caldonia. She served the rest of the war on that ship until a Jap suicide plane crashed into it in April of 1945. It evidently was a bad scene, with many dead and wounded. She was hurt in the resulting explosions, and they evacuated her back to the States. When peace was declared that August, she was still in the hospital. When she had fully recovered, they promoted her to Captain and assigned her to the Pentagon where she served briefly before resigning her commission. She used the GI Bill to study and take a Masters Degree in English and Comparative Literature at the University of Georgetown. Then she accepted a position teaching English at Saint Agnes School for Girls in Alexandria, Virginia. After twenty years of teaching there, she retired four years ago. She has a pension and social security, and those seem to be all she needs. She lives simply, doesn't even have a car. Takes the bus to the store. As far as I can determine, there is no man in her life, and I could find no children. She lives on Woodland Terrace, off Russell Road in Alexandria, just three blocks from that Saint Agnes school."

The detective's report was all Andy needed. In October of 1974, he went on a shopping spree, the first in years. He bought several new outfits. He needed to. His waist was smaller, and his neck was larger. Most of what he bought was casual but classic, but he included one suit for evening wear. He needed shirts and ties, as well as new loafers and dress shoes. He even bought new underwear, socks, and handkerchiefs. Wardrobe ready, he packed his new luggage carefully and drove to Mobile, where he boarded a flight for Washington. At National Airport, he rented the best car he could find and drove to a motel just off I-95 in Arlington.

Unpacking, he walked a few miles to shake off the effects of the plane ride. He quit when it was dark. After showering and resting, he made the call.

"Helen Vincent," she said. He took a deep breath. "Helen, this is Andy Walker."

She paused for what seemed several minutes. "Is it really you?" she asked.

"Yes, and everything has changed," he said. "Would you have lunch with me tomorrow so I can explain?"

Again a pause, but then she accepted. That was really all there was to it.

Just before noon the next day, he drove to her place. It turned out to be a quiet, crowded neighborhood with twisting roads, mature lawns, and large trees. Well established, it looked as if it had been that way for a hundred years. He was nervous. He felt as if he was fifteen once more and at that Cincinnati recruiting station, but again taking that deep breath, he walked up to the door. He wore one of his new sports outfits, and there was a spring in his step. In spite of having spent a restless night, he looked trim and clear-eyed as he rang the bell.

She must have been watching for his arrival, because she opened the door almost immediately. Time had served her well. Her skin was clear and her eyes sparkled. Her short hair was not quite as white as his, and she was as wide-eyed and beautiful as ever in a light-cotton, casual dress. He handed her a small bouquet of flowers. She hesitated, but then took it with a shy smile and a thank you. When she did, the most difficult part was over. He cleared his throat.

"You look great," he said. "You too," she said.

He took her to lunch at the Army Navy Country Club where he had activated his long dormant absentee membership. Over a leisurely meal, he brought her up to date.

"Penny died in a car crash a year ago," he said. "She'd been living in New York and dating General Bob Harrison. You remember, he was the one who led the military police during the killings at the airfield."

"You were still married?"

"Yes, but separated since the war," he said. "Where did you go after Fiji?" she asked.

"Built a road in New Guinea for two years, then airfields and other roads on Leyte and Luzon. We were in the Philippines about to invade Japan when they dropped the atomic bombs. I went into Japan immediately after the surrender. You wouldn't believe the destruction. And the effects of blast, fire, and radiation on the people. I don't think I'll ever forget the women and children. It was horrible."

"When did you retire?"

"After MacArthur kept me out of Korea," he said. "I was fed up, so I went down to that cottage in Destin and brooded."

"MacArthur kept you out of Korea?"

"It's a long story," he said. "But how about you? What did you do after you left Fiji? I heard you went into the WACs."

"I joined the Women's Army Auxiliary," she said. "We were trying to be part of the Army, but nobody wanted us, so they gave us some uniforms and called us Second Officers. Those who were not officers were not even called soldiers. They became 'auxiliaries.' The Army gave us half pay and no benefits."

"But what about the WACs?"

"That happened in mid-1943. Congress passed and FDR signed a bill that made us a separate part of the Army, and I became a First Lieutenant, with all the right pay and benefits. I tried to join the Army Nurse Corps, but I would have had to come back to the States for training, and I was too busy to leave."

"But you got a Commission?"

"That was because the Red Cross was responsible for all recruiting for the Army Nurses. Through the home office, I was able to get a Commission without going back, but I couldn't be a nurse, so I joined the Transportation Corps as a part of the cadre on a hospital ship."

"Which one?"

"The *USS Comfort*. We evacuated wounded from the islands back to base hospitals in the New Hebrides and New Caldonia."

"When I was on Leyte," he said, "some of my men were sent back to that ship. I heard quite a few died."

"The Leyte campaign had the highest wounded-to-dead ratio in the war, something like 1:3. It was pretty bad. The Japs attacked our hospital ships even though we were painted white with large red crosses on the sides."

"Your ship was hit?"

"In 1945, a Kamikaze scored a direct hit on us. It was a mess, but we limped back to Guam."

"You were hurt?"

"Not bad. Some burns and minor gashes. Nothing permanent." "But a Purple Heart?"

"That, and a Commendation Ribbon." "Then what?"

"I thought I might stay in the Army," she said. "But service in the Pentagon convinced me the Army wasn't ready for women, so I resigned to use the GI Bill. I decided to teach."

By the time lunch was over, they were both pretty much up to date. When he dropped her off at her house, he asked if she would accompany him to the Army-Navy club that Saturday evening, for a dinner-dance. She accepted.

For that occasion, he was more confident. He wore his new suit and again brought flowers. She had on an apparently new cocktail dress and was waiting at the door. She accepted his flowers without hesitation, and this time she invited him in while she arranged them in a vase. Her place was a small, two-bedroom bungalow. It was clean and tastefully, but modestly decorated. She had a small television set and a good record player with a stack of seventy-eight rpm records. The titles seemed to be of a World War II vintage that he remembered well. The absence of ashtrays indicated she neither smoked nor permitted smoking in the house. Outside, the neat, well- kept garden revealed she had a green thumb.

Due to the threat of rain, the dinner dance at the country club was not held on the roof under the stars. Andy would have preferred the stars, but the weather was turning a bit colder, so he accepted the dining room. He ordered her a bourbon, and he asked for a glass of wine.

"Good memories," he said, and raised his glass. "Long life," she said.

"You said earlier that the Army wasn't ready for women. What did you mean?"

"Well, the Red Cross was responsible for nurse recruitment, and we had only a thousand nurses on December 7th. By the end of the war, fifty thousand were serving, so we had a big challenge to find qualified women. The problem was made more difficult by the attitude of the Army. It reflected society in believing women had no business in the war zones, so it dragged its feet as long as it could."

"But you didn't go into the Army Nurse Corps?"

"No, the nurses had to have formal medical training that I lacked, and they weren't given Commissions until 1944. So I went into the WACs."

"As an officer?"

"At first, I was what they called a Second Officer. Later, I became a Lieutenant, and I finished the war as a Captain."

"Were the WACs more accepted?"

"Not initially. Congresswoman Edith Rogers had to lobby hard, but finally General Marshall came over to her side and supported her. Then Oveta Culp Hobby, who eventually became the first Director of the WACs, had to convince both Congress and the public that women wanting to serve in the armed forces were actually not prostitutes and were really needed to free men for combat."

"How many WACs were there?"

"By the end of the war, we had 150,000 on active duty. A year after the war, ten thousand."

"How many Blacks?"

"Only about five hundred nurses and a couple thousand WACs. Black nurses were trained separately and only allowed to treat Black soldiers, and the Black WACs were gathered at separate sites and segregated in separate battalions like the postal units in Europe."

"Why do you say the Army wasn't ready for women?"

"Some parts of the services were ready. The Army Air Corps wanted as many as they could get, not only for things like typing, but also for important tasks such as the Aircraft Warning Service and aircraft supply and maintenance. Some women even flew transports. General Eisenhower wanted women for his headquarters, and General Clark asked for them on his staff. On the other hand, General MacArthur was firmly opposed. When WACs finally did come into the Southwest Pacific, he had them bivouacked behind barbed wire that was patrolled by armed guards. It was humiliating. Whenever a WAC left the compound, she had to have an armed escort. That was why I worked my way onto that hospital ship. The Army Medical Service desperately needed anybody who could wrap a bandage so we were treated with more respect."

"Tell me about your ship being hit by a suicide plane." "Twenty-nine were killed, and six were my nurses."

"And yet you wanted to stay in the Army after the war?"

"Sure. I felt women had earned respect, and I wanted to build something more permanent. That was when I determined that the Army really wasn't ready for us. At the Pentagon, I was treated like a glorified typist instead of a veteran commander. So I got out, went back to college, and taught English at a girls school. But that's enough about me. Tell me about you and MacArthur. He kept you out of Korea?"

"It goes back farther than that," Andy said, and he spent the rest of the supper telling her stories about MacArthur at West Point, during the war in the South Pacific, and in Japan after the surrender. He brought up MacArthur's reaction to Andy's interview about dropping the atomic bombs on Hiroshima and Nagasaki, and she was very attentive, so that led him to the atomic tests in the Marshall Islands. They had finished their meal before they could do more than start a discussion of the Vietnam War, so he left that for another time.

Over coffee, she seemed at ease, so he signaled to the bandleader and asked her to dance. As they went hand in hand to the floor, the band struck up the strains of "Sleepy Lagoon." She melted into his arms and closed her eyes. The music took them back thirty-two years. The rest of the evening, they danced to songs of the Second World War. Saying good night on her doorstep, he kissed her on the cheek and asked if he could come by the next day to tell her about some plans.

He arrived just before cocktail hour on Sunday. She met him at the door, and they settled down to a glass of wine in her living room. He began immediately.

"I'm going to sell the beach cottage in Destin and move to Mobridge, South Dakota," he said. "I want to be near the Indian Reservation at Standing Rock."

"Why there?" she asked.

"It's a Sioux Reservation," he said. "My family goes back a long ways with the Sioux, and I want to help them."

"Back a long ways with the Sioux?" she asked. "What do you mean by that?"

"My grandfather first fought them on the Bozeman Trail in 1866. He didn't stop until Wounded Knee in 1890, and my father was with him there. I met one of their chiefs in 1926."

"If you fought them for so long, why help them now?"

"Two reasons: First, we were part of a system that broke many promises to them over the years. We took advantage of them, and in some small way, I'd like to make up for that. Secondly, one of their great Chiefs put a curse on my family, and I'd like to show he was wrong to do it."

"A curse? You're serious?"

"Completely. Someday I'd like to tell you the full story. But cursed or not, I want to help them."

"How would you do that?"

"Find a way to fight against poverty, corruption, and government violations of their rights. But that's only part of it; I'm also going to work out a project to find a way to make up for the damage we did to that holy site on Viti Levu in the Fiji Islands. Maybe move the graves or build a chapel near the airport. Whatever I can work out with the church people we hurt when Harrison attacked their defenders."

"A chapel in the Fiji Islands. Won't that cost money?"

"Money won't be the problem," he said. "I have plenty of that. The obstacles will come from government bureaucrats who have never dealt with someone like me before."

"You have money?"

"Yes, Dad left Kate, Jeanette, Rose, and me twenty-five thousand dollars each when he died in 1926. My share has been untouched in a mutual fund ever since then. And when Mom died, she split what she had from Dad between us kids."

"But how about your sisters? Are they okay?"

"Yes, they are well married. I do not need to help them, and Kathleen and Sandy are well off. She married a fellow student from the University of Florida. They have a successful real estate business on Hilton Head Island. Walter's widow, Cathy, and her children are with them. Sandy is about to retire from the Army, and he and Nancy are going into real estate with Kathleen. Sara is working with them. No, I am free and clear to do as I wish."

"But you are talking about spending a lot of money."

"Wait, there's more," he said. "When Penny died, Sandy, Kathleen, and I each received a third of her estate. After we sold the Westchester house and New York law partnership, each of us had more than a million dollars. You can see why she never asked me for any money. And now a Florida developer wants to buy my place in Destin for a couple hundred thousand dollars. He wants to build a high rise on the oceanfront. And I never spent even half of my army pension, so I have more than enough money."

She sat back, obviously amazed.

"Why are you telling me all this?" she asked.

He rose from the coffee table, removed a diamond ring from his pocket, knelt on one knee, and said:

"I want you to marry me."

She burst into tears as he took her left hand and slid the ring onto her finger. It was a bit too large, but it went on as if it were always meant to be.

"Please share the rest of my life," he said. "We need to make up for what we have missed. Come with me."

She nodded through her tears.

CHAPTER FOURTEEN

Helen was in a state of shock. For the last twenty-eight years she had lived a quiet, almost reclusive life. After the terror of that suicide air attack on her hospital ship and the pain of her subsequent hospitalization, the desk job at the Pentagon was boring. Staff work was so dull and unsatisfying that she decided to resign her Captain's commission and take a Masters Degree in Literature at Georgetown University. Then for twenty years, she had taught English at Saint Agnes. In all that time, she had never owned a car, choosing instead to walk to her job and take a bus elsewhere. She had never traveled. Nothing in her routine had prepared her for the major disruption that Andy had just caused, and she was having second thoughts.

"I don't think I can do this," she told Andy. "What's to do?" he asked.

"The house, the furniture, all those address changes, my pension, my social security checks, my friends here: it's just too much. I don't know where to start."

"Let's take it one step at a time. First thing, I'll call that developer who wants my cottage, and then we'll put your house on the market."

"But I've accumulated a lot of junk over the years."

"So have I. And much of it is excess baggage. We'll give it to the Salvation Army or Good Will. What we really want to keep, we'll ship to temporary storage in South Dakota. We have a lifetime ahead of us."

"At age seventy? Aren't we being foolish?"

"Not for a minute," he said. "Benjamin Franklin dominated the Continental Convention when he was in his eighties, and Frank Lloyd Wright designed the Guggenheim Museum when he was almost ninety. And Martha Graham danced until she was older than either of us."

"Those are exceptions."

"Then how 'bout these? Grandma Moses did her best work in her eighties. Marshall Tito was a major force in Europe until he died at eighty-eight, Goethe finished Faust at eighty-two, and Charlie Chaplin got a special Academy Award at eighty-three. I could cite many more, but you get the idea."

"But those people were doing their life work," she said. "We are talking about making major changes."

"You want changes? Albert Einstein became an American citizen at age sixty-one. Golda Meir was Prime Minister of the new Israel in her seventies. And Buckminister Fuller almost committed suicide before he changed his life. He ended up still building geodesic domes at age seventy."

"You're very persuasive," she said.

"Who was it that said 'Grow old along with me, the best is yet to be'? Let's do it."

"Browning," she said. "Rabbi ben Ezra. I think he meant that all our lives, we prepare for our final years."

"A good idea," he said. "But we've done enough preparation. Let's start living."

She gave in. The next day, they studied the papers to find out what her house was worth, and then she called a realtor and began to sort out what to keep. That same day, Andy called the developer who wanted to buy the cottage in Destin.

"I may sell after all," he told the man. "Great. Name your price."

"Three hundred thousand, if you can settle in less than thirty days."

"We'll settle in two weeks," the man said.

Andy flew down to Florida the following day to arrange the closing. For the next week, he sold, threw out, or gave away whatever he would not need in South Dakota. He shipped clothes to Helen in Alexandria and sent the rest to storage in Pierre. He sent out cards changing his address to hers, but he wrote only one letter, to Sandy offering the briefest of explanations. By now, most of his family considered him eccentric anyway, so he did not bother to rationalize his actions. When he had the check after the closing, he called Helen.

"I'm done here," he said. "How're you doing?"

"We're getting lots of lookers," she said. "The agent says we'll have a good offer very soon."

"Ask for a sixty-day closing. I'll fly out to Pierre and find a place we can rent temporarily."

"But we aren't even married yet."

"Call a judge and set it up. I'll be there in a week."

He spent a day in Pierre uncovering the best realtor in town, and made an appointment.

"Find us a ranch in the vicinity of Mobridge," he told the man, "near Sitting Bull's grave if possible. We can fix up the house if we have to, and we want a stable and enough pasture for several horses. We'd like some good trails to ride and someone to help us take care of the place. Mrs. Walker wants a garden, and I need an office in the house. We'd like a family room and a big stone fireplace. While you're hunting, find us a temporary rental in a nice place in town. We'll sign a year's lease."

He flew back to Alexandria, and they signed the necessary papers so that the judge could marry them. When that occasion arrived, the jurist seemed inclined to lecture them about the sanctity of marriage, but their white hair must have flustered him, for he faltered on the parts about "so long as you both shall live" and "till death do you part." Then he signed the marriage certificate, and the deed was done.

She had a contract on her house the following week. The location was so close to everything that the buyer did not quibble on price, and they had sixty days to sort out her possessions. They went to work with a vengeance. He had just gone through the process down in Florida, so he was able to expedite some of the details, although he felt a little foolish in sending out a second change of address for himself in less than a month. He was sure the recipients would think he had gone entirely off his rocker, but he did not care. They gave her excess possessions to charity and threw away much of the rest, not even bothering to hold a garage sale. What she really wanted to keep, they shipped to the rental address in Pierre.

After the closing in January, they flew out to meet with the real estate agent. He had found nothing up at Mobridge that appealed to them, so they settled as well as they could in the rental. Then, leaving their ranch request open with the agent, they set out on Pan Am for a honeymoon trip to the Fiji Islands. When they left South Dakota, the temperature was twelve degrees; when they landed at Nandi Airport, it was eighty.

Viti Levu had changed. In the late sixties, the previously peaceful island had been engulfed in race riots between native Fijians and immigrant Indians. The causes went back at least to World War II, when the growing population of Indians had refused to serve with the Allied forces while the Fijians had provided a battalion of infantry that fought well in the Solomon Islands.

As independence approached, however, the immigrants outnumbered the natives, and that fact complicated the process of becoming independent from Britain. Finally a system had been set up that gave the power to the minority natives as long as they remained unified, and in 1970 the Fiji Islands were on their own. The process, however, left a simmering resentment among the majority Indians, who felt sullen and disenfranchised.

Andy wanted no part of Fiji politics, so he found a quiet hotel along the southern coastal road to Suva. There, they were able to rent a small cottage just off the white beach adjacent to the hotel and the warm blue waters. A constant offshore breeze carried the fresh smell of the sea and made the place a delight. Although the cottage had its own kitchen, the main hotel had an excellent dining room, where fresh fish was an obvious and delicious specialty. The bar had a picture window from which to watch the dramatic sunsets and listen to a jazz trio. After Andy taught the pianist to play World War II songs like the perfect "Long Ago and Far Away," they danced nightly to their favorite music. It became a ritual that the hotel staff looked forward to watching. For three weeks, they acted just like honeymooners. During the days, they sailed the blue waters, fished the quiet lagoons, or swam off the sandy beaches. Her anxiety left her, and she embraced their new life. When he brought up his plans for the Fijians and the Sioux, however, she was curious.

"You have an obsession with them," she said. "It's more than wanting to do good. What's really behind it?"

"It's a family thing that goes back to 1890. Just before he died, Sitting Bull put a curse on Joseph and Junior, and ever since then, we've had more than our share of bad luck."

"What do you mean?"

"We were involved in some pretty bad scenes: Wounded Knee, No Gun Ri, and My Lai for example. And I hate the idea we might have been even remotely connected with the slaughter of the Moros in the Crater, the hanging of the Buffalo Soldiers at Houston, the obliteration of the Japanese in those heavily populated cities, or the contamination of the Marshall Islanders by atomic testing. And the government we've served for so long has not done well by people of color."

"Or women either," she said. "But you want to help the Fijians and the Sioux because you think you're under some sort of Indian curse?"

"No. I want to help because it's right and I can. But some strange coincidences in dates worry me. Joseph, Junior, and Walter all died on September the fifth. That was the same day that Crazy Horse died back in 1877 and Sitting Bull pronounced the curse in 1890. And it doesn't seem to stop there either. It turns out that Paul was born on March 16th, the date of the My Lai massacre. And I don't sleep well. Every now and then, I dream about the curse and what has happened. That's probably what you mean by an obsession."

"Obsession or not," she said, "it's something we ought to talk about and deal with, and we will."

After that, because she would listen and not laugh, Andy felt better. So he was able to move on and begin implementing his plan to restore the religious site near the airport. Thus he asked the hotel manager to identify a trustworthy island cleric who had the best interest of the Fijians at heart. Without hesitation, the manager named a specific pastor. After talking to some local government officials, the police, and the American consulate, Andy arranged to meet at the church. In his office there, the reverend listened to Andy's account of the killings at the airfield back in 1942. After a few questions, he agreed to find out what he could. In a month, he had assembled data that showed the site was indeed considered a holy place by islanders, but that no graves had been located there. Andy asked what he could do to make amends for what had happened. The man suggested the possibility of a commemorative chapel, and Andy asked him to come up with a proposal. After two more meetings at which both natives and local politicians provided input, they agreed on a concept. Then Andy talked to a local architect and consulted an attorney who drew up a trust to oversee the project. Having done everything he could think of to start the chapel project in the right direction, Andy wrote the first check for $100,000.

After four months, construction was well underway and they received word that their real estate agent had found something for them near Mobridge. Vowing they would come back to Viti Levu every year, they returned to South Dakota in May.

Their agent had located a ranch whose owner had just died. The heirs wanted to sell. One hundred and ten acres, it had a garden for Helen, a horse barn and pasture for Andy, and a separate cabin for a live-in couple, Reva and Joe Bearclaw, who agreed to stay on and help. Joe had the smooth, dark skin and straight, black hair of a full-blooded Sioux. At about one hundred and seventy pounds, he was deceptively smooth-muscled, hiding his impressive strength behind a soft-looking body. He usually wore jeans, a denim jacket, and a black hat that resembled a flat-topped bowler. His normal conversation was a grunt that could be both affirmative and negative. Reva was his female equivalent, with a square body used to hard work. Andy and Helen were delighted to have such promising help. They moved their belongings from the rental house and storage, started renovation of the buildings and fences, and became ranchers. After selling their houses, moving to Mobridge, buying the ranch, and paying the first installment on the chapel in Fiji, they had a little less than three million dollars in bank and mutual funds.

As the place began to shape up, Andy had more time to do some on-site research into the problems of the Sioux on the Standing Rock

Reservation. He found that alcoholism among adult males there approached ninety percent. Their unemployment rate was over fifty percent. And their children had the highest rate of teen suicide in the nation. When he discussed statistics with the Indian Agents, they seemed universally frustrated by the situation but reluctant to do anything at all to solve the problems. Initiative lacking, they mostly processed routine paperwork and responded to federal inquiries. And the Sioux themselves seemed to distrust all White men, especially one with the name of Walker. A year of research and questioning produced no answers.

During that time, Andy and Joe Bearclaw became friends. Joe would not let Andy do any of the tough work, but he was willing to discuss what had to be done. They went together to buy four riding horses, but Andy let Joe buy the tack, and when they had agreed on what was to be done on the farm, he let Joe select and purchase the equipment. Reva worked in the house and garden with Helen, and gradually a mutual trust and understanding developed. Most of all, Joe came to understand that Andy was frustrated by not being able to find answers to the Standing Rock puzzle.

"There may be a better way," he said one day. "Such as?" Andy asked.

"Our real leaders are the shamans. They can help you with the Tribal Council."

"How do I find a shaman?" Andy asked. "I'll take you," Joe said.

Andy volunteered his Jeep, but Joe said it would be better if they went in his old pick up. They drove to the western side of Mobridge, crossed the river, left the asphalt, and took a dirt road farther west up into the hills. There, a split-rail fence surrounded a clapboard house that needed paint. The uncut yard was a mass of weeds and unruly bushes. A ten-year-old Ford pick-up truck without wheels was propped on cinder blocks in the driveway, and a middle-aged man sat in a rocker on the porch. He wore the jeans and jacket of a farmer, and streaks of white were starting to show in his black hair.

"His name is Tashunka," Joe said.

Joe sat on the front steps, and Andy took a chair near the rocker.

An Indian woman brought them Cokes. "You a Walker?" Tashunka asked.

"My grandfather was Joseph Walker," Andy said, "The Angry White Chief Who Fights The Sioux."

"The Walkers were our enemies."

"That's what Chief Whitefeathers said. He also repeated a curse on my family. We don't deserve that. I want to prove it by helping your people."

"How?"

"You tell me. I have resources. Let's find a way."

For three hours, Tashunka asked questions about Andy's life, career, and family. Most of the questions had to do with character and sincerity. Frequently, he referred to treaties the White Men had broken. Again and again, he mentioned trust. The man's quiet voice had a hypnotic effect, and Andy felt as if he was in the presence of a powerful force. Finally, Tashunka announced that he needed to meditate and pray for guidance from the Great Spirit. He asked that they meet the following month. On the trip home, Joe said that Andy had done well, but he would not elaborate. The intervening time went by slowly, but then, back on the run-down front porch, Tashunka lit his pipe.

"The Great Spirit has revealed that your family is indeed under a black cloud," he said. "But you seem to be standing alone in a ray of sunlight. I will help you."

He suggested that some members of the Tribal Council might agree to meet Andy and parlay in the hope of finding a way to better conditions on the reservation. He would send out feelers if Andy wished. Thus, in August of 1978, seven members of the Council joined Andy on Tashunka's front porch. The weather was hot and dry, the flies buzzed incessantly, and not even a hint of a breeze stirred the air. This time, Andy brought a cooler full of cold Cokes.

Tashunka broke the ice by introducing and indorsing Andy, and then Andy repeated his purpose in coming:

"I have resources," he said, "and I want to help."

They all knew the problems. Over the years, the government had tried job training, but no jobs materialized, and the effort dwindled away. Subsidized housing was made available, but the units were not well done, and the Indians let them deteriorate. Social workers offered counseling on alcohol and substance abuse, but few cared. Welfare money went for liquor and drugs. Nothing had worked, and the future seemed dim. There had to be a better way. They turned to Andy.

"You need to break the cycle, change habits," he said. "How do we do that?"

"Maybe education," he said. "But we have tribal schools."

"I mean you should send kids to good, mainline American colleges and universities. If you are going to compete, you need a level playing field."

"Our kids feel out of place there. And we want to stay on our lands. If we leave, the Great Spirit doesn't go with us. Besides, those schools are expensive."

"Don't worry about the cost. Try to find kids who can handle the change, prepare them for the transition, and try to make sure they'll come back."

"I suppose some would go."

"If you'll recommend promising youngsters," he said, "I'll pay their expenses to prepare and attend good schools in any fields they want. What about that?"

"But how will that help?"

"If you can find the right kids, they'll come back and be your leaders of tomorrow. They'll break up the old patterns and shape your future. Can you identify good ones?"

"Maybe."

"Then why not have each Council member recommend one kid to the Council. If the Council accepts the choices, I'll pay their room, board, tuition, and other reasonable expenses at schools they choose. Once every Council member has recommended one, we'll go through the process again and again until the money runs out. What about that?"

"How much money are we talking about?"

"I'd guess we could budget between ten and fifteen thousand dollars per youngster, per year. Why don't we try to identify twenty-five to fifty kids?"

The Council members thought the idea had merit, so they began to discuss checks and balances to insure that the system would be fairly managed. Once they established the details, each Council member agreed to recommend a young person. That took two months. Then the Council chose twenty youngsters from the bunch, and Andy interviewed them. He set up a system to send off applications to the schools they had chosen, and the Council renewed its search for additional candidates.

Andy had plenty to do in making sure the Fiji chapel was properly run and the Sioux scholarships were fairly implemented, but he made time each day for Helen and the ranch. After the renovations were well along and Helen's garden was prospering, he began to teach her the basics of horseback riding. Whenever time and weather permitted, they worked in the ring. Soon they and the Bearclaws were riding the many nearby trails. When the weather turned cold, he and Helen returned to the Fiji Islands. Life was full, and Andy was at peace.

He could not escape the tragedy of the Marshall Islanders, however, for in 1975 the United States declared Bikini to be unsafe again, and the islanders had to evacuate once more. It was too late. By 1976, sixty-nine percent of islander children had thyroid tumors. Nasty rumors began to circulate that the United States had intentionally exposed the natives to radiation in order to observe its effects. Class action lawsuits started, and Congress began to pay compensation awards that threatened to amount to a billion dollars.

Helen too had her moment of triumph, for in 1978 the Army finally followed the lead of the Navy and the Air Force by reluctantly abolishing the WACs as a separate organization and fully integrating women in combat support roles, although they were still prohibited from serving in combat.

"And long overdue," she said. "How's that?" he asked.

"Forty thousand women served in World War II and fifty thousand in Vietnam."

"But not in combat."

"Close enough for plenty of medals. The first woman to be awarded the Purple Heart was at Pearl Harbor."

"Okay, they served in wartime, but they didn't like it. After the war, they got out. You did too."

"Not all. Some stayed on. In 1971 the Air Force promoted its first female Brigadier General. The first woman Admiral was two years ago, in 1976, and the WACs have had a Brigadier General since 1970."

"So now you're happy?"

"No. Because the Army will still not let women serve in combat units."

"Makes sense to me. Combat requires strength and aggression that most woman don't have."

"Both of us have seen a lot of men who didn't have that combination either. The test ought to be whether or not the individual can do the job. If a woman isn't strong enough, she should not qualify, but neither should a puny guy. The Army ought to have physical, mental, and psychological tests for every skill it requires. The qualified should get the jobs, and their sex shouldn't matter. If you were a commander, you'd want the best person in each position, wouldn't you? And you wouldn't care about size, color, or sex."

He had to agree, so he did not argue.

After four years, the renovations to the ranch were almost finished, and the chapel in the Fijis was up and running. So in July, they decided to hold the first of a series of annual cook-outs for the Tribal Council and students they had helped. Andy invited prominent businessmen, job recruiters, and college counselors. As a sweetener, Joe organized simultaneous hunting expeditions with the Indians from Standing Rock. When the men met the youngsters Andy was supporting, job offers materialized, and West Point recruiters even persuaded two boys to try for the Academy. These were years of great joy.

After spending almost half a million dollars on the chapel project in the Fiji Islands, and working forty-seven Sioux youngsters into his scholarship program, Andy still had not exhausted his funds.

The stock market boom ignited during the years of the Reagan Administration actually had resulted in an increase in his holdings. He could do more. He was glad to be alive.

Andy's happiness was shattered in 1989, however, when Helen returned from a hospital appointment to announce that her doctor had found a lump in her breast and taken a biopsy. When the sample was reported to be malignant, they went to the Mt. Sinai Medical Center to confirm the terrible diagnosis and discuss alternative treatments. She decided to start chemotherapy treatments that soon sickened her with debilitating nausea and terrible pain. When she also lost her hair, she fell into a fit of depression. Andy was devastated and frantically searched for a way to help her. Then, one day Joe Bearclaw approached him with some cookies.

"Give her these," he said. "They are a special mix of herbs we know about."

And help they did. Her nausea and pain soon disappeared, and her morale immediately improved. As she brightened, she began to voice hope they could beat the disease. And as she improved, so did Andy, and he was grateful to Joe. But a gnawing suspicion and some quiet research told him that Joe's cookies were not really herbal remedies, but actually marijuana. Joe would not confirm the suspicions, but Andy began to study the question of medical use of cannabis. He learned that there were severe penalties for simple possession of pot, and the country was squandering great resources in prosecution and imprisonment of offenders. He also determined that the effects of alcohol were far worse than those of pot. And there was considerable empirical evidence that marijuana significantly helped alleviate the effects of chemotherapy, just as Joe's cookies had helped Helen. So Andy began to study the arguments for the decriminalization of simple adult possession of marijuana, especially for medical purposes. It was clear to him that anybody who dealt in pot for minors ought to be put in prison for a long time, but he wondered if the money being spent on prosecution of adult possession could be spent for more deserving purposes. It was a puzzle he could not decide.

Helen lingered for over a year, but the shattering end finally came on August 4, 1990. Andy was devastated. Almost four hundred people paid their respects at the funeral home and attended her memorial service. Even though Iraq had just invaded Kuwait and the Pentagon was in an uproar, the military was represented by a Brigadier General from the office of the Deputy Chief of Staff for Personnel and a Colonel from the South Dakota National Guard. The Fiji Islands sent a Military Attaché, and the Department of the Interior sent a Director from the Bureau of Indian Affairs. As it was summertime, most of the almost fifty Indian students Andy had helped through scholarships were out of school and able to be there. A few Indians from Standing Rock attended the services, but mostly they came quietly to the ranch and sat for hours on the porch with Andy, Reva, and Joe.

Andy arranged a quiet burial service by her grave on a ridge just off a trail ride she loved. It was at a point that overlooked her favorite lake. On a quiet afternoon when all the outsiders had gone home and the ranch was deserted once more, Andy saddled old Buck and rode slowly out to the ridge. He gave Buck the reins, and the horse seemed to know the way. Andy found a good sitting rock near the site and tethered Buck so he could graze nearby. At first, the sky was a mottled red and purple, and the lake was crystal blue. But soon, storm clouds began to descend from the hills ten miles west across the valley. Then, in the gathering darkness, lightning flashed from the now black clouds, and thunder rolled around the heights like the crashing of a great artillery barrage. Old Buck whinnied and stirred nervously, but Andy did not notice. As rain began to pelt him, he lowered his head onto his arms and wept.

CHAPTER FIFTEEN

On August 7th, President Bush directed his Security Council to deploy advanced elements of the 82nd Airborne Division to Saudi Arabia, and the implications of war in the Middle East began to shock Andy out of his deep depression. In late August, when the Administration ordered a selective call-up of reservists, Andy had to know if Walter's son, Paul, would be going to fight in the desert. For sixteen years, Andy's only contact with his family had been an annual exchange of letters at Christmas. From those, he knew that Paul was in the Army and stationed in West Germany, but now he wanted more particulars. For the first time in years, he called Sandy, but as soon as he heard Sandy's voice, his needs changed:

"Helen is gone," he said. "Please come."

Sandy arrived from Hilton Head the following week. Joe met him at the airport at Pierre with a big "Walker" sign and Andy's Jeep. During their two-hour drive up to the ranch north of Mobridge, Sandy probed Joe for information about Andy, Helen, and the ranch, but he received monosyllabic grunts in response. Joe did give him one complete sentence:

"Colonel Walker is a good man, needs help."

A whitewashed fence bordered the long, gravel driveway to the house. By the time he was halfway up the drive, Sandy could make out his father sitting in a rocker on the front porch. When Andy rose to greet him, Sandy fully comprehended how the man had aged. Andy looked every bit of his eighty-seven years. He was stooped as if his back was stiff and hurting, and his sallow complexion was set off by stark white hair. He seemed frail and hesitant.

"It's been a long time," Andy said. "Too long," Sandy replied.

"Let's sit awhile and talk," Andy said, turning to the Indian woman who had come out to the porch. "This is Reva. She'll bring us Cokes."

"Tell me about the family," Andy asked as they settled.

"Well, you probably recall that I retired at Fort Jackson as a Colonel fourteen years ago. Nancy and I then went down to Hilton Head to earn real estate licenses and work with Kathleen and Dan. She turned out to be a real dynamo, and their business was a great success. They've just now retired to slow down a bit. You'll be happy to know they're healthy and well off."

"What did they do about the business?"

"Nancy and I have bought them out, and Sara and Cathy have agreed to stay on with the firm."

"And Walter's kids, what about them?"

"Beth is just finishing her undergraduate work at Clemson. I think she went there just because Sara did, but now she wants to stay on and take an advanced degree in something to do with computers. It's the place to be."

"And Paul?" Andy asked. "What does he do in the Army? Is he going to be sent to the Middle East?"

"He went into the Army right after high school. He had never traveled much after Walter was killed, and I think he simply wanted to get out and see the world."

"Drafted?"

"No, he was a volunteer, so they let him pick and choose. He went through Airborne and Ranger training, and then he chose Special Forces and was assigned to Fort Bragg. Just before he went over to Germany, they made him a Buck Sergeant, and he married a girl from home. Her name is Jo, and she just had a boy they named Steven."

"What does he do in Germany?"

"His primary job is to carry and emplace the SADEM. That's the atomic demolition munition two men can carry into combat by parachuting behind enemy lines. They use it to demolish avenues of communications and force enemy attacks into routes where they can be destroyed."

"What a crazy idea. But surely we wouldn't use such a thing in Arabia. So he won't be going to the Gulf War."

"Not with his bomb, but every Special Forces team has an area specialty, and Paul's is the Middle East. We think he's probably over there already. The mission of his team would be deep penetration behind Iraqi lines."

Andy seemed to sink into his rocker. Lost in thought, he stared off into space. After a time, Sandy interrupted him.

"Tell me about Helen," he said. "How did she die?" "Breast cancer," Andy said. "It was pretty bad." "How did you two meet?"

"In the Fiji Islands during World War II. She was a Red Cross volunteer there during the time I was working on that airfield so we could take the offensive against the Japs at the Coral Sea and Guadalcanal. We met when I went to the aid station for treatment."

"And you stayed in touch all those years?"

"No, she went to Australia and I went to New Guinea, and I lost track of her. I didn't try to find her again until after your mother died. Even then, because it seemed right, I waited a year before I hired a detective to locate her. I used that time to sober up. She had been teaching at a girl's school, but was retired up in Alexandria, Virginia. We married on Thanksgiving Day in 1974, because I thought it was an appropriate choice."

"And you were happy?"

"Very. We had almost sixteen good years," Andy said. "I had hoped it would never end. Foolish, I guess."

"It was breast cancer?"

"Can we talk about that some other time?" Andy asked. "I seem to get tired very easily. I'd like to lie down now, but I hope you'll be able to stay awhile."

"As long as you need me," Sandy said.

For the next several days, Andy did little more than eat and nap. He seldom left the house and did not want to talk. Sandy was on his own, and he spent the time with Reva and Joe trying to find out how the ranch was run, if the bills were being paid, and what was the state of Andy's health. At first, they were hesitant to answer, but gradually they opened up. All this time, the mail was piling up unread, and

Sandy was amazed at the sheer volume. Then one morning, Andy said he would like to take a ride. Joe went with them, and they slowly traveled the trail west to Helen's grave. There, Joe took care of the horses while Andy settled on his rock above the beautiful lake. After a few moments of silence, he began to talk.

"I had no idea," he said, "what a terrible thing breast cancer would be. She suffered terribly from the chemotherapy until Joe found some marijuana. That eased the pain and nausea. Even then, it was horrible to see such a beautiful woman deteriorate like that."

He paused to regain composure and let the emotion pass while Sandy took in the dramatic view of the lake below with its reflection of the hills to the west.

"I'd like to do something in her memory," Andy finally said. "Maybe give some money to help find a cure for breast cancer. Help me do that, will you?"

"Sure, Dad, but wasn't the marijuana a risk?"

"A great risk indeed. Responsible, tax-paying, family men in this great nation have been put in jail and their homes have been seized because they smoked a joint alone out in their garages. Alcohol is far more dangerous and does more damage, but pot is illegal. I've never tried it, but I'm glad Joe made it available to Helen. We spend twenty billion dollars a year on the problem of adult possession of marijuana. That seems a lot."

Sandy did not answer, and they sat for a time in silence. Then, in the gathering darkness, they made their way back to the ranch. The effort seemed to take a lot out of Andy, mentally and physically, and he went to bed for several days. Then one day, he returned to his rocker on the porch, and Sandy was able to again ask about Helen.

"She was an unusual woman," Andy said. "She was a Red Cross volunteer in a combat zone, then an officer in the Woman's Army Auxiliary, and finally a Captain in the Woman's Army Corps who was wounded in combat. She believed strongly that women could serve in a war zone, and as it turned out, she was right. If things heat up in the Gulf, a lot of women will be serving out there. I'd like to help that cause too. Trouble is, I want to do so much, and I have very little time left. I really need you to help me."

"I'll do whatever I can," Sandy said. "But women in combat. Isn't that pretty risky?"

"Women have been in combat at least as far back as the Greeks," Andy said. "Did you know that a woman won the Medal of Honor in the Civil War?"

"No, I didn't. Are you sure?"

"Yes. She was a nurse, just like Helen in the Fijis. You know, we went there every winter for fifteen years."

"To get away from the Dakota cold?"

"That, and to make certain a chapel we had built there was doing what it was supposed to do."

"You built a chapel in the Fiji Islands?" "It's a long story. Let's talk about it later."

The opportunity to do that came when Andy asked Sandy to help clear up the accumulated pile of unopened letters. Many were sympathy notes expressing sorrow at Helen's passing. What was interesting was their diversity. Sandy divided them into stacks. One group came from the Fijis and their diplomatic representatives in Washington. The second appeared to be from Indians, many of whom seemed to be students writing on college stationery like Minnesota, North Dakota State, Oregon, and even California. The military stack came from the Pentagon and many retired servicemen and women. Several clergy and local officials were represented, as well as ordinary citizens from Mobridge and Pierre. The rest were bills, periodicals, solicitations, and advertisements. Sandy was intrigued by the large correspondence from Fiji and the Sioux.

"You want to tell me about that chapel, Dad?"

"You probably should know. Back in '42, some troops under Penny's friend, Harrison, killed some islanders at the airfield where my battalion was working. It was a fight over a religious site, and I wanted to make amends, so when Helen and I went back to the islands in '75 for our honeymoon, I set up a trust to build a memorial chapel."

"And what about all these letters from students?"

"When Helen and I moved here, we wanted to do something to ease the deplorable conditions on the Standing Rock Reservation.

After we talked to a lot of people, scholarships for their young people seemed to be one way we could make a difference. So we started back in 1977 giving annual gifts to deserving students."

"But there appear to be a lot of them."

"Almost fifty. At the start, some only needed a few years help, but now we are picking some really good ones as early as the seventh grade."

"But what does that cost?"

"It's not a fixed figure. Expenses vary, but in the past they have averaged between ten and fifteen thousand dollars per student per year."

"But that's half a million dollars, and a chapel in the Fiji Islands must have cost a bundle."

"Not as much as you think, but I still have enough left for you to work on some of the things I asked you to."

"Where did all the money come from? Did Helen have a lot?"

"Not much. The real gem has been the stock market these last nine years. Even after all my expenses, I have more than when I started."

Andy went on to explain about money from Joseph, Junior, Kate, and Penny, as well as the sale of their houses in Destin and Alexandria. Couple that with his modest life style for over forty years, he explained, and he had quite a bundle.

"I had no idea you had money like that," Sandy said. "And I can see why you might want to build that chapel. It obviously had significance for you and Helen, but why this emphasis on the Indians and the Standing Rock Reservation?"

"That's a story I never told you," Andy said. "But you should know that in a final confrontation a hundred years ago, Sitting Bull, the old Sioux medicine man, put a curse on your grandfather and great- grandfather. He said that because they and the Army they served had slaughtered so many Sioux women and children and lied to the survivors, the Walkers and their children would never sleep until people of color killed every one of them. I want to put that evil to rest."

"What on earth are you talking about?"

"Massacres at Sand Creek and on the Washita. You've heard of Wounded Knee, but maybe not the nine hundred Moros who died in The Crater. You should know about the hangings of the Buffalo Soldiers and the sacrifice of the Marshall Islanders to atomic tests. I just told you about the killings in the Fijis, and you have first-hand knowledge of No Gun Ri and My Lai. And those are just the tip of the iceberg. That's what the curse was about, and we wanted to change it."

"No Gun Ri was nothing like My Lai, and even if a few bad apples have been involved in some terrible things, that is no reason to condemn the great majority of servicemen. Bad things happen in combat, but most soldiers are honorable men who don't deserve that kind of stigma. And what makes you think our family is cursed?"

"I heard it from my father, who was present when his father met Sitting Bull for the third and last time. Dad quoted the curse for me. And years afterwards at Fort Smith, I met an old Sioux Chief who repeated the curse almost verbatim. And just a few years ago, I consulted a Sioux shaman who confirmed the entire story. That is why I wanted to do something to try to remove the curse, to save our family, you, Paul, and now Steven."

"But this is nonsense," Sandy said. "Why on earth would you believe trash like that?"

"If you believe it is trash," Andy said, "answer me this: what date did Penny and Walter die?"

"September 5th."

"Both Joseph and Junior died on that same day." "Coincidence."

"Hardly. And what day did you arrive here?"

"September 5th," Sandy admitted. "But what does that prove?" "That was the date the government agents murdered the great Sioux War Chieftain, Crazy Horse." "But no Walker killed him?"

"Wait, there's more," Andy said. "Helen died on August 4th, the same date that Joseph first met Sitting Bull back in 1873 on the Yellowstone River."

"This is crazy," Sandy repeated.

"If it is crazy nonsense, tell me how it would happen that Paul was born on March 16th, the date of the My Lai massacre."

"But surely you are grabbing at straws."

"Except that Steven was born on December 15th, the date of Sitting Bull's murder in 1890. It is enough for me to wonder if something strange is going on."

"But why would that be? What have we done?"

"Joseph was the first object of the evil. He had fought the Sioux for twenty-five years before that, and Sitting Bull must have considered him symbolic of his enemies." "But what about Junior?"

"He was at Wounded Knee, and he was in the Philippines for three years. And remember, he felt responsible for the trials and hangings of the Buffalo Soldiers."

"But what did you do to merit a curse?"

"It was my battalion that started the trouble that resulted in those deaths in the Fijis."

"And you think I am cursed too?"

"You were at No Gun Ri when those South Koreans died in that tunnel, and you fought in Vietnam against people of color. That is the repeated theme of all this."

"And you think Walter died because of My Lai?"

"Yes, and now Paul is fighting in the Middle East," Andy said. "Don't you see, it is always against another race."

"I see only the selective use of history, and it doesn't convince me.

If there was a curse, you would be dead by now."

"You must ask Tashunka about that," Andy said, and he would discuss it no more.

The following week, Joe Bearclaw drove Sandy west across the Missouri, first past Sitting Bull's grave, and then up into the hills west of Mobridge. Tashunka was waiting on his porch. After introductions, Joe took his place on the steps, and an Indian woman passed the Cokes around.

"Educate me," Sandy said. "What is a shaman?"

"A priest, or perhaps a pastor," Tashunka said. "Someone you can turn to."

"You have a congregation?"

"No, I just help those who need help." "How?"

"I rely on the collective wisdom of our people, and I pray often to the Great Spirit for answers."

"Did you consult the Great Spirit about my father?" "Yes, and what he has told you is true."

"If it is true, why is he still alive?"

"It is because he has done many good things for so many people; he is an exception. Others of his family are not as fortunate. You and they remain under a dark cloud."

"And is that inevitable?"

"Probably not. Follow your father's lead." "But how do you consult the Great Spirit?"

"There are many ways. Some have found answers in visions brought about by rituals like the Sun Dance. Prayer, meditation, or abstinence can sharpen a person's senses. Some use drugs. No one knows all the paths."

"So you learn through visions?"

"Visions, dreams, and even stories. Andy's father used to tell him stories. Great wisdom can be found in them too."

"What kind of wisdom?"

"How to live your life. What the good things are. What to look for as you pass through this world. Values. Much more."

"Can you give any examples?"

"To listen well. To walk in a soft breeze and savor the red and purple sunsets of a mottled sky. To find peace that comes only through silence. To be able to love and express that love. To rise and rest with the sun. To walk life's journey but leave no tracks. To accept responsibility. To have eyes that see and the wisdom to understand. Those are some."

"But how does a person find these things?"

"Clean the waters. Replenish the earth. Restore humanity. Speak the truth quietly. Respect your brothers. Realize we are all related, every rock and leaf. Seek the strength not to judge or criticize your neighbors. Walk a good road until on that final day of quiet, you go to the Great Spirit without shame. For he is our Father and the Earth is our Mother."

"And did Andy do these things?"

"Yes, and it saved him. He did what was right. He dedicated a part of himself to a greater good. He led a remarkable life. He was a warrior, and he fought many battles, but he chose to be an engineer, one who built things. And he could love with a love that lasted over a long time. My vision showed him standing in a single ray of sunlight while surrounded by great clouds of evil and darkness. In the midst of chaos, he remained untouched."

As Tashunka talked, his voice took on a singsong, hypnotic quality. Sandy felt as if he was in a dream, and he was not sure how long they spent on that porch. When he left, he only knew that he had experienced something unusual. And when he next spoke with his father, Sandy was less critical.

"Tashunka is a remarkable man," he said.

"He and his people have endured much," Andy said. "Yet they are good human beings. Reva and Joe have been a great blessing to me. I hope you will take care of them after I am gone."

He seemed reconciled, almost eager, to follow Helen, as if she was waiting for him to join her down a long, lonely road or perhaps just around the next bend. So they sat down and worked together to carry out Andy's wishes. They arranged for periodic gifts for cancer research. Sandy came across a foundation that was setting up a memorial in Washington to honor women who had served in combat, and they budgeted contributions to that cause. The Fiji chapel needed little more than maintenance money, but the Sioux scholarships were a full time job. Andy amended his will and gave Sandy a durable power of attorney to carry on with both of those. Once the arrangements were made, Andy grew weaker by the day, as if he was ready to move on. Sandy tried to tell him how much everyone loved him, and that helped, but he evidently missed Helen very much and wanted to be with her. He died on December 15, 1990, exactly one hundred years after Sitting Bull had been killed at Standing Rock. Somehow, Sandy knew it would turn out that way.

www.ingramcontent.com/pod-product-compliance
Lightning Source LLC
Chambersburg PA
CBHW060449310726
48977CB00001B/372